Aware of growing stiffness in his fingers, the numbness of his cheeks, he lumbered to his feet, boots squeaking in the powdery snow. He was tall and slender, but in the bulky clothing—boots, fur coat, and cloth cap with wolfskin border pulled low over his ears—he looked like a grizzly. Pondering, he stood for a long time, glasses dangling from his neck by their leather strap. Now—or was it better to wait for a while before attempting to make friends with them? For days, ever since he located Big Hail's camp, he had delayed making himself known to them. For days he had wandered on the fringes of the village, keeping out of sight, downwind, hesitating to commit himself. After all, they were savages. But his time was running out. Soon he would have to make the deadly plunge.

THE GALVANIZED REB

ROBERT J. STEELMAN

CHARTER
NEW YORK

A Division of Charter Communications Inc.
A GROSSET & DUNLAP COMPANY
51 Madison Avenue
New York, New York 10010

An Ace Charter Book published by arrangement with Doubleday & Co., Inc.

First Ace Charter printing: December 1981
Published simultaneously in Canada

Manufactured in the United States of America
2 4 6 8 0 9 7 5 3 1

"While the written word has done much to preserve history, pictures are necessary to supplement the printed page. No other section of the American frontier has been so richly endowed with a pictorial record of its past as has the area encompassed by the headwaters of the Missouri River and its tributary, the Yellowstone. For almost a century, beginning in the 1830's, artists with pencil and brush added to this record. Although paintings and drawings often provide a valuable record, when pictures are considered from the standpoint of exactness the work of the photographer must come first. Only the camera can make a precise record of a scene or subject."

The Frontier Years
Mark H. Brown and W. R. Felton
Henry Holt and Co.
New York, N. Y. 1955

"The very things which an artist would leave out, or render imperfectly, the photograph takes infinite care with, and so renders its illusions perfect. What is the picture of a drum without the marks on its head where the beating of the sticks has darkened the parchment? In a perfect photograph there will be as many beauties lurking unseen as there are flowers that blush unobserved in forests and meadows."

Oliver Wendell Holmes
Atlantic Monthly
Vol. III, p. 746, 1859

CHAPTER ONE

The Oglalas were camped on the Tongue, several miles below its confluence with Otter Creek. The river was frozen hard to a depth of several inches, and the Fahrenheit thermometer in his wagon showed minus ten degrees that morning when he awoke. But now he was not in the wagon. The mules, Nig and Pansy, and the photographic wagon were back across the frozen Tongue. He had crossed the river to lurk in the ice-spangled box elder, cottonwood, and willow lining the far shore. Now, teeth chattering and feet numb, he knelt in the snow to focus field glasses on the distant encampment.

There were many lodges—tall, conical shelters, smoke-blackened at the top. Tendrils of smoke rose from the noon cooking. Reaching upward to an unseen ceiling, the smoke flattened out and drifted toward him in the wind. He was hungry. So close to the hostile camp, he had not dared to start a fire. Instead, he had settled for a mouthful of cold fried potatoes and hunks of bread torn from a frozen loaf softened by holding it between his shirt and his body. Now there came to him from the Indian camp the smell of cooking meat. His mouth watered; the moisture on his lips instantly froze.

With mittened fingers he adjusted the glasses. Spidery lodgepoles sticking from the tops of the tipis made a good target to focus on. But the lubricant in the glasses was gummy from the cold, and it was hard to turn the lens barrels. Swearing, he breathed on them, tried again. Details swam into view. A woman came to a door flap to hack meat from a frozen carcass hanging on a rack; children played in the snow; a dog looked up the river toward him and sniffed, nose high and inquisitive.

It was ridiculous, of course; he was a good mile or two from their camp and downwind. Nevertheless he felt the elation of danger as the dog seemed to watch him, continuing to sniff a foreign scent. He gripped his carbine hard and half raised it, but finally a stripling boy cuffed the cur and it slunk away.

Slowly he swung the glasses this way and that. They were good glasses, the best the Council had been able to buy. But, then, the Council had plenty of money and was willing to spend it to arouse the tribes against the government. He counted the lodges, estimating when some were half hidden in the trees or beyond the towering butte that gave the Oglala camp shelter from the probing winds of the Idaho Territory, the vast northwestern land containing the thousands of Sioux and Cheyennes who could make the finest irregulars in the world if properly incited, encouraged, armed, and led.

Watching them as he had for several days, scanning the activity of the camp, he had begun to feel almost an affection for the fierce Oglalas. Their camp reminded him in a way of Big Oaks, his father's plantation on the banks of the Mississippi, in Claiborne County, fifty miles below Vicksburg. Even now the blacks would similarly be going about their nooning: cooking, washing, throwing out debris, kicking at the fice dogs that always hung around the slave quarters. The old woman in the lenses of his glasses, the Indian woman with long braids and bosoms like sacks of grain, reminded him of black Aunt Ella, the nurse who had suckled both him and Wade. Aunt Ella liked Wade best, he remembered. But, then, Wade generally got the best of everything.

Aware of growing stiffness in his fingers, the numbness of his cheeks, he lumbered to his feet, boots squeaking in the powdery snow. He was tall and slender, but in the bulky clothing—boots, fur coat, and cloth cap with wolfskin border pulled low over his ears—he looked like a grizzly. Pondering, he stood for a long time, glasses dangling from his neck by their leather strap. Now—or was it better to wait for a while before attempting to make friends with them? For days, ever since he located Big Hail's camp, he had delayed making himself known to them. For days he had wandered on the fringes of the village, keeping out of sight, downwind, hesitating to commit himself. After all, they were savages. But his time was running out. Soon he would have to make the plunge.

Again he became aware of the gnawing in his gut. He was ravenous. Certainly it would be better to approach the camp after he put something nourishing in his belly. Maybe he could risk a small fire with the patent Swiss alcohol stove in his wagon. Perhaps he would even warm frozen stew, boil coffee. Yes, that was it! Go back to the comfort of the wagon for now, eat, warm himself, plan exactly how to enter the camp! Since the old treaty had expired, the Oglalas were very distrustful of white men, he had been informed. During the summer, the Council experts said, the hostiles came in to Elk City and neighboring Fort Zachary Taylor to trade for powder and ball, sugar and tobacco, bolts of cloth and sacks of beads. But in the winter season they remained in snow-locked camps. They did not welcome white men while they pursued their ancient winter ways. So now he decided with relief to go back to the photographic wagon, eat, feed the mules, and rest for a while.

Crossing the slippery ice on the river, he stumbled and fell, swearing when he thought he had damaged the precious field glasses. But they were intact; he struggled on, working up a clammy sweat in his thick clothing. Consumptive lungs labored; he puffed clouds of vapor; moisture condensed on his lips and cheeks and beard, quickly freezing into a glasslike shell so that he had to grimace to break it loose. The sun had disappeared, its station marked only by a faint luminance in the clouds. For days the weather had been raggedly overcast, and now that he neared his wagon, gasping for breath and stumbling, a light rain of snow descended.

In a kind of white vapor, he approached his camp. Nig and Pansy stamped in recognition and whuffled. In the rocky hollow where they had sought shelter the night before, the wind, at least, was broken. Exhausted, he slumped on the wagon tongue. It was then he saw the bearded face topped by a weathered felt hat bound around the ears with a ragged shawl. The man's nose was red and bladelike, and the malevolent eyes squinted down the chill iron blackness of an ancient Hawken rifle to center on David Chantry's chest.

"Who the hell be you?" the rifleman demanded. "And what in hell you doin' in my territory?"

He was too tired, too utterly weary, to do anything but sit and stare at the intruder. The man was old and lean, stringy in soiled buckskins, with a thicket of pepper-and-salt beard and beetling brows almost covering the angry eyes. A shaggy Indian pony was tethered to David's wagon, and two stolid pack mules pawed the snow in a search for grass.

"I said," the apparition insisted, "what in hell are you doing here on the Tongue?" Moving closer, he prodded David's chest with the muzzle of the rifle. "Speak up, now! What's your handle?"

"My name is Chantry," David said. "David Chantry." His voice emerged thin and husky; he was still out of wind. He cleared his throat, and when he reached for a handkerchief the old man started and waved his weapon in alarm.

"Stop that, now! What you doin'?"

David cleared his throat again, spat into the handkerchief. "It's my lungs," he explained. "I've got a weakness of the chest. Exertion makes me bleed a little, inside."

"It ain't catching?"

"No, it isn't catching."

The old man prodded him again. "Got a gun on you?"

"No."

The man touched David's thighs, patted him under the arms, finally seemed satisfied.

"So what in Tophet you doin' out here—in winter? You look kind of frail to me."

"I'm a photographer."

"A what?"

"I take pictures. Surely you've seen photographs?"

The old man scratched a bristly chin, pondered. "Like—dagooro-types?"

"Better than daguerreotypes," David said. "I use the collodion process." He gestured toward his wagon. "Wet glass plates, developed in nitrate of silver. All my gear is in there."

"Pictures, eh?" The old man was still uncertain. Keeping a bead on David, he said, "Take my picture, then! Prove it!"

David folded the handkerchief, put it away. "Too cold."

"Eh? Why too cold?"

"When the weather is this cold," David explained, "the chemicals don't work right sometimes." Slapping his arms against his sides, he felt snow on his eyelashes, drifting on his blond mustache. "Look here," he said. "I'm about frozen! If you'll put down that blunderbuss and let me boil some coffee—"

Satisfied, the old man propped his rifle against the wagon and stuck out a gnarled hand. "Blossom," he announced.

"Who?"

"Blossom—that's all the name I go by." He pinched his nose and blew into the snow, wiping afterward with a sleeve. "I'm a wolfer."

David helped him into the canvas shelter of the wagon. "Sit there," he invited, pointing to the sagging wicker chair that had somehow made the long journey up the Missouri and been sold to him for five dollars in Elk City. That was a lot of money for a secondhand chair with a split-cane bottom. But then, he had plenty of money! It was nice, after all these years, to be working for a good salary and expenses, though there was certainly little to spend it on in the Idaho Territory.

"What's a wolfer?" he asked, busying himself with the patent stove.

Blossom slumped into the proffered chair. "This cold always hits me right in the sitting bones," he observed, settling back with a sigh. "By God, I ain't sit in a proper chair since last September, when I put up for a spell at Dooley's Hotel in Elk City!" Sticking his shabby boots out before him, he inspected the crowded contents of the photographic wagon. "What in tarnation is all this claptrap?"

David got out the frozen loaf of bread. The coffee water was hot, and he set the pan of rock-hard stew on the flame.

"I said I was a photographer. For Horace Kinnear's *Illustrated Weekly News*, back in Washington, D.C. Those are my chemicals in the cabinet there. Then, my cameras in the boxes—I've got three of them, including the big red one there with the ground-glass screen. That's made by Anthony and Company in New York City and cost two hundred dollars. Most of the rest is just my personal stuff—clothes and books and things—and supplies, like canned goods and dried beans and bacon and sugar."

Blossom accepted a cup of coffee and sipped greedily. "I marvel," he exclaimed, "how you got all them traps in this little wagon!"

There was more in the wagon, too. David did not mention the

rifles in the compartment underneath, between the springs. Instead he remarked, "You were going to tell me about being a wolfer."

Blossom nodded. "After I get me a lining of that stew in my belly."

In the fading light, they sat across from each other, eating luke-warm corned-beef stew cleaned up with chunks of thawed bread. The flame of the alcohol lamp together with the warmth of their bodies made the interior of the wagon almost comfortable.

Blossom belched, finished his coffee, lit an ancient pipe.

"I trap wolves," he explained. "That is, I *used* to trap 'em. Now I find these work better." Digging into a dirty sack, he brought out a handful of greasy yellow pellets.

"What are those?"

"Tallow balls," the wolfer explained. "Mutton tallow mixed with strychnine poison. Ain't *anything* a wolf loves better in winter than a nice, fat sheep-tallow ball!" He giggled, put the deadly things away. "Wolf hardly swallers it till he goes crazy for water. Staggers around whooping and hollering, then lays on his back, griped at the guts, pawing in the air! Oh, it hits 'em fast, you better believe!" Wiping his hands on the buckskin shirt, he asked, "You got a little swallow handy? Rum, say—or brandy? It's comin' on a cold night."

David Chantry was not a drinker. The penitentiary surgeon in Columbus who had discovered his prison-born consumption had for-bidden alcohol as well as tobacco, but for emergencies there was a bottle of Clubhouse gin on a shelf. He poured Blossom two fingers in a tin cup.

"Thanks," the wolfer said. He tossed off the gin, belched, patted his stomach. "Wolf skins," he went on, "prime ones, that is, brings ten dollars apiece at the steamboat landing in Elk City. Then the Territorial Legislature pays me another ten dollars for each varmint. Oh, it ain't a half-bad business for an old geezer!" He stuffed the pipe with tobacco again, stared at his host from under the beetling brows. "You're a young feller, Chantry. Why ain't you back there?" He jerked his head. "In the war, I mean?"

David was amused. "I was."

"Wounded, was you? Invalided out?"

Wind sifted through a gap in the wagon canvas. David plugged the hole with a dirty shirt. Disregarding the surgeon's warning, he took a long nine from a box, chewed the end off, and extended another to the wolfer. Blossom declined, preferring to puff at the evil-smelling pipe.

"Was you wounded?" he insisted.

The stogie was Connecticut tobacco, not at all like the golden North Carolina weed sold in Biloxi. David made a face as he drew on the cheroot. "Not exactly. The Army turned me down. Our Army, I mean. The Army of the Confederacy."

"You a reb?" Blossom's voice was chill.

"Actually, I was never even a soldier. At home they turned me down on account of I was too tall or too skinny or something or other, said I couldn't go for a soldier."

"So?" Blossom's eyes were bright, ferret-like.

"At college I'd learned something about chemistry, so they let me work as a civilian with Julian Vannerson, the South's battle camera-man. People are already beginning to call him the 'Mathew Brady of the Confederacy.' Anyway, Mr. Vannerson taught me a lot about cameras. At Manassas Junction I was out in the field, taking pictures, when the Sixth Ohio captured me and all my equipment." He grinned. "I was too busy taking pictures to notice them sneaking up on me! They put me in Fort Delaware Prison, in the middle of the Delaware River, but I escaped with some of Jo Shelby's cavalrymen. Then they caught me again and sent me out to the Ohio State Penitentiary, in Columbus. That's where they sent the most dangerous prisoners, they said. Lordy, I didn't think I was so dangerous, especially after I got a good look at the North and decided we didn't have a snowball's chance in hell! So that was the end of the war, as far as I was concerned."

Blossom's face turned sly. David could imagine the wolfer thinking of a reward. "You escaped again, then, and come out here!"

"Lord, no!" David chuckled.

"But you said—"

"You needn't worry. I've been galvanized."

"Gal—galvanized? What in suffering Jesus does that mean?"

"A galvanized reb, that's what they call me now. I finally took the oath of allegiance to the North and they let me out of prison when I promised not to fight them any more. Anyway, they thought I was going to die of the consumption." He felt a twinge of conscience, as always, but went on. "Someone said galvanizing was a '. . . thin coat of loyalty to the Union covering an unreconstructed rebel.'"

"That so?" Blossom asked, still suspicious.

"It was in Columbus that I finally saw the light. Good Lord, the South can't possibly beat a country with all those factories, coal mines, iron foundries! I learned that right quick!" It was deception, but he was fast learning to live with deception.

"Hmmmm," Blossom murmured. He seemed disappointed. Sighing, he reached for the gin bottle. Before David could circumvent him, he poured himself a tin cup full of gin. "Prime stuff," he wheezed, wiping his mouth. "Sure better 'n the horse piss I usual get."

"Horace Kinnear," David went on, "heard about me, staked me to come out here to the Territory and do a collection of photographic studies of the Indians and their way of life." This much, at least, was true.

"Pictures?" Blossom snickered. "Who in hell wants pictures of mangy savages? Brutes, that's all they are!" Again he reached for the gin bottle, but David anticipated him. Blossom turned sulky.

"Kinnear wants pictures of Indians—savages—whatever you want to call them. He's a rich man and fond of nature. He thinks the Indians are a great people and the government—the Union, that is—is mistreating them, taking away their rightful lands and cheating them with pieces of paper called treaties."

Blossom grunted morosely. "I kin just see old Spotted Horse or Bobtail or Ghost Bull or any of those saddle-colored sons of bitches sitting still to have their picture took!" Casually his eye fell on the case hanging from the oaken roof bow. "What's that?"

"A violin."

"You play it?"

"A little," David admitted.

Blossom's rheumy eyes watered. He wiped his nose with the liver-spotted back of a hand. "Play me something, then."

Carefully David took down the instrument, opened the case. "What would you like?"

Blossom toyed with the empty cup. "Do you know 'Faded Flowers'?"

There had been a free Negro groom at Major Garrett's big house on Third Street in Columbus who sang "Faded Flowers" incessantly. It was a lugubrious song; the words were about a disappointed maiden left with only a bouquet of faded flowers to remember her lover.

"As I remember, it goes like this," he said, tuning the violin. Bowing with fingers stiff from long disuse, he played the melody. Stroking a lingering conclusion, he asked, "Recognize it? I haven't played for a long time."

A tear sparkled on Blossom's weathered cheek.

"I recognize it," he said. He rubbed at his red-veined nose. "There was another song—my kid used to sing it before she—before she—" He broke off, dabbing at his eyes. "It was called 'Run, Little Rabbit.'"

"Sounds like a nursery rhyme," David observed, trying to remember the tune.

Blossom was suddenly, unexpectedly, belligerent. "What the hell's the difference? Play it!"

Half amused, half annoyed, David managed to recall a fair semblance of the tune, judging from the tears that ran down the wolfer's cheeks. Outside, the wind rose to a half gale. Wagon canvas rippled and slapped, the flame of the alcohol lamp wavered, smoked low, sprang up again.

"Mattie," Blossom quavered.

"Eh?"

"Mattie—that was her name. My kid, my girl. After her ma died, there was only little Mattie and me. Mathilde, her ma named her, after a lady she read about in a French novel." For a long time, Blossom remained silent, staring abstractedly into the flame of the lamp. "I come out to Omaha, took me a job of work in a tannery there. They wasn't no money in it, though, and Mattie and me took the stage to Yankton, in the Dakota Territory. They'd told me there was a need for wheelwrights there, and I'd apprenticed to the trade. But there wasn't no jobs, and we moved on."

Blossom picked up his empty cup, dangled it between his fingers.

"Moved here, moved there—Mattie was always sweet and cheerful, no matter how bad things was." Blossom swallowed painfully; the lean Adam's apple bobbed up and down. "It was along the Niobrara I lost her."

David put the violin carefully away, hung the case back on the wagon bow. "The smallpox?"

Blossom shook his head. "No. If 'twas the pox, then that would have been God's will, I guess. But it was the damned Injuns stole her! They come on us in a gully, just the two of us and a buckboard and team I'd bought in Yankton with the last money I had. I don't even remember where we was headin' for." He buried his face in his hands. After a while he said, "Knocked me over the head, left me for dead. They stole the team, carried Mattie away."

The wagon was quiet now, and warm. The winter dusk was already settling in. David heard an animal pawing the earth. Old Nig broke wind, a sign he was hungry and demanded attention.

"When was that?" David asked.

Buckskin arms dangling between skinny knees, Blossom looked up, face haggard. "That was in '50. Mattie was—let me see—three or four, I disremember which. Travelin' around the way we did, I kinely lost track of dates."

"I'm sorry," David commiserated. "I truly am. There's never been any word of her, then?"

Blossom shook his head. "Nary word, nary solitary word." He fished a tallow ball from his pocket. In the flickering light it shone greasily, evilly. "I went to wolfing then, so's to be able to foller the tribes around, keep an eye peeled for Mattie. Since then I killed me a passel of wolves, got a dozen years older. The sun's come up and gone down thousands of times, and I still ain't found my little Mattie." He held the tallow ball to the light, examining it as if it were a crystal sphere that could show him his daughter's whereabouts. "Probably she's long since dead. They likely cut her throat when they got tired of her, that little child, and threw her on the prairie. Well, I suppose her bones has long been moldering. But they took white children, sometimes, and brought 'em up like their own. That's the only reason I keep on."

David was touched by the old man's burden of grief.

"I'm sorry," he said again.

Blossom stirred painfully, stretched his booted legs. "Ah, it's hard to keep these old shanks in motion, David Chantry or whatever your name was in the States." He blinked, yawned a gap-toothed yawn, drooped. In minutes he snored, head between his knees.

Poor old wretch, to have so much grief! David thought also of his own childhood, when he had been Mattie's age—four or five, maybe six. The early memories were dim. Wade had been about ten then—acknowledged leader in the escapades of his younger brother and the black children who were their friends and accomplices. Wade was always the leader—dark, incisive, graceful as a fox even as a child, and so unlike David's towheaded awkwardness. Wade favored the Walton side of the family. Their mother's great-grandfather Walton had signed the Declaration of Independence. Now Wade Chantry was the youngest line colonel in the ranks of the Confederacy, while he—David Chantry—could only nurse sick lungs in the Idaho Territory. Horace Kinnear had made it all sound so attractive, so romantic; the publisher thought, too, that the cold dry air would be good for David's lungs. But David had failed. He was too frightened to enter the Oglala camp. What did he know of Red Indians? He must have been insane to volunteer for Kinnear's secret assignment!

Carefully, so as not to disturb the snoring Blossom, he left the wagon. The wind had finally abated, the sky was clear. Over his head wheeled Orion, the hunter. The night was pierced with diamond-like pricks of light; from north to south stretched the long luminosity of the Milky Way: Only the distant yapping of a band of coyotes broke the silence. They were probably pursuing a rabbit. Wryly he thought to himself that he was a rabbit also.

Later, he fed Nig and Pansy. On Blossom's pack mules he found a sack of corn and poured out measures for the mules and for the wolfer's patient buckskin pony. Backs and manes mounded with snow, the animals pressed warmly against him. In compassion he brushed them off with his hand. They seemed restless; prowling animals nearby, he guessed. But a mule could probably defend itself against anything.

From the position of Orion, it was midnight when he finally wrapped himself in his blanket to lie down in the wagon. Blossom still snored. For a time, that kept him awake. He listened to the stirring of the animals, an occasional *thunk* as fresh snow slid from a tree or bush. Later—he did not know when—he slept, a drugged and weary sleep. He dreamed of Big Oaks; of the river and the boats, of Wade and his father's niggers jumping over a fallen log and running, ever running. He tried to catch up with Wade, but his brother had already disappeared in the moss-hung trees. Furious, he sank to the ground and wept.

In winter dawn he awoke. The sagging chair where Blossom had slept was vacant. Sunlight filtered through scrub oaks surrounding his wagon, dappling the canvas. For a moment he lay listening, and heard nothing. Scratching and yawning, he got to his feet. Still in the bearskin coat, he shuffled to the door flap and looked out.

The land sparkled with sunlight on new snow. The brilliance hurt; he winced and shaded his eyes. There were tracks, doglike prints, all around his wagon. Examining them, he heard a distant whoop. Blossom waded through knee-deep snow, holding aloft his bag of tallow balls.

"They was all around us during the night," he chuckled. "This here is the best place for wolfing I come on in a month of Sundays!" Panting for breath, he paused before David Chantry, grinning. The wolfer's nose was chapped and peeling, the smile marred by missing teeth, but age was almost transformed to youth by ecstasy. "This wind sure peels my bark," he said, "but I baited all around—under every bush, in every rabbit hole, wherever the brutes are likely to pee!"

David looked dourly at him. Enthusiasm, he did not understand early in the morning; he was a slow riser.

"I know this Sioux country like I know the palm of my hand!" Blossom exulted, "and I ain't *never* seen such a gathering of wolves! Why, it's like a political convention of the varmints!"

Something stirred in David—an idea. He stopped yawning. "Come in," he said, "out of the cold. I'll make some tea."

When the water was hot, they sat in the wagon, sipping tea and chewing on half-frozen strips of dried meat from Blossom's saddlebags. David gnawed on the stuff gingerly, fearing it was contaminated with the mutton-tallow balls. But the wolfer had said strychnine worked fast. After they had finished the meat and tea, David still had no cramps, did not crave water, in fact felt well. He broached his subject casually.

"Know the country well, you said. I suppose you're familiar with the Sioux, and the Cheyennes too."

Blossom poured himself another cup of the scalding brew, dumped half the sugar bowl into it, stirred.

"Know 'em all—Yellow Knife, Ice, Big Hail, Ghost Bull, all the high mucketymucks!"

"Look here," David said, leaning forward with hands clasped around the steaming teacup to warm them. The sun was still low and slanting, without warmth. "I came out here on a commission to make pictures of these people, but I must admit I haven't had too much success. It's—" He broke off, uncomfortable. "Well, I just don't know how to approach them, these savages. After all, they *are* dangerous."

Blossom watched him over the rim of his cup. "Meaning what?"

David plunged ahead. "*You* know them—the Sioux along the Tongue. Take me into that camp down there." He nodded toward the river. "Introduce me, tell them I mean no harm, explain what I want. I'll make it worth while for you."

Blossom bit off a morning chew from his plug of Wedding Cake. "How much?"

"Fifty dollars."

Blossom shook his head. "'Tain't enough."

"But—"

"I suppose," the wolfer said, "I know Sioux and Cheyenne as well as any man in the Territory. But this time of the year they spook easy. They're in winter camp, see? It's a private time, and they don't favor white men around. They got ceremonies—dances, meetings, stuff like that—no white man ever laid eyes on, including me. So it ain't all that simple."

"Sixty dollars?" David offered.

The mules whickered nervously; old Nig finally broke into a bray. Blossom's face grew covetous. He licked his lips, tweaked the beak of a nose. "After all," he said, "you're askin' me to risk my giblets, too."

"Seventy-five," David said with finality.

Blossom pondered. Then he reached out and clasped David's hand. "All right—done!"

The bargain was academic. When they stepped out of the wagon, they found themselves ringed by Sioux. Tall, implacable-looking men on wiry, barrel-chested ponies, the warriors had silently surrounded the wagon. That was why old Nig had tried to warn them.

Blossom stood stock-still in the snow, fingering his chin. David paused on the iron wagon step, blinking in fear and surprise.

"Don't say nothing," Blossom muttered. "Just act natural." He turned to the silent horsemen, raising a hand, palm out.

"*Haul!*"

No one spoke. The tall men, their gaze severe, continued to stare. The scowling brave with a V of yellow paint across the bridge of his nose made an undoubtedly obscene gesture toward Blossom the wolfer, clenching his fist and allowing his thumb to protrude between index and middle fingers.

"*Oh*-oh!" the wolfer murmured. In an aside to David he muttered, "That there is Big Hail! He don't like me for sour apples." He slid the old rifle into the crook of his arm, ready.

"But I don't understand!" David protested. "I thought you were friends with the Oglala Sioux!"

"I know 'em," Blossom agreed, "but I never said anything about bein' friends, did I? Wolves is their big totem, and they don't favor me killin' so many."

"But—"

The wolfer pulled David off the step and shoved him forward.

"Might be trouble," he said. "See what you kin do with 'em, pilgrim! I'll cover your backside."

CHAPTER TWO

Secretly, as always, the Council met to carry out its objective of bringing confusion and defeat to the forces of the North and to "the gorilla in the White House," as Abraham Lincoln was called by many people. The Council met at Horace Kinnear's estate on New Hampshire Avenue near Rock Creek, in the nation's capital.

Carriages crunched up the gravel driveway to deposit elegant ladies and Dundrearied men in stiff-bosomed shirts. The weather was cold and clear, with none of the rain that had drenched the city a few days before. A string orchestra played discreetly; the rooms buzzed with polite conversation; liveried black servants passed trays of glasses with imported champagne. John Welcher's restaurant on the Avenue catered a dinner of oysters on the shell, chicken cutlets, sweetbreads and game, ices, jellies, charlottes, and coffee, along with four different kinds of French wine. After dinner the ladies exchanged titbits of Capitol gossip while the gentlemen withdrew for cigars and cognac. Certain selected gentlemen withdrew even farther, into a former summerhouse along the creek, now converted into a library and private office for Horace Kinnear, publisher of the prestigious *Illustrated Weekly News*. There the members of the Council were safe from prying eyes and hungry ears.

"You'll keep the minutes as usual, Catlett," Kinnear instructed. "Eleventh meeting, December second, eighteen hundred and sixty-two."

Kinnear was a ponderous man, with steel-rimmed spectacles and a grizzled beard lying like a blanket over his chest. He made a great deal of money with the *News;* he knew what the public wanted.

Even more, Kinnear knew what he wanted, and intended to get it. The Council was his invention toward that end.

Rapping for order, he introduced the new participants: Mr. Roland Dillard-Hume, the British ambassador's private secretary, and John W. Ashmore, the Confederate major who was ostensibly in Washington to supply the North with mules.

"Gentlemen," Kinnear began, "our task is onerous, but being called a Copperhead is a small price to pay for stopping this ruinous war! Someday we shall be called patriots, and enshrined in the Capitol!" He raised his glass. "Success to Robert E. Lee!"

Mr. Dillard-Hume spoke quickly. "Her Majesty's government joins you in that sentiment! It is no secret that English sympathies lie with the South, and the Trent affair has exacerbated the situation. Our mills must have southern cotton, and this war is disrupting our supply. But I hope you will all understand that we must be circumspect about our participation in the affairs of the Council."

"Agreed," Kinnear said, rubbing his hands together briskly. "That is understood, sir, and we are honored to have this expression of interest from your government." He looked about the room. "Now may we have reports from the chairmen of the various subcommittees?"

The president of a Washington bank gave a summary of the current state of hostilities. "Burnside has changed his headquarters to Aquia Creek. To counter this move, General Lee has taken up new positions on the Fredericksburg heights. If Burnside tries to cross the Rappahannock, Lee will slaughter him."

There was applause; the Council toasted Robert E. Lee, that master of strategy who would ultimately prevail. "Although," Kinnear admitted, "we do not know much about Ambrose Burnside. I personally felt much better when McClellan was commanding the Army. Mac was, as you know, a damned tin soldier, with no get-up-and-go to him. Burnside could be more effective."

Others made their reports. An official of the Baltimore & Ohio Railroad had managed to divert and misroute northern troop trains. The owner of an iron foundry had delayed the casting of an order of large howitzers. A broker had been successful in persuading his directors not to buy Federal bonds. Kinnear himself had published a probing series of articles in his *News* questioning whether the war was necessary, or even worth while. Response, he reported, had been surprisingly favorable. Between McClellan's blundering on the one hand and Lee's crossing the Potomac and occupying Maryland on the other, the public was apprehensive and discouraged.

A servant brought more cognac and cigars, and Kinnear turned to another matter. "As you know, we have a promising plan to incite the hostile tribes in the West to divert Federal troops to that area. So let us now hear from the Indian Subcommittee how our western operations are proceeding."

Mr. Gosling, head of a large wholesale grocery company, spoke. "As we can now report, the massacres of Minnesota settlers last fall were brought about largely by our people in the Indian Office delaying promised annuities to Little Crow and his Sioux. Now we have arranged through various channels open to us to get General Curtis —S. R. Curtis—assigned to the Platte District. Curtis is a pompous fool, ignorant of Indians. He is bound to cause a lot of trouble with them and help our cause. We also have in hand a scheme to get Colonel Chivington assigned to the field. Our people in the territorial governor's office in Golden are working on it. Chivington is a bloodthirsty rascal; maybe we can stir up something."

Another man reported on the dispatch of large numbers of guns to the Idaho Territory. "This is illegal, of course, but we have found no lack of traders willing and eager to defy the Army and sell guns to the Sioux. An Indian will give anything for a Henry magazine rifle."

Kinnear nodded approvingly. "Thank you, gentlemen."

He himself read a letter from David Chantry, the young photographer he had hired to go out to the Powder River country. The letter had been forwarded by a long and devious route. Chantry had not yet made contact with the Sioux but hoped soon to do so.

"Promising, very promising, David Chantry and his activities," Kinnear concluded. "The proper man—even one man—can sow seeds of restlessness among the tribes that will flower into full-blown rebellion!"

There was a slight stir. Kinnear's dispatching Chantry without Council approval had ruffled some feelings.

"I have this day," Kinnear continued, "arranged for another operative to go out to the Cheyennes along the Upper Missouri and stir up trouble there, as Chantry is instructed to do among the Sioux. Benjamin Berrisford Sears is a young man, vigorous and articulate. He is the son of an old servant of my family, and devoted to our cause. Three of Benjie's brothers have already been killed in what he considers an evil and pointless war."

There was more uneasiness, more stirring, but Kinnear went determinedly on. The Council was his creation; success in that cause could make him a power in national politics, a goal that so far eluded him.

"Benjie went briefly to seminary in Utica but was expelled for a youthful prank. It is my opinion the boy deserves another chance. I have instructed him to deliver some photographic supplies to David Chantry at Elk City—covertly, of course—and then proceed to the Missouri, near its juncture with the Musselshell." With a pointer the publisher indicated on a wall map the confluence of the two rivers. "There, in the guise of a Church of the Redeemer missionary, Benjie will work mischief among the Cheyennes."

The restlessness came to a head. A man with a wen asked, "Horace, are you sure we can trust this Sears feller? After all, none of us knew this turncoat Chantry you hired, and we sure as hell don't know any Benjamin Sears! Suppose one of 'em is caught, and blabs?"

Kinnear was finally forced to recognize the rebellion. He dealt with it deftly. "I will vouch for both young men. I am also their only contact. If anything happens, I am ready with a plausible denial. Who is to believe their incredible story against the testimonial of Horace Kinnear?"

"Well," Gosling grumbled, "it's just that whole rigmarole is getting dangerous! Working on our own, that's one thing. But an Indian plot, with hired agents and everything! We could *all* hang if something went wrong!"

Kinnear shook his head. "There is no connection to any of you. This is my own, and—I think—valuable, contribution to the cause." He looked challengingly about. "After all, I am not a fool! There have been prepared certain papers which, if necessary, can prove I am not involved, and give further damaging evidence against Chantry and Sears. I hope, of course, not to be forced to use the documents, but they are at hand, ready." He slapped his hand on the table. "Trust me, gentlemen!"

Still, the prospect of a mass gallows hung over the room. There was moody silence, not broken until Mr. Dillard-Hume consulted a large gold watch.

"I would suggest we hurry along with our business. Our absence from the rest of the guests may soon be noticed, and commented on."

Kinnear agreed. In a final word he warned, "Remember, gentlemen, we must, as Benjamin Franklin said, hang together, or we shall all hang separately! And we must *certainly* not allow small differences among us to obscure the main objective!" Consulting the papers at his elbow, he said, "Finally, there is the matter of the proposed treaty with the tribes. As you know, our informers in the Indian Office have for some time been aware of rumors that the government is seriously considering a great convocation of the tribes on the Powder River when spring comes and the Indians emerge from their winter camps. They hope to convince the Sioux and the Cheyennes to remain neutral so long as the war continues—to buy peace from them with blankets and liquor and lavish presents. We must—the Council must—discourage the prospect of such a treaty meeting."

For the first time, the Confederate major Ashmore spoke. "Sir, I cannot agree too heartily! The South is counting heavily on an uprising of the western tribes to divert Federal troops from the battlefield!"

Kinnear nodded, went on. "A certain Lieutenant Colonel Owen Garrett has recently been sent out to command Fort Zachary Taylor, on the Yellowstone. Garrett is a skilled and capable man, and we suspect it is his assignment to see that the Indians are in place along the river to discuss a treaty if the Indian Office goes ahead with the plan."

Major Ashmore dropped his slender stogie, bent to retrieve it. "Owen Garrett?"

Kinnear turned. "Yes. Do you know him?"

"I suppose it's the same man. Owen was my classmate at the Academy in—let's see—'42. He served with me at Fort Gibson for a while. Black Irish, from Boston. Family had a lot of money from the liquor-importing business." Ashmore drew hard on his cigar; a reminiscent smile came to his lips. "Cassie," he murmured. "Cassie Garrett!"

Kinnear blinked, looked puzzled.

"Excuse me!" Aware of the silence, Ashmore recovered himself. "You must forgive me, gentlemen! I was thinking of Owen Garrett's wife. She was a wild one, I can tell you!" He chuckled. "Cassie led Owen a merry chase!"

Kinnear smiled, stroked his beard. "Perhaps we can use that information someday to discredit or embarrass Colonel Garrett, perhaps distract him. We must not hesitate to take advantage of the most minuscule weapons." He continued, referring to a notebook. "My information indicates that Garrett was wounded at Ball's Bluff. Later he was sent out to the State Penitentiary at Columbus, Ohio, on a convalescent sinecure to command a detachment of troops guarding Confederate prisoners. Garrett has now recovered his health, it appears, and probably has been chosen to superintend any treaty proceedings at Fort Taylor." He looked up from his notes. "In view of this recent development, I think the Council extremely fortunate in having David Chantry and Benjamin Sears—two trusted agents—on the site out there to scotch any treaty preparations!"

There was still muttering at the publisher's highhandedness, but the rebellion was defeated. After all, the Council *were* committed; they would indeed have to hang together.

"I will entertain a motion to adjourn," Kinnear offered.

There was a grumble from the back of the room.

"Second?"

The man with the wen nodded. "Second, I guess."

"All in favor?"

There was a quick show of hands.

"I declare this meeting adjourned," Kinnear said. "Catlett, please make copies of the minutes in cipher and see they are properly distributed in sealed envelopes. Two copies to the British Embassy, care of Mr. Dillard-Hume. Mr. Ashmore—Major Ashmore—thank you for coming. I will be in touch with you further, you may believe me!"

Afterward, Horace Kinnear bent over his wife in the ballroom and brushed her cheek with his whiskers. Startled, she turned, smiled.

"Horace, whatever have you and those men been doing for so long in the library? I declare—people were beginning to talk!"

He sat beside her and picked up a leg of pheasant, John Welcher's specialty, the flesh tender and juicy under a crisp brown skin.

"My dear," he smiled, "you know how men are! They love to get together and tell jokes, stories hardly proper for the delicate ears of the ladies! I am afraid we quite forgot the time! I must circulate about and tender my apologies."

———◆———

David Chantry was startled. "Wait a minute," he protested. "Don't leave me now!"

Muttering curses under his breath, Blossom scowled. "No matter what he says," he protested, gesturing toward Big Hail, "them wolves don't belong to *nobody*! I got as much right as anyone!"

An ancient musket was slung over Big Hail's back. He unlimbered it, cocked it. By menacing signs he made it known the wolfer was unwelcome in Oglala territory.

"Damned brutes!" Blossom snarled. "You'd think they owned this country!" Crossing his arms defiantly, he spoke to the Sioux in what David assumed was their own language, a choking sibilant tongue embellished with anger. Finishing, he picked up his Hawken rifle again and growled an aside to David Chantry. "They better not cross *me*, or there'll be trouble! I got friends in high places out here!"

Big Hail was unimpressed. Sitting statuelike on the paint pony, moccasined legs dangling below the animal's belly, he raised his musket and aimed, squinting along the barrel at the wolfer's whiskered face.

"Now, just a minute." Blossom raised a placating hand. "Let's talk this over!"

Big Hail's finger tightened.

"No need to get mad!" the wolfer pleaded. "I like to be friends with the red brothers!"

Big Hail's finger curled around the trigger; the mechanism of the musket squeaked faintly as the pressure grew.

"All right, all right!" Blossom scurried to pick up his effects, throw his packs on the mule, mount the shaggy pony. "God damn it, they don't *want* to be friends! I'll leave, all right, but I won't never forget this!" He turned to David Chantry. "Remember—you owe me seventy-five dollars!"

David was astonished. "But—"

A grinning brave stepped forward and slapped Blossom's Indian pony on the rump. Startled, the beast plunged forward, nearly throwing its rider. Big Hail pulled the trigger. There was an ear-shattering roar, a great plume of smoke, the stench of burned powder. A gout of snow erupted at the pony's heels as it plunged into the cover of a stand of trees. Even after the little train disappeared, they could still hear Blossom cursing steadily at the top of his lungs.

To David Chantry it was all a bad dream. One moment, he had gained a friend and counselor to arrange for him an entry into the Oglala world; the next—he was alone, surrounded by hostile Red Indians.

Big Hail, amused, slung the gun across his back again. David did not know Indians smiled. Trembling and apprehensive, he remained on the step, watching them. They stared back, expectant, waiting—for what, he did not know. There were perhaps a dozen of them, dressed in wild and barbaric clothes that would be exotic in an encyclopedia illustration but were somehow appropriate to the frontier wilderness. They wore shirts of skin, trailing fringes decorated with beads, and quill-like needlework across shoulders and chests. Some had leggings of buckskin with a broad, beaded stripe down the leg. In this winter weather others had bare brown legs and chests, though they wore colored blankets over their backs in a kind of toga style to befit their Roman dignity. One brave sported a leather hat decorated with beads and feathers. Black hair was adorned with eagle feathers at various angles; one man had long braids wrapped in fur.

David cleared his throat. "I am a friend." Remembering Blossom's gestures, he held out his hand, palm up. "How!"

He wondered if they were going to harm him. After all, he had been a friend of the wolfer. They obviously hated Blossom.

"I—I take photographs," he stammered. An idea came to him. "Would you like to see a sample of my work?" Turning suddenly, he entered the interior of the wagon, half expecting to be pierced with an arrow from one of the decorated bows. But they were patiently waiting when he emerged.

"There!" he exclaimed. "How do you like that?" Knee-deep in the snow he waded about, holding up the photographic study of Cassie Garrett, the one he had worked so hard at, trying varying camera angles, differing exposures, new developing solutions, and finally discovering how to tint the lips and cheeks and hair with water colors. He was proud of it, though a paper print could hardly do justice to the major's wife. "I—I want to take pictures of *you* people, if you'll let me," he said, suspecting they understood no English but hoping the earnestness and goodwill of his manner would impress them.

Big Hail took the picture in brown hands and stared at it. He grunted, showed it to another man. Others urged their ponies closer, looking at Cassie Garrett. Cassie was probably not the Sioux ideal of beauty, but perhaps the Oglalas would appreciate workmanship. Or had they never before seen a camera portrait?

"*Pick—sher*." Big Hail nodded.

David was encouraged. "Yes, that's a picture! A photograph!"

"Pick—sher," Big Hail repeated, nodding.

"Be careful with it!" David cautioned. "That's just thin paper, and wrinkles very easily!"

Unnoticed, one of the Oglalas had dismounted and entered the wagon. Now he emerged, dipping a casual hand into a bag of raisins from David Chantry's stores. Others prowled about the wagon, lifting the flaps, staring within. One brave, a large red hand painted on his chest, found David's violin. He squatted in the snow, opening the case. Another man plucked a string and they both jumped at the twang, then laughed uproariously.

"You—make—picksher?" Big Hail inquired.

So Big Hail had a little English! That would make things easier.

"I do, indeed," David admitted. He went to the wagon and got the big red Anthony and Co. camera, setting it on its tripod in the snow. In his preoccupation as photographer he almost forgot to be afraid. It was cold; a gun-metal-gray haze enveloped the sun, and the wind rose, sighing through the pines with a mournful keening. But now he was neither cold nor afraid.

"Look here," he invited, beckoning.

Big Hail slid off the pony, approached warily. He was skittish about having the black cloth placed over his head, but David persuaded him, speaking softly and soothingly as to a child.

"There! See that, on the ground-glass screen? See your pony standing there in the snow?"

Big Hail seemed perplexed. Finally he snatched off the black cloth, grabbed the camera on its tripod and turned the whole assembly upside down, staring again at the glass plate while the legs of the tripod trembled in the air like a gigantic insect.

David understood. "No, no!" he protested, wresting the camera away from Big Hail. "That doesn't do any good! The—the image is just upside down, that's all! It's—well, it's just the law of optics!" He himself was so accustomed to seeing the focused image inverted that it had not occurred to him the Oglala would be startled and attempt to remedy the situation.

Reluctantly Big Hail allowed himself to be coaxed once more under the black cloth. David showed him how to turn the knurled knob to focus the image. "Look how sharp and clear! I know your pony is topside-to, but see how every detail comes through! You can count the hairs in his mane! That camera is the best you can buy! It cost two hundred dollars."

Big Hail happily twisted the knob, entranced by the way the image of the pony swam in and out of focus. He called to the man with the raisins, munching a few himself while his friend played with the knob.

"You see," David explained, "I put a sensitized glass plate in the holder here. Then I take off the lens cap, count two or three or ten or whatever time it takes, and I have a picture. Of course, I've got to develop it! Sulphate-of-iron solution and acetic acid—then wash and fix with cyanide of potassium. It's a tricky process, but no painting can compare with the realism of a photograph!"

Big Hail seemed to understand a great deal of what David said, nodding and grunting, apparently comprehending the connection between the camera on its tripod and the photograph of Cassie Garrett.

"I—me—" He placed a clenched hand against his chest. "You—make picksher—me!"

David shook his head. "I'm afraid that's impossible. It's—well, you see, it's too cold. When the air is this cold, the chemicals don't work right."

Big Hail frowned. He pounded himself on the chest again. "Me." He pointed to the camera sitting on its tripod in the snow. "Picksher!" He waved the portrait of Cassie and thumped his chest again. "Make picksher of me!"

The rest, attracted by Big Hail's loud voice, clustered about. The man with the raisins chewed steadily; the bag was almost empty. The warrior with the violin stopped plucking the strings. They looked from Big Hail to David Chantry, then back again.

"But I can't—"

Big Hail's gesture was so imperious, so commanding, the scowl so ferocious, that there was no remedy for it. Indians, David remembered from his brief study before coming out to the Territory, could be mercurial. Friendship quickly evaporated when passion surged into savage breasts.

"I—I'll try," he agreed.

While they waited, squatting in the snow, he went into the wagon and prepared the glass plate. Though he was expert at the task, his fingers trembled. Taking an eight-by-ten plate from its storage box, he carefully cleaned it. Mixing a batch of collodion in a tray, he measured out the excitants—the bromides and iodides of potassium—and added them to the syrupy collodion evaporated to the right degree of stickiness. Then he lowered the plate into the silver-nitrate solution to create the proper light-sensitive condition. With bated breath, mindful of Mr. Vannerson's repeated warning that the very slightest breath might carry enough "poison" across the plate to make it produce a blank spot, he finally tested the edge of the plate with his finger and found the collodion set. Sliding the prepared plate into its holder, he climbed from the wagon.

"Please stand there," he instructed Big Hail, pulling the black cloth about his shoulders.

The Oglala warrior's figure was proud and erect on the glass focusing screen, coming into sharp focus as David adjusted the knurled brass knob. Big Hail was certainly six feet in height, almost as tall as David Chantry, and sinewy and muscular. The features were prominent, sharp, and regular; cheekbones high, lips thin and severe. Scars of some sort—perhaps from the tortures of the Sun

Dance David had read about—were prominent on his upper arms and chest, revealed where the Oglala had thrown back the scarlet blanket. Big Hail stood gracefully, one foot slightly before the other, musket cradled in his arm. However the portrait turned out, the subject was magnificent. David felt a thrill of excitement as he removed the lens cap and counted.

One. . . . Two. . . . Three. . . .

Gray light could fool a photographer. Sometimes the harsh overcast affected a photographic plate more than bright sunlight.

Four. . . . Five. . . . Six. . . .

His whispered numbers kept pace with the dull thudding of his heart. He did not want to overexpose, yet there had to be sufficient light to bring out the image.

Seven. . . . Eight. . . . Nine. . . .

A load of snow slid from a branch. Somewhere a jay scolded.

Ten. . . . Eleven. . . .

At twelve he stopped, replaced the lens cap, emerged blinking into the hard daylight. Making reassuring motions to Big Hail, he clambered into the wagon and submerged the plate in developing solution. Washing and fixing it, he opened the curtains and held the plate up to the light.

Disaster! The plate was fogged! Perhaps there had been too much light in the wagon. Perhaps the chemicals had been too cold. Perhaps he had inadvertently "poisoned" the plate. Whatever had been the cause, the developed plate showed only a faint, patchy luminance.

For a long time he sat in the wagon, staring at the ruined plate. What an opportunity lost! If only he had been able to show Big Hail his picture, the Indian's own portrait! That might have insured his entry into the Oglala camp, perhaps even as a person of importance. But now—

"Eh?" He looked up as the wagon canvas was lifted. Savage faces were all around him, staring, inquisitive. Big Hail reached within. "Picksher?"

David shook his head. "It didn't work out. The chemicals were too cold—or something."

Big Hail held out his hand. "Picksher!" His voice was imperious, demanding.

Listlessly David handed over the fogged plate. Big Hail stared, turned it over to inspect the back, reversed it again. His visage darkened; the thin brows drew together.

"No picksher!"

David agreed. "It didn't come out. I'm sorry!"

Big Hail raised the glass plate high above his head and smashed it on the iron wagon step.

"No picksher!" he howled. "Where picksher?"

"Listen," David pleaded. "I'm sorry, very sorry! These things happen sometimes! If we were in the city, in a proper studio—"

The Oglalas became ugly. Taking a cue from Big Hail the rest of the band prowled about him, making menacing motions, pulling at his clothing, shoving him. The man with the raisins dropped the empty bag, unsheathed a knife, held it near David Chantry's throat. Big Hail himself spat into the snow, cocked his musket, scowled.

David was a sophisticated young man. He had been to college, slept with women, had already fought an abortive duel. He knew that many of the things valued by men were not worth valuing. But two things were important to him: the Confederate States of America and his reputation as a photographer.

"If you came to me at my studio at home," he insisted, "I'd give you your money back! What do you expect me to do now? I told you —these things happen sometimes to the best of photographers!"

The raisin eater pricked David's chest with the blade of his knife. David pushed the man's hand away in annoyance. He had always had a temper—perhaps his childish frustration by Wade had nurtured it—and he felt his face flushing.

"What do you expect—miracles?" Professional pride stung, he railed at them. "Julian Vannerson himself couldn't work with cold chemicals!" They had barged into his camp, eaten all his raisins, pawed his violin and probably damaged it—now they were criticizing his photography. "Give me that!" he demanded, snatching his violin from the hands of the startled brave. When the man snarled and drew a feathered hatchet from his belt, David suddenly recalled epithets learned from a sergeant of Jo Shelby's cavalry. In utter frustration at their unreasonableness he embarked on a string of curses, delivered almost like an incantation.

Mouths open, the Oglalas stared at him. Probably they believed him taken with a fit of madness. One man made an uneasy gesture as if warding off an evil spirit. Big Hail himself looked uncertain. The muzzle of his musket sagged; his glance wavered. Finally, almost spent, David paused. Surprised by the effect his profanity had produced, he came at last to see that they were cowed.

"That's better!" he snapped. "Now, if you'll just give me another chance—"

He hurried to the wagon. Carefully he repeated the lengthy preparation of the glass plate, cautious to divert his breath from the sensitized surface. When he came out again, clutching the plate in its holder against his chest to warm it, Big Hail was standing puzzled and motionless in the snow, watching him. The other braves crowded around Big Hail as if to draw some assurance from mutual proximity.

"Stand there," David ordered, pointing.

Big Hail complied.

Taking off the lens cap, David counted again. Replacing the cap, he hurried back into the wagon, slid the glass plate from the holder and into the developing bath. Washing and fixing, he opened the canvas flap to look at the negative image by daylight.

Beautiful! This time, everything had come out as it should! The little group filled the scene. Sharp and clear the images stood out— Big Hail in the center, face anxious and a little uncertain, the rest of the band gathered around like a family portrait of a Biloxi planter, all leaning slightly toward the center of the photograph, craning their necks at the camera. Elated, he slipped a piece of black cardboard behind the glass plate to give the proper reversal to a positive image and stepped down from the wagon.

"Picksher?" Big Hail's voice was almost polite.

David handed him the photograph. "It's still a little damp—be careful! Hold it by the edge, like this."

There was a muffled chorus of exclamation. One man's mouth dropped open; he put his hand quickly over it as if to prevent the entry of some white man's devil. Big Hail's eyes widened. He held the picture stiffly, at arm's length, almost as if it might sting him.

"Look there!" David pointed out the sharp detail of a string of beads, quills on a jacket, the detailed lock mechanism of Big Hail's musket, feathery outlines of pine boughs behind. "Now, that's photography, fellows! That's what a two-hundred-dollar Anthony camera can do!"

The Oglalas were entranced. By gestures they made David Chantry know they were inviting him to their camp. He hitched up Nig and Pansy; Big Hail's band tried to help him but the mules were skittish of Indians. Packing things away, he mounted the high seat. They drove away across the ice of the river, the little group escorting him in a triumphal entry into the Oglala camp, Big Hail riding before with the picksher carried like a totem.

CHAPTER THREE

Their quarters at Fort Zachary Taylor were crude, hammered together of whipsawed cottonwood logs, and not at all befitting a lieutenant colonel. The house was *certainly* not appropriate for the commanding officer. Cassie had tried to persuade Owen to have additional rooms built by the post carpenter, but her husband was too busy with treaty plans to listen to her, to look at her penciled sketches. The treaty, always the treaty! She was tired of hearing about the damned treaty! Plans for the forthcoming talks took all his time, every day and far into the evening, though the meetings with the hostile tribes were not scheduled until late spring at the earliest. Now, in the bleak dawn of a winter morning, Cassie Garrett lay in the big brass bed they had brought from their last duty station, in Columbus, Ohio, and listened to Owen snore. Did all men snore? It was not an attractive sound.

Even when the bugle blew reveille, Owen did not awake. He was exhausted, she knew, but she desperately wanted to talk to someone. In Columbus, at least there had been parties, dancing, the buzz and hum of conversation laced with gossip. Though Columbus *was* a bit provincial after their tour of duty at the War Department in Washington, the Ohio capital was preferable to this bleak frontier post with its stockade of cottonwood logs, endless vistas of snow, and only the village of Elk City on the frozen Yellowstone for shopping and social contact, limited as was the selection of both.

Gray light leaked through lace-curtained windows. She had brought the curtains from Columbus, too; every amenity had to be shipped in, by steamboat in summer, in winter by Diamond R ox teams toiling over the frozen landscape from Omaha. Carefully, so as not to disturb Owen, she stood up, yawning and stretching like a cat.

It was cold in the room. A rime of ice veiled the window, but she was still warm from the heavy buffalo robe they slept under. Standing before the pier glass, she turned this way and that, examining her outline, arms gracefully over her head so her breasts showed— fetchingly, she thought—under the flowered flannel shift. She twisted her body again, watching the breasts press delicately against the thin fabric. They were her best feature, really, but since he was wounded Owen often did not notice her for weeks. In a sudden effort to reassure herself, she pulled the shift over her head and stood naked before the mirror.

She was a little tall for a woman, she had to admit that, but she and Owen made a handsome couple. Her face she had always considered aristocratic, in spite of her youthful poverty as Cassandra Sadler. The large, blue eyes were set well apart, cheekbones high, the lips wide and full perhaps, but disciplined. Her shoulders were somewhat narrow for the broad and fecund hips, but she prided herself on the twenty-two-inch waist, the slender legs, the narrow and well-formed feet. Smiling at her image, reassured, she postured and pirouetted before the mirror until she began to shiver. Quickly she pulled out a drawer in search of her robe, washed only yesterday by the Indian woman. Trembling with the chill, she found it and snatched it out, only to have the damned little derringer pistol fall out, too, thumping on the floor. Owen was a fanatic about guns. He had guns, which were a mystery to her, all over the house in racks and chests and standing in corners. Horses and guns, horses and guns—that was all he ever seemed interested in! She hated guns, but Owen insisted she keep the short-barreled derringer close at hand. "For," he explained, "this is the frontier, Cassie, and violence is apt to be a much closer neighbor that it was in Columbus." Holding the pistol gingerly between thumb and forefinger, she dropped it back among her underthings and hurried into the makeshift lean-to off the bedroom to make her toilette with a basin of warm water brought by the Indian woman.

At breakfast Private Dobbs, the terrierlike enlisted man detailed as cook, groom, butler, and general factotum to the commanding officer's household, brought her fried meat and warm biscuits and coffee, along with a jar of wild-sage honey traded from the Rees, who hung around the post.

"Thank you, Dobbs," Cassie murmured. She did not favor the heavily floured side meat, but ate a mouthful to please the gray old man. Crippled by rheumatism, Dobbs was to be discharged, unable to stand the winter rigors of Fort Taylor. "I will want you," Cassie told him, folding her napkin, "to bring around the cutter in a half hour. I am going in to Elk City to buy a few things this morning."

Dobbs raised thatched eyebrows toward the bedroom.

"The colonel is very tired," Cassie said. "He will probably be getting up soon. Leave coffee for him, and I will write a little note."

Elk City was not large, but it was lively in a vulgar way. On the Yellowstone, between O'Fallon Creek and the Powder River, it lay on the wagon road leading eastward. When the river was free from ice, the paddle-wheel steamboats—the *F. Y. Batchelor, Key West, Peninah, Josephine*—brought in freight from St. Louis and the East, returning downriver with deckloads of hides and robes. That was the good time for Cassie; evenings visiting with Owen in the grand saloon of the *F. Y. Batchelor* and the *Peninah*, listening to band concerts on the parade ground, buying such long-denied luxuries as laces and ribbons and face powder come up on the boats. But in winter Boreas laid his icy hand on the Territory. Few bull trains cared to risk the arduous passage to Elk City. There was not enough money in it, they said. That was true; there was not enough anything in Elk City to please Cassie's cosmopolitan tastes.

The town sprawled along the frozen Yellowstone, a huddle of raw-wood storefronts, shacks, tumble-down lean-tos—even tents. Whatever else Elk City lacked, there seemed always, even in the dead of winter, plenty of rum, beer, and whiskey. Dance halls, saloons, and hurdy-gurdies flourished for the entertainment of the soldiers, trappers, and the miners who only last fall had discovered promising "color," as they called it, in the sands of Big Dry Creek.

The population, exclusive of the soldiers at Fort Taylor, was six hundred and eighty. Though the wants of the citizens were simple, Elk City now boasted a hotel of wood salvaged from the wreck of the *Eliza Tate*, a bank, a wagon builder, two Chinese laundries, a general mercantile store, and a brewery offering in the Elk City *Gazette* ". . . beer absolutely free from drugs and adulterations."

Leaving Dobbs to wait in the cutter, Cassie bought a tortoise-shell comb in Riker's Mercantile, along with two pounds of precious onions—Owen loved buffalo-hump steak with fried onions—and a tin dipper to replace the rusted one in the kitchen.

Hands in her muff, precariously balancing the sack across her arms, she stepped out onto the boardwalk. The day was cold and gray, the thermometer hovering at only a few degrees above zero. During the night, snow on the walk had frozen into rippled ice. Vision obscured by the sack in her arms, Cassie caught the heel of her boot on the step and toppled forward. Trying to regain her balance, she sprawled headlong on the frozen boards. The little fur hat she so fancied sailed in one direction, a torrent of onions in the other; the dipper and muff departed she knew not where. Furious, she muttered an obscenity.

"Ma'am, are you all right?" A whiskered drover helped her to her feet.

"Mr. Riker," she said through set teeth, "will have that walk cleared of ice by noon today, or my husband will declare his store off limits to military personnel!"

"Yes'm," an off-duty corporal agreed, handing her the fur hat. "Yes, indeed, Miz Garrett."

Someone else retrieved the onions and put them back into the sack. Old Dobbs, from afar seeing her fall, hurried through the icy muck of River Street and tried to take the sack of onions, but a tall man in a bearskin coat held on to them, saying in a gentle drawl, "Mrs. Garrett, I sure do hope you haven't hurt yourself, ma'am."

Surprised, she looked up. The stranger, bulky in the bearskin coat, with sweeping blond mustaches and gentian-blue eyes, smiled.

"Mr.—Mr.—"

The mustache was new to her, and under the earflapped cap the blond hair was long and shaggy. His cheeks were raw and red, with peeling skin that must have been frostbite. But a great surge of recognition welled in her.

"David!" Quickly she looked around. Dobbs was retrieving the dipper. "Mr. Chantry!"

He continued to regard her with that gentle smile. Her heart lifted. David Chantry! It had been a long time.

"It's you," she said softly. "What in heaven's name brought you here? However did you come to Elk City, in this frozen waste?"

Chantry relinquished the sack of onions to Dobbs and accompanied her back to the cutter. "I knew you and the colonel were here. I read it in the *Army and Navy Register*." After the surprise of their encounter, he was again the diffident and awkward young man; she wondered if some of the tint in his cheeks was not the blushing she used to tease him about when the towheaded young Confederate prisoner had been assigned to the Garretts' big house on Third Street in Columbus to take care of the gardening. David Chantry's behavior in prison had been so model that Owen Garrett did not hesitate to recommend him as a trusty.

"But I—I never figured to run into you this way, ma'am," he went on. "Are you sure you didn't hurt yourself? That was a nasty fall."

Stopping before the cutter, she looked down. "Perhaps I bruised my knee a little, but it's nothing serious. I'll have Dr. Symonds at the post look at it when I get home."

At the mention of her knee, he did indeed blush. Even in their closest moments David had always been uneasy at mention of a lady's anatomy. Did not southern ladies have knees? she had once asked him. At his confusion she laughed, the deep hearty laugh the Sadlers had. Laughter was about all the Sadlers had owned. There certainly wasn't any money in the family, at least not until she married Owen Garrett.

"But tell me—what *are* you doing in Elk City?"

"After they let me out of the State Penitentiary, when I signed the oath of allegiance to the North," he explained, "a man called Horace Kinnear—he publishes the *Illustrated Weekly News*—hired me."

"I know Horace," she said quickly. "We used to go to parties at his house on Rock Creek when Owen and I were at the War Department."

"He wanted a photographer," David went on, "to come out to the Territory and do studies of the Oglala Sioux, their way of life, their customs, the children, how they built lodges. He's very interested in primitive man. Well, he saw some of my pictures and liked them and commissioned me. That's it, I guess."

It began to snow, a soft feathery sprinkle. The sky darkened. Lamps winked on in the stores and shops and gaming houses, though it was not yet noon.

"There aren't any Oglala Sioux in Elk City," she pointed out. "Why, then—"

"I've spent the last month or two with Big Hail, down on the Tongue, maybe thirty miles south of here. Got some good photographs, too. But I ran out of chemicals. In October I tried to drive across Clear Fork in my wagon and the ford was deeper than I thought. A lot of my bromides were spoiled. So I rode all the way into Elk City to pick up a shipment supposed to come in on the stage last week."

"You rode all that way in this weather?"

He shrugged. "It was no lark, but Big Hail gave me an Indian pony that's a marvel! Star Boy reminds me of the Morgans my father used to raise at Big Oaks."

"Where are you staying?" she asked.

"I've been at Dooley's Hotel. But if I can locate my chemicals I'm going back to Big Hail's camp in the morning."

"Why, you'll *freeze!*" His cap was already high-piled with snow; it lay on the blond mustache, the uncut curling hair. His hair, she recalled, had been shining and golden. Now it was weather-bleached and unkempt. "You mustn't think of it!"

He grinned. "Star Boy travels through snow like a catfish in the Mississippi!"

"At least you mustn't leave without coming out to see me and Owen! He'll remember you, I know. He's busy all day—every day, it seems—with plans for the big treaty meeting this summer. But come to supper, *do!*"

David did not remember Owen Garrett being particularly fond of him in Columbus, but Mrs. Garrett had been kind, very kind. Though he was anxious to locate Benjamin Sears and get the chemicals and his latest instructions from the Council, there was the matter of courtesy to be considered. Too, a visit to the commandant's house might yield a few crumbs of information about the government's plans for the treaty, something the Council might be interested in.

"Well?" Her eyes sparkled. She stood on tiptoe with excitement. "Say you will, David!"

It had been a long time since anyone had called him David. At home, at Big Oaks, everyone knew him as David; at least those who didn't simply identify him as Wade Chantry's little brother.

"All right," he agreed. "I'll come."

"At six, then! Owen may not be home till later. But I have an Indian woman who takes care of the house, and Private Dobbs, in the cutter there, does all the cooking, so we shall be properly chaperoned until Owen comes home."

"Yes, ma'am."

"You don't know how people gossip in this miserable little frontier town. And an army post is *always* a hotbed of rumor!"

"Yes, ma'am," he said again. "Until tonight, then."

Dobbs took her elbow, helped her into the cutter. In the feathery downpour they drove away, runners squeaking in the snow, team breathing clouds of steam. He watched them go until the cutter veered off River Street and took the road to the post, lined now with leafless cottonwoods, stark and bare.

Going back to the hotel, he dined on venison chops and boiled beans and corn bread. Mrs. Major Garrett! Mrs. Colonel Garrett now; of all people! For a long time he sat in what passed for the lobby of Dooley's Hotel, reminiscing. He was sure his assignment to the Garretts' big house had been her doing. Mrs. Garrett had at first frightened him with her free-and-easy ways, her generosity to a prisoner. Mrs. Garrett was blond and vivacious. Columbus gossip whispered she led the sobersided Major Owen Garrett a merry chase before he managed to slip a ring on her pretty finger. Before, he thought pleasurably, and after, too.

He found himself becoming annoyed with Sears, or whatever the man's name was. Smoking the thin cigar the doctors had forbidden, he scowled through the smoke. His cipher instructions from the Council required him to put up at the hotel and wait for Sears to approach him. There was a password and other mumbo jumbo. But the stage had arrived the day before. So far, no Sears had appeared on the scene.

Drumming on the arm of his chair, he stared out the window. Through the streets ox teams toiled, wheels crunching in liquid muck slowly turning to iron-hard ice. Soldiers in buffalo coats and fur caps, mufflers wrapped around ears, strolled about, planning the evening's rowdiness. A grizzled trapper with a pack-mule load of pelts plodded by; a gaggle of the harmless Rees, wrapped in blankets, stood like statues against the weathered buildings. The snow had stopped; it was now probably too cold to snow.

Opening the door of the potbellied stove, the hotel swamper shoved in an oaken billet and clanged shut the door. In the iron echo of the sound David heard a man's voice raised in what sounded like a Hindoo chant. The cry was high-pitched and nasal, exhortatory.

". . . and that same loving Jesus can save you, too, friends, just like he saved me, a miserable sinner!"

Intrigued, David put on his coat, walked outside. On a wooden box stood an itinerant preacher, haranguing the Rees, who stared back with opaque eyes.

"I tell you—throw away your savage gods! Accept the Lord in your hearts, come to know His love and His forgiveness for all the dirty tricks you undoubtedly done in your lifetime, like scalping your enemies and eating their giblets!"

Passers-by paused to listen, grinning and whispering to each other. A weaving farrier sergeant called out, "Hallelujah, Rev! Tell 'em all about hell-fire and damnation!" Jostling and pushing, the good-natured crowd pressed close as David approached.

"That's right!" the evangelist cried. "That's the Lord's very truth! Fire and brimstone, that's what's waiting on them careless souls that don't heed the warning!"

The preacher was a young man, tall and ungainly in a rusty black coat, with a thatch of blue-black hair under a shapeless black hat with a broad brim. His jaw was long and bony, and there was a mad and gleeful look in his eye.

"But never say the Lord ain't merciful! His mercy lays all around us, like the snow in these here streets! And be you white or black or red or green, he's willing to fold you in his ever-loving arms, no matter how black and stinking your soul!"

"Amen!" someone shouted.

The preacher looked at David Chantry. His eyelid suddenly lowered with a prodigious wink.

"Yes, sir, and yes, ma'am—it don't signify a bit whether you're drunkard or Temperance, Republican or Democrat, Union soldier or in Confederate gray—"

David worked the remnant of cigar around his lips, watching, listening.

"YOU CAN BE SAVED!"

With his bony-fingered hand the preacher made an almost imperceptible gesture toward David Chantry. David nodded, ground out the cigar butt in the mud, and sauntered back to the Dooley Hotel. Later, in almost full dark, the preacher threw open the door and stamped in, scraping mud from his boots. Seeing David in the seat-sprung leather chair, feet on the hob of the stove, he bustled over, drawing long knitted gloves from chapped hands.

"The Lord's grace to you, mister! Ain't it one hell of a day?"

David looked up from his newspaper. He paused a long moment before speaking. Then he said, "The storm is rising."

"True, true!" The preacher unbuttoned his coat, blew on his fingers, flipped coattails and exposed his lean backside to the cherry-red stove. "It will blow away a lot of things before it's over."

Nodding cheerily to the desk clerk, the preacher clumped up the stairs, across the balcony, and turned a corner into a dark hall. After a seemly interval David rose, stretched, folded his paper, and followed the preacher, pausing to say to the indifferent clerk, "Guess I'll take a little snooze before supper."

In the dark hallway the preacher waited for him. "Benjie Sears," he said, shaking hands. He turned the key in the lock and they went in, Sears pausing to strike a match and light a coal-oil lamp. Hurrying to the window, he drew the tattered curtains.

"So you're Chantry."

"That's right."

In the yellow glow of the lamp, Benjie Sears looked even younger. There was a wisp of black beard; David suspected Benjie did not yet even shave.

"Where in the hell have you been?" David demanded. "I've been cooling my heels for two days!"

Benjie chuckled. "Been about my preaching! After all, I got to get into practice, don't I? Mr. Kinnear said I was to be extra-careful, make sure folks accepted me as a real man of the cloth before I took off to minister to the Cheyennes!" Reaching into a pocket, he brought out a sealed envelope. "These here are your latest instructions from the Council."

Still annoyed, David slipped the envelope into a coat pocket.

"I must say you don't make a very convincing minister. You don't convince *me*."

Benjie chuckled again. "I don't have to convince *you!* You look like a gentleman, Mr. Chantry. All I got to convince is these roughnecks and chuckleheads and Red Indians out here."

"You're pretty young," David said doubtfully.

"Twenty-three," Benjie said, "and old for my age." Digging into a brass-cornered trunk, he brought out a bottle. "Hell, I seen the devil and been rode by witches already! But I got to warm up gradual to my preaching; I do better that way. In seminary, old Dr. Vowles always said I was a real stem-winder once I got started. When they throwed me out of seminary, found that silly girl in my room, old Vowles cried. Said if the devil hadn't cotched my coattails, I'd of been the everlasting pride of the Blood of the Lamb Seminary and Christian Agricultural College!"

David sipped the proffered bourbon whiskey. "You sound like a heathen to me!"

Benjie was delighted. "I am, I am!"

"How did you ever come to attend seminary?"

Benjie gulped the whiskey, quickly poured himself another. "We was nineteen in our family—ten boys and nine girls." He giggled. "Pa always read the Good Book, and where it said 'Be ye fruitful and multiply' he didn't just multiply—he squared and cubed his brats!"

David declined another drink.

"Pa and Ma," Benjie went on, "they took their savings—they worked for Mr. Kinnear on his farm most of their lives—and sent me to seminary. They hoped I'd amount to something, where the others wasn't likely to." A shadow crossed his face. "I was sorry to be throwed out of seminary—sorry for Pa and Ma, that is, not for me. Anyway. . . ." He downed the rest of his drink. "Now I figure to make me some money and pay Pa and Ma back for their bad investment. Pa, I mean. Ma died." He stared into the lamp, momentarily sober. "Maybe do a little something in memory of Buck and Elrod and Jim Will, too." He glanced at David. "They were my brothers. They was already killed in this damned war that nobody except old Lincoln wants."

"I'm sorry," David said.

Benjie sighed, shrugged. "Well, how's things going with my brother agent?"

"Fair," David admitted. "I got along pretty well with Big Hail, down on the Tongue. Got his people stirred up a little, hope for bigger things soon. I learned some of the lingo, too; kind of feeling my way along."

"I admire anyone can speak languages," Benjie said.

"Next stop for me is Ghost Bull's camp, on the Powder. He's the big nibs around here, I guess. All the Oglalas listen when he talks."

Benjie rummaged in the trunk, brought out a box of green and brown bottles wrapped in straw. "Looks like they're in pretty good shape," he volunteered, passing them to David.

David held the bottles to the lamp one by one to examine the liquids, the crystals, the powders. "This ought to put me back in business," he said. "For a while, at least."

Benjie grinned wryly. He held up his Bible. "There was plenty of room in my old trunk for your stuff. This is about all my baggage, except for another collar and some socks, though the Council told me there'd be a shipment waiting for me at the Diamond R freight office." He pulled the cork out of the bottle. "Have another swaller! It's a cold night out."

David shook his head. Carefully he repacked the bottles in the straw, wrapped twine tightly around the box. "I've been in here with you too long already. Someone might be watching us."

Benjie took another drink. "Spies watching spies?"

David was annoyed at his levity. "A person can't be too careful. This is a high-stakes game we're playing, remember that!"

In spite of his brashness, Benjie Sears seemed reluctant to see David leave. "Well," he said, shaking hands, "I been glad to meet you, Mr. Chantry. See you in Washington when old Robert E. Lee marches in, eh?"

In the hallway David paused, looked around. Nothing. From

below he could hear the room clerk telling a raucous joke. A man laughed; a piano tinkled. The tinny noise ceased when the door slammed shut. Everything was business as usual in Elk City. No one suspected a Copperhead plot.

With a selection of Oglala photographs on albumenized paper to give a pleasing sepia tint, David Chantry rode out to Fort Zachary Taylor on his Indian pony. The commandant's house of sawed lumber had a wreath of green boughs and red berries on the door. When he knocked, an Indian woman came to the door and ushered him into the parlor. In a corner was a small Christmas tree festooned with strings of popcorn and paper cutouts of angels. A cheery fire burned on the hearth of the stone fireplace. The Indian woman lit a lamp. While she padded away to call Cassie and the colonel, David wandered about the room, stopping before the Brady photograph of the couple on their wedding day, taken in Brady's own studio on the Avenue in Washington. With professional interest he examined the work. Owen sat, dour and inflexible, head clamped in the Brady "immobilizer." Cassie, blond and beautiful in her white gown, held a bouquet of roses. It had been a June wedding.

"Mr. Chantry!"

He turned, took her hand in his.

"Owen," she said, "here's David Chantry, come all the way out to the wild frontier!"

Garrett, chewing on a cigar, shook hands with David. He was much as David remembered: thickset, with bowed cavalry legs in shiny boots, heavy black brows, and the short determined nose of the Irishman.

"Good to see you again, Chantry. Cassie, here, tells me you've come out to the Territory to take pictures for Horace Kinnear."

"That's right, sir."

Mrs. Garrett made a little face, waved a lacy handkerchief at the colonel's cigar. "He *will* insist on smoking, though I've told him countless times it yellows the curtains!" They sat down, Garrett in a sagging leather chair, Mrs. Garrett perched on a hassock, David at one end of a flowered wicker settee that had seen better days. Cassie laughed. "It's not much but it's home now!"

The Indian woman silently brought a tray with whiskey and some glasses. The colonel poured, and Mrs. Garrett handed David a drink. "And what do you have in that package, David?"

He unwrapped it. "Some of my pictures. I thought you and the colonel would be interested to see how the Oglalas live in their winter camps. I don't mind telling you—since I've lived at Big Hail's camp I've gotten quite fond of the Oglalas, really. They've been very hospitable to me, and their customs are fascinating. I'm studying their language, especially the beautiful *wibluta*—the hand language."

Colonel Garrett seemed bored but his wife was encouraging. "Yes, indeed—do let's see them! Owen, pull your chair a little closer and put out that frightful cigar!"

She came to sit beside David on the sofa as he held the paper prints close to the round wick of the Argand lamp. "This," he explained, "is a panoramic view of Big Hail's village on the Tongue River. This next one is his lodge—his *tipi*, as they call it. Next to it is the one where Rain Coming, the shaman, talks to the spirits— makes magic powders and brews drafts and prays to the gods for good hunting and things like that. Now, here's a picture of some kids playing on the ice of the Tongue. Do you know—they make sleds out of buffalo rib bones! And here's Deer Woman. She's one of Big Hail's wives."

Mrs. Garrett was shocked, or pretended to be. Archly she asked, "You mean they have more than one wife—like the sultans in Turkey?"

"They're savages, Cassie," Owen Garrett grunted.

David smiled. "Sometimes they have three or four, depending on how many they can support."

"And what is this picture?" Cassie touched the print with a delicate fingernail.

"I took that one at night. It was a difficult job, technically speaking. I exposed it for over three minutes." The scene was a picture of the Indian camp, a low moon caught in the branches of the snow-laden trees. "You know," he mused, "it's actually beautiful. I mean— look how the camera caught the fires in the lodges shining through the skins, and the tipis glow like big candles! At night Big Hail's camp seems almost—almost like a fairyland!"

Garrett fidgeted. "It's well to remember they're not exactly little elves in gingerbread houses, Chantry! They're dangerous people, bloodthirsty people! That's why I'm assigned out here to keep the peace, stop the God-damned traders from selling them guns to work their mischief, breaking my butt to keep some crazy medicine man like Rain Coming from getting the tribes all upset and onto the war-path! The Army needs every man it can spare to fight the War in the East!"

"Yes, sir," David agreed. "You're absolutely right, Colonel. I'm aware of the potential danger. Sometimes the most beautiful things can be the most deadly." Carefully he stacked the prints, slid them back into their wrappings. "Let's hope you're successful, Colonel."

He hoped to elicit some comment from Garrett about the treaty prospects, but Mrs. Garrett interrupted, poking him with her fan. "Don't be so formal, David! Call him Owen, as I do! I'm sure he won't mind! We're all friends here, old friends."

Private Dobbs came in, awkward in dress blues, to announce supper.

"There's pork," Mrs. Garrett beamed, "with applesauce! Creamed onions, too, and a dried-apple pie for dessert!"

"We don't usually eat this high on the hog," Owen said dryly. "But Cassie was anxious to please you."

While they dined they talked of many things. Cassie remembered with pleasure the huge farmers' market on Third Street in Columbus: mounds of yellow cheeses and squash and fresh berries dew-wet from the country. Colonel Garrett recalled his duty on General Sheridan's staff. "You know," he said, "Phil Sheridan was from Ohio; born in Somerset. Knew Phil when he was only a quarter-master officer in Missouri."

He poured wine for them. Mrs. Garrett drank hers quickly. "Do you still play the violin?" she asked David.

"A little," he admitted.

"Sorry we don't have a fiddle here," the colonel said, and did not seem sorry at all. He poured more wine while Mrs. Garrett signaled Dobbs to bring dessert and coffee.

"And Franklin Park, out on the East Side." She smiled. "Ah, the picnics we used to have there! But there are no parks in the Territory! A person is afraid to go to the countryside for fear of the hostiles—the Indians."

When a knock sounded at the outer door, Dobbs left his station, soon returned with a folded sheet of paper. "Telegraph message, come from Department for you, sir."

Garrett read the message, sighed, folded his napkin. "I'm afraid, Cassie, I'll have to leave for a while. This is from the Department of the Missouri, and ought to be answered at once."

She frowned, tapped a wine glass with her folded fan. "Owen, I *don't* think it's right for you to leave Mr. Chantry and me and hurry down to headquarters this evening! After all, we haven't seen David for a long time!"

"But—"

"Have Dobbs tell the orderly you'll be down later, after dinner." Her cheeks were touched with color. "I don't see how an hour or so can make all that difference!"

"Cassie—"

"I have hardly seen you at all lately, much less to dine together like civilized people. And we *have* a guest."

David was uncomfortable. "Really," he murmured, "it's getting late, ma'am. I've got a long ride back to Big Hail's camp in the morning. Perhaps I'd just better—"

"You will stay," she said, leaning forward and putting her hand on his. Her eyes were bright. "Owen and I have our duty as hosts— don't we, Owen?"

The colonel nodded to Dobbs, and the old soldier shuffled back into the hall to bear the message.

The pie was good. "Our Indian woman," Cassie explained, "is not a cook but a maid. However, Dobbs is quite expert; he used once to work in a restaurant in Chicago. When he retires, next fall, we shall be sorry to lose him."

Owen Garrett, moodily champing a fresh cigar, said, "I hear your brother Wade distinguished himself again at Fredericksburg. His cavalry gave that old fuddy-duddy Burnside a buffeting." He blew a reflective smoke ring, ignoring Cassie's disapproving stare. "Wade Chantry is a good cavalryman—maybe a great cavalryman, almost of Jackson's stature. I only wish he was on the Union side, damn it!"

David nodded. "Even though I signed the oath and consider myself a Northerner, I'm proud of Wade. I only wish I had been there, at Fredericksburg, to take a photograph of him."

"Photographs are all right," the colonel said heavily, "but I prefer a good painting. There's something missing in a photograph. No color, no appearance of life, no real beauty—just a record, you might say. At least, that's my opinion."

"A lot of people agree with you," David said politely. "A certain critic once called photographs '. . . something painted by the sun without instruction in art.' But we're just beginning, you know. Someday there may be photographs to compare with the old masters: Rembrandt, Rubens, Raphael. Color photographs, perhaps —actual colors, pink cheeks, a red shawl, green grass, the colors in the setting sun."

The colonel was tired of polite conversation. "Cassie," he said, pushing back his chair, "I've got to go! That was an important dispatch and can't wait much longer." While Mrs. Garrett pouted, he gave David a firm handshake. "Sorry about this. Meant, actually, to spend a quiet evening at home for once. But duty calls—it always does, it seems."

With her husband gone, Mrs. Garrett signaled the Indian woman to clear the dishes. Private Dobbs remained mutely in the corner, staring straight ahead.

"In Washington," she said, "Mr. Brady, whom Owen and I got to know quite well, had occasional showings—exhibitions—at his salon on the Avenue. David, your photographs are so beautiful, so unusual —why couldn't you do the same thing right here in Elk City? Perhaps arrange it with Mr. Dooley at the hotel? I'm sure he would let you have a showing in the hotel."

He sipped a blackberry cordial. "I don't know—"

Again her hand touched his. It was warm, vibrant. "But you must! You can't imagine how tiresome life is here! No dances, no parties, no fun! It's as dull as ditchwater! Say you'll do it, pray! The officers from the post and their wives would come—every woman here is as bored as I am—and we could have a reception, with champagne from St. Louis, and a tea dance afterward, honoring the distinguished photographer Mr. David Chantry—" She threw back her head and laughed. "Why, it would be the social event of the year!" Cheeks flushed, bosom rising and falling under the lace ruching, her eyes sparkled. She drank more cordial. "Say you'll do it next time you come to town!"

At this early stage of his mission, he did not want to attract attention, and so demurred. "I'm hardly well enough known for that, ma'am."

"Think about it!" She glanced at Dobbs. The old soldier swayed slightly on his feet, appearing to have gone to sleep. The Indian woman had gone into the kitchen. "Think about it," she repeated. She pressed his hand hard. "David, you are too modest about your gifts!"

Later, Private Dobbs helped him into the bearskin coat, went around to fetch Star Boy from the stable. They stood together for a moment on the porch of the commandant's quarters. Winter-killed plants were brown and sere in hanging pots. From the parade ground came the muted and mournful whisper of taps. Cassie Garrett stared at the brooding bulk of the Wolf Mountains, the range the Oglalas called the *Chetish*.

"It's so lonely here," she sighed. "Sometimes I wish even for Columbus, provincial as *that* was!"

Feeling uncomfortable, he looked into his fur cap. "Ma'am, you're a soldier's wife, and a good one too, I'm sure. I know it's hard, but you're bound to be a credit to the colonel. It helps, you know, to have a—a—"

When he paused she looked at him, eyes searching.

"I mean—" he stammered. "I mean—well, it helps to have a *pretty* wife, like you! In promotions, I mean, and duty assignments. Next tour of duty, I wouldn't be surprised if the colonel were made military attaché at Paris!" Quickly he drew on his gloves. "Now you must go in! It's freezing out here on the porch, and your arms are bare! Look how our breaths show—like smoke!"

She seemed almost not to hear him. "Smoke," she murmured, looking at the distant glimmer of light in the headquarters building. "Smoke—that's right. And look how they seem to flow together, mingling—"

He was about to step from the veranda when he saw a man in the shadows, leaning against a post supporting the porch roof. The stranger was smoking a pipe; the coal flared red as he puffed.

"Who is that?" David asked.

Cassie turned quickly, then seemed to draw away from him, wrapping bare arms about her against the chill. Then she said, "That's

Chris. Chris Rowley. He's Owen's chief civilian scout." She stepped forward, called. "Chris, is that you?"

"Yes, ma'am."

To David she whispered, "He sleeps in the stable." Aloud she asked, "What are you doing out there? Do you want anything?"

Rowley continued to lounge in the darkness. "No, Miz Garrett. Just having me a good-night pipe. It's a beautiful night out, ain't it? Just look at them stars!"

"Chris was a soldier," Cassie murmured, "till his feet got frozen, up in the Badlands, they call them. The surgeon had to take off the front parts of both his feet. He sort of hobbles, but he can ride and shoot, I guess. Owen depends on him a lot."

The pipe glowed briefly, then winked out as Rowley banged it against a post. The dottle fell in a shower of sparks. Private Dobbs brought Star Boy, and David said good night to Cassie Garrett.

"You'll come back?" she asked wistfully.

He rubbed the pony's firm neck. "I don't know, ma'am. My work will keep me busy for quite a while. When the weather gets better I may come in to Elk City for supplies. It all depends."

"Come soon," she urged in a whisper, as if fearing to be overheard.

Throwing a leg over the pony, he trotted out to the road. "Goodby!" he called. As he rode away toward town he was aware Chris Rowley was watching him, also.

CHAPTER FOUR

On his last night in the Oglala camp David Chantry lay for a long, sweet time with Pretty Nose, Big Hail's niece. It was The Moon When the Raccoons Come Out, and the Tongue River country was locked in the grip of a fierce winter. Winter was one of the great Sioux gods, along with Rock, Thunder, Sun, Buffalo, Earth, and the other primal deities. There was scanty food for the horse herd, but the sturdy beasts—small, tough, deer-legged, with the fantastically flared and blotched hides so dear to the Sioux—made do with a diet of cottonwood bark and twigs, together with tufts of frozen grass uncovered by sharp hoofs.

David knew good horses; he knew breeding among women also. It was a sign of Big Hail's present favor that he had given Pretty Nose to David as a bed companion. But Big Hail's favor was mercurial; he could quickly turn from the large-minded and generous camp chief, the *wakicunza,* to a cranky and sullen despot. David knew he was in the camp only on Big Hail's sufferance. Though he had made many friends among the Oglalas, he comported himself with great caution. Indians were, after all, primitive people, with savage customs.

"Eh?" he asked, roused from his reverie. He had been gazing into the red eye of the fire, bemused by the yip of a prowling coyote, the occasional pistol-like crack as a tree froze in the great cold, congealed sap expanding and splitting the woody fibers.

Pretty Nose repeated her question in the Sioux tongue, rising on her elbow from the warm robes to sign the question also.

"Yes," he answered simply. "I am very glad." He made the sign he had learned, *sunshine in the heart;* right hand, index finger curled to represent a small heart, carried over to the left breast, then both hands outswept to greet the rising sun. "I am glad you came back."

During the menstrual period the Oglala women were considered unclean, banished to small and dreary lodges to wait out their period. Now Pretty Nose had returned, soft and warm and loving. She had taught him much hand talk. Her fingers were long and slender; like birds, they fluttered in the firelit gloom of the lodge. Even the harsh and sibilant Sioux tongue seemed softened and made musical in her mouth.

"But you must not go away." Like an animal she wriggled against him, pressing her body against his.

"It is necessary," he said. He tried to think of the sign for *work;* finally it came to him. Extending his hands before him, fingers widespread, he moved them back and forth in a chopping motion. *Work. Cutting wood.* "I have work to do."

Pretty Nose did not speak again, only held him tighter, and finally slept. In the darkness he grinned wryly. What would Wade Chantry think, seeing his younger brother, the shy and diffident one, lying in the arms of an Indian maiden in Sioux country?

After a while David slept also, but woke near dawn with a fit of the coughing that plagued him. Pretty Nose sat near the replenished fire, heating water in a battered tin pot for the breakfast coffee—*pazuta sapa,* the Sioux called it. Indian women never squatted as the men did, considering it undignified and unfeminine. Instead, Pretty Nose sat gracefully beside the fire, bare brown legs on the same side, watching him with concern.

Again he coughed, the old deep-welling cough that shook him as with the ague. In habit he put a hand to his mouth, but there was no banner of fresh blood. He stared at his hand in surprise. "No blood!" he marveled.

Pretty Nose rose and hurried to him, kneeling beside him.

"You say?"

She did not understand his words but knew from his manner he was pleased. She was pleased also. She kissed him, in that foreign gesture he had taught her, and laughed.

Maybe the cold dry air of the Territory *had* started to heal his prison-ravaged lungs. In sudden elation he caught Pretty Nose around the slender waist and whirled through the lodge in a mazurka. She still did not understand what so delighted him. But he had never had his brother's grace in the dance. David's moccasined feet became entangled with her bare brown legs. Laughing, they fell together into the tumbled furs that had been their bed. The paper photographic prints he had hung on a cord to dry were dislodged in the wind of their passing, raining down on them like giant snowflakes.

While Pretty Nose cooked a morning stew of brisket hacked from the frozen quarter of venison on the meat rack outside, he picked up the prints, sorted them, hung them up again. He was proud of his pictures, and stepped backward the better to inspect them: a group of the six- and seven-year-olds of the Strong Hearts Society, solemn and dignified in newly sewn ceremonial shirts; an old woman, face lined and seamed like crazed crystal, chuckling as he snapped her sewing moccasins; a boy cutting an iron trade skillet into arrow points while his grandfather straightened red-willow arrow shafts with a cylindrical tool made from the vertebra of a deer. David was particularly pleased with a photograph of Big Hail's best war pony, an animal so intelligent it had seemed almost to follow his muttered comments as he set up his tripod in the snow and pulled the black cloth over his head. *A little to the left—so! Raise your head, beast, cock it a little to one side. Perhaps spread the front legs a little more apart. There—that's it! Perfect!*

Bemused, he went to the door flap and held it aside to get a better light on the print. The pony stared back at him with glints of light in the large, dark eyes. On the muzzle the network of veins was clear and distinct, like the traceries of rivers on a map. The Sioux slit the nostrils of their mounts, believing this permitted the entrance of greater volumes of air, and so more endurance. Big Hail had painted wavy lines on each foreleg from hoof to shoulder, a hand on the pony's flank to show the animal had been struck there by the enemy, several tracks in the shape of hoofprints to indicate he had captured that many enemy ponies. All these carefully fashioned marks were distinct in his photograph, but the print cried out for color—the brilliant yellow of the wavy lines, the dripping blood red of the hand on the flank, the intense blue of the hoofprints. Someday, perhaps, there would be chemicals that—

"What is it?" He turned.

"You eat," Pretty Nose urged.

She sat in silence, hands clasped in her lap, bringing more coffee when his cup was empty, afterward taking away the bowl and the cup to scrub with sand and water. Replete, David took out his code book and fell to preparing his monthly report to the Washington address given him for the Council. It was a 1700 number on F Street, around the corner from the War Department itself; a curious irony. On his coming trip to Ghost Bull's camp, in the shadow of the great buttes along the Powder, he hoped to meet a Diamond R bull train or a government mail rider to forward his letter informing the Council of his favorable reception by Big Hail and his people, his gifts of the .52-caliber Sharps carbines to the savages, along with a plentiful supply of linen-cased cartridges.

Sealing the letter, he put it back into the rawhide bag he carried on his pony. Now he had to say his farewells to Big Hail and the Oglalas. Stepping outside, he blinked in the early-morning sunlight. The sky was already a bowl of eye-hurting blue. Rising sun cast a sheet of brilliance across the crusted snow. The air smelled sharp and invigorating, laced with the vinous scent of pine. Not bothering with his bearskin coat—his blood no longer seemed so thin and unsupportive—he walked around the great circle of lodges, greeting new friends, pausing for a joke, accepting a friendly puff from a pipe. Men sat in the sunlight painting themselves, braiding hair, painfully removing whiskers with the aid of a clamshell tweezer. Children slid down a nearby hill on a makeshift sled. Others rolled a ribboned hoop down a slope and threw stick spears at it, shrieking with excitement when someone pinned the hoop to the ground with a well-aimed shaft. Altogether, it was not too different from a winter scene in Columbus, Ohio, at Franklin Park, on the East Side.

Big Hail and the elders awaited him. Politely he scratched at the door flap before entering the great lodge. Inside it was dim, lit only by a smoldering buffalo-chip fire. Face impassive, Big Hail sat on an ammunition box, bearing like a scepter the new carbine David had presented to him. The rest sat like courtiers, watching David—Rain Coming, the shaman, with the stuffed skin of a yellowhammer on his head as badge of office; High Bear, leader of the Grass Dancers; Little Hawk, Smoke, Poor Buffalo.

"Hau!" David raised his hand in salute.

Big Hail nodded gravely, motioning him to a thick-furred robe at the chief's feet.

"Hie," David said. *"Hie. Hie.* Thanks."

In the circuitous way of Indians, they all sat for a long time in silence, passing around a feathered ceremonial pipe loaded with finely chopped red-willow bark. In the winter they had run short of the trade tobacco they favored. David took the pipe from his neighbor, blew the required four puffs to the various quarters of the compass, then a final wavering circle high into the blackened lodgepoles. This last was a propitiatory offering to the Great Spirit, the Father of All, who loved the smell of tobacco. David had learned their customs not only for his own convenience and safety among the Oglalas but because the rites were colorful and interesting, impressive also.

In spite of the winter chill, the tipi was warm and smoky. Drops of sweat stitched down David's cheeks, bathed his chest under the beaded buckskin shirt Pretty Nose had sewed for him. From a distance he heard the shrill voices of the children, a woman singing, the squawk of a jay. He did not move, continuing to sit silently in what he hoped was a manner as dignified and serene as the old men, as stone-faced and immobile as Big Hail himself.

The smoking took a long time. The Oglalas stared somberly at him. In spite of his resolve he twitched, brushed at a fly on his nose, cleared his throat. Finally Big Hail took a last puff at the feathered pipe, laid it carefully down, gestured to David to speak.

Feeling shy and awkward, he rose, painfully aware of his gangling height. The Oglalas were tall men; some were big and powerful by any standard. But David Chantry towered above them all. His long blond hair Pretty Nose had attempted to braid in otter fur, but the hair was so fine that she had finally despaired. His shabby and worn white man's clothing was pieced out with Oglala moccasins and a red blanket. Wishing he had his brother Wade's facile mind, he cleared his throat again and began, in a halting mixture of Sioux, hand signs, and occasional English words to thank them for their hospitality. Now, he told them, he was about to move on to the camp of the great Ghost Bull, friend of Big Hail and leader of the Sioux nation in the Powder River country. Big Hail and his people had welcomed him, David Chantry, a stranger, to their lodges with traditional hospitality and generosity, posed patiently for his pickshers.

Warming to his task, encouraged by their attention, he went on. *The Oglalas are a great people, I will remember them always. They lived on this land since the Great Spirit gave it to them countless moons ago. They were here long before the white men came.* But now, he reminded them, the white men were trying to push them off their ancestral lands. The white men might promise the Sioux many blankets and red paint and whiskey if they would permit the settlers, the farmers, the miners, to enter the Powder River country to hunt, plow the fields, dig in the earth for gold. But that was all a trick. *Listen to me. Listen!*

Cupping a hand behind his ear, one old man leaned forward. Another scratched his nose, but the black eyes never left David Chantry. A third stared watchfully through the curling smoke of the pipe and seemed to nod in agreement.

It is all a trick, a trick they play like Iktomi, the trickster god you all know. Recalling the fable of the camel getting his nose into the Bedouin's tent, David improvised. *They are like the buffalo that got cold in winter and wanted to put just his nose into a Sioux lodge. Then he asked to put his shoulder in, then his hump. At last he got his backside in, and all of the buffalo was inside and the man had to go out and get cold himself. He could not get into his own lodge any more.*

Appreciating the fable, the elder with the pipe grinned, nudged his neighbor. Someone grunted approval also, but Big Hail's face was somber.

Finished, David signed, and sat down.

Big Hail waved his new carbine at David Chantry. "Friend," he grumbled, "why do you tell us all this? You are a white man, too. Why do you speak against your own color? I do not know if the Oglalas should trust you or not!"

The change of manner, the quick and incisive demand unsettled him. Really, Big Hail's questions forced him unwillingly to examine his own motives, to justify to them, if not to himself, his position. Actually, he had never wanted to sign the damned oath of loyalty. For days in Columbus he had struggled with the decision when Major Garrett offered him the papers. After all, he was—or had at least been born—a gentleman. Gentlemen in the South did not break a solemn oath. But, then—greater things were at stake, were they not? A man, he told himself, a Southerner, had a right, even a duty, to compromise himself for the Stars and Bars of the Confederate States of America. Deception, admittedly, but both sides practiced it. So he had signed the parole. Now he was committed. There was little point in worrying further about it.

"There are," he explained, standing again, "different kinds of white men. I am a white man from the South"—he gestured—"and we do not want your lands. But the northern men are greedy. They have sent their walk-a-heaps and their pony soldiers out here to make war against you, drive you away. When the winter god leaves this land, I know they plan to come against you, set fire to your lodges, rape your women, and shoot your children. I speak this truth because I love my brothers the Oglalas." He gestured with his thumb, the ritual sign for *speak truth,* and sat down again.

Staring with obsidian eyes at David Chantry, Big Hail pulled thoughtfully at his lip.

"We listen. We hear. The part about the buffalo coming into a man's tipi we understand. Maybe you have a good heart. Maybe you are a friend. But maybe you other white men, you men from the South, are just trying in your own way to get our lands, too." He fell silent again. Looking down at the precious carbine, he rubbed the polished stock with a brown thumb. "Winter is ending soon. We think about all these things you have told us. Before the ice in the rivers goes away we will decide what to do." He rose, dismissing the council.

Well, David thought, *it is as good as could be expected, for a first try, anyway.*

"Hie," he said again, "hie, hie."

Shaking hands with them all, he finally persuaded them to come outside for a group portrait, standing in the snow before Big Hail's great lodge decorated with moons and stars and sticklike figures of men and horses. While he focused under the black cloth the elders stood patiently, countenances grave and dignified. The people came to surround the group, silent and impressed. He took off the lens cap.

One. . . . Two. . . . Three. . . . The moment was congealing in collodion as bright winter sun burned the chemicals of the wet plate.

Four. . . . *Five.* . . . *Six.* . . . Pretty Nose came to stand beside him, watching with round, soft eyes the magic of the big-barreled Anthony camera.

Seven. . . . *Eight.* . . . *Nine.* . . . That ought to be enough. Replacing the lens cap, he went to his wagon to develop the plate. Pretty Nose accompanied him, sitting beside him in the wicker chair to marvel as the glass plate emerged dripping from the developing bath.

"The best I've done yet!" David exulted. "Look at it, will you? The depth, the detail—"

"You say?" Pretty Nose asked.

In his enthusiasm he had spoken in English. He looked up and saw her eyes filled with tears. She looked away then and murmured, "Pretty—very pretty." He had taught her a little English, including the important words *love* and *kiss* and *you are beautiful.*

"You're crying!" With his finger he touched the shining drops on her cheek.

"You go—you go away."

"Yes, I go away."

In English she asked, "You 'member me?"

He kissed her cheek. "I 'member you, my sweet. I will always remember you."

When he left, driving the mules Nig and Pansy with Star Boy tethered behind the camera wagon, the weather had undergone another of its quick changes. The sun was gone, gun-metal clouds filled the sky, wind howled in the trees. Big Hail's Oglalas stood in the snow, watching his departure. Searching the silent figures, he looked for Pretty Nose but did not see her. Waving in farewell, he slapped the reins over the broad backs of the mules. Easily they pulled into the harness, drawing his wagon crunching across the snow to the frozen Powder River, where Ghost Bull's camp lay.

"Yes," he murmured, "I 'member you indeed."

That first day, he enjoyed immensely the freedom of being again out on his own, enjoyed even the downy flakes sifting on his cheeks, tickling his nose, dry and powdery on his uncut beard. The distance to Ghost Bull's camp among the buttes was perhaps forty miles, due east, and he anticipated no difficulty. But the snow grew heavier, the wind blew it into giant drifts that made hard going. Nooning, he boiled up tea, ate some dried meat, and put nosebags of grain on Nig and Pansy and Star Boy. While they crunched corn he consulted his map and compass, squinting toward a distant saddle in the mountains only dimly seen in the downpour. Mizpah Creek, according to the map, should lie below that saddle, on the far side. Ghost Bull's camp was only a few miles farther.

Hurried by the falling snow, dusk came early. That night, his little party found shelter in a tree-ringed cleft in the hills where the searching wind did not reach. For supper he brewed more tea, thick with sugar, and munched the flat meat cakes Pretty Nose had packed in his leather war bag. Out hunting or on the war trail the Sioux depended much on small cakes compounded of dried plums, chokecherries, and currants pounded fine and mixed with shredded dried buffalo meat and tallow. They were nourishing, and kept well even in warm weather.

Silently he sat in the wagon, wrapped in the bearskin coat, staring into the flame of a candle. After the cheery bustle of the Indian camp, after those many nights with Pretty Nose warm and soft in his bed, he became suddenly, incredibly lonely. He thought nostalgically of Big Oaks, Biloxi, black old Aunt Emma, his father, his mother. How he would love to see Wade, tell Wade what he was doing to help the Cause, maybe even brag a little! He thought also of Benjamin Sears, Benjie's long and bony jaw, the wisp of beard, the gleeful—almost devilish—glint in his eye as the young man preached to the heathen in Elk City's rutted River Street. He wondered idly how Benjie was doing with his missionary work among the Cheyennes. Benjie was articulate, you had to give him that, but he was a bit of a fool. Still, the Council would hardly have picked him for such an important task if Benjie had not come with good recommendation.

In the morning, the snow had ceased to fall, but drifts still made going difficult. Nig and Pansy strained into the collars, moist breaths puffing in clouds like the steam from twin locomotives, while the pony followed patiently behind. The wagon rocked and swayed and once almost tipped over on an unseen rocky ledge. But the distant saddle grew nearer, and a luminous glow of colored rings marked a hesitant sun.

Now he was even more conscious of the enormousness of the land, the insignificance of himself and his little train. Shrouded in the anonymity of the snow, they labored across a great rising moraine. The wind had died; there was no sound but the heavy breathing of the mules, the crunch and squeak of iron-shod wheels in crusted snow. Once, a hawk dived from the heights like a bullet, braking suddenly almost before his face with a flushing of powerful wings, then soared skyward with a squawk, bird curiosity satisfied. Startled and nervous after the experience, he felt also comforted. There *were* other living things in this snow-blanketed wilderness.

In late afternoon the sun emerged from a rack of clouds and briefly shone. There was no warmth in it, only a metallic sheen. In the wan light, he sensed, far to the north, a disturbance prickling the edges of his vision. Snatching up the field glasses, he trained them on the distant, antlike figures. They were soldiers—cavalrymen —riding hard toward Elk City and Fort Taylor, accompanying a wagon.

"Hey!" Remembering his unposted letter, he stood on the seat, waving his hat. "Hey! Halloooo!"

Of course it was foolish. At that distance they did not see him, certainly could not hear him.

"Hey!" he shouted again, the sound relieving his loneliness. "You fellows! Hey!"

Nig turned his big barrel of a head and stared at him. The Indian pony neighed shrilly and pawed the frozen ground. Perhaps the animals thought he was crazy. Maybe he was. Prolonged isolation made people act strangely. But he did feel better. It had, in a way, been talking to someone. Feeling better, he watched the distant specks until they dipped into a depression and were lost to view.

That night, they camped in the hollow of the saddle above Mizpah Creek. Ghost Bull's camp could not be more than another ten or fifteen miles, at the foot of the distant buttes. The sun was well up in a brilliant sky when he awoke, roused by Nig and Pansy snuffling and stamping as they rooted through the snow for tufts of grass.

Mizpah Creek was frozen hard. The camera wagon slipped and slid as the mules drew it across, Nig and Pansy and the pony spreadeagling on uncertain hoofs. Safe on the far bank he reined up, listening. Against the murmur of water trapped under the ice he heard a faint whimpering. A baby? Of course, impossible. But the whimper persisted, laced now with a bubbling, coughing sound.

Taking his carbine, he got down from the high seat and cautiously approached what he took to be the source of the queer noise. Pushing aside the tangle of brush caught among the cottonwoods and willows from the last rise of Mizpah Creek, he saw a huge gray wolf, belly up in the snow. The animal squirmed in pain, paws helplessly aloft. Saberlike teeth grinding together, the animal made bitter mewling noises, diminishing even as David watched.

Blossom? The wolfer with his balls of mutton fat and strychnine? Was Blossom near?

He could not stand the slavering agony of the wolf. Quickly he shot it through the head. For a moment, the great, furry body stiffened, paralyzed into the grotesque position. Then, as the echoes of his shot died away, the tortured muscles relaxed. Rolling over, breathing what seemed almost a sigh of relief, the giant animal lay still.

Blossom—it had to be Blossom! Reloading, David looked around. Of course, the wolfer covered a lot of the Territory in his activities. He might be dozens of miles away, and not come on the carcass of this particular wolf for days. David had not liked Blossom; the old man promised to help him with Big Hail's Oglalas, then abandoned him when danger threatened. But Blossom would be someone to talk to.

Actually, he did not find the wolfer until the next morning. Winding in and out of the flat-topped buttes on a trail that seemed to bear toward Ghost Bull's camp, David came on Blossom and his pack mules loaded high with pelts.

"Well!" The wolfer hunched himself up in the saddle, fists on the saddle horn, staring. "If'n it ain't the picture man!"

David reined up Nig and Pansy, got stiffly down.

"That's right."

"Ain't been et by no grizzly, I see, nor froze to death in that last storm! And ain't busted your parole, neither, I hope!"

"No," David said coolly. "I survived. Spent a few weeks with Big Hail and his Oglalas and got along just fine. Got some fine photographs, and managed to learn a little of the lingo." Unpacking his alcohol stove, he swept a rocky ledge clear of snow and placed it beneath a protected outcropping. "I was just about to boil up tea. Care to join me?"

"Don't mind if I do." Blossom slid off his pony, grimacing painfully and favoring his back, and hunkered down with David over the tiny, bluish flame. "I got to admit I didn't think you'd still be wearing that mop of yeller hair."

David grinned, shrugged. "How's wolfing?" he asked, shaking tea into the tin pot.

Blossom looked proudly at the high-piled bales of hides, edges dark with frozen blood. "Not half bad! I'm gonna take me one last swing along Mizpah Creek to look at my baits, then make a flat coattail downstream to Elk City and really tie me one on! Them pelts ought to bring six, seven hundred dollars."

David remembered his unposted letter. Soon he would reach Ghost Bull's camp, and would probably not have another chance for weeks, perhaps months. The Council, he knew, was anxious to hear from him. Maybe Blossom could be prevailed on to take the letter back to Elk City for posting, though David would have preferred another courier. Still, the letter was composed in the Council code, which was unbreakable. What harm could Blossom do him?

"You're the first white face I've seen for weeks," he told Blossom, burning his lips on the rim of the tin cup but grateful for the warm flush in his gullet. "Except maybe for some soldiers yesterday heading toward Fort Taylor. They were riding fast, escorting a wagon."

"Paymaster," Blossom grunted.

"Paymaster?"

"Oncet a month he comes out from Fort Kearney to pay off the soldiers. Carries a lot of money with him—maybe ten thousand dollars. *That's* why they wasn't wasting no time."

David took out the letter. "I wonder if you'd post this for me when you get to Elk City? I'm headed for Ghost Bull's camp now, and won't have an opportunity myself."

Blossom's long nose twitched. "What is it?"

"Just a letter to some old friends back East. They haven't heard from me for a long time, and they'll be worried."

Blossom put the letter into his war bag. "Always glad to oblige a friend." He spat a gout of tobacco juice. "I guess, friend, you ain't forgot you still owe me seventy-five dollars?"

David frowned. "For what?"

"Why, for makin' you acquainted with Big Hail and his Oglalas that day!"

David was astonished. "You didn't help me at all! They threw down on you, and you ran away!"

"Didn't neither!" Blossom snarled.

"You did too! You lit a shuck and skedaddled!"

"Don't make no never mind, does it?" the wolfer demanded. "I was willing to carry out my part of the bargain! No fault of mine they wasn't willing to palaver!"

David shook his head, threw out the dregs of tea. "I don't owe you anything."

Blossom's rheumy eyes turned vicious. "Them's your last words?"

"Absolutely."

The wolfer snatched up the old Hawken rifle and pointed it at David. "This here is *my* last word, then! You just fork over that money you owe me. Be quick about it if you don't want your head blowed off!"

David stared at him, unbelieving.

"I know you got plenty of money!" Blossom squalled. "A dude like you, fine and fancy manners, carried on a chip all his life—you got to have money, plenty of money!" He rolled his eyes virtuously skyward. "Seventy-five dollars, that's all I'm asking. I'm a poor man, but I don't want no more than my just due!"

Indignant, David backed away. But there was no mistaking the mad light in the wolfer's eyes. "I— I— there's some money in the wagon," he admitted.

"I'll folly you," Blossom said coldly, "just to see you don't come across a pistol in there and try to bushwhack me!"

Furious, David climbed into the wagon. Blossom poked his grizzled head through the curtains, watching. With his back to the wolfer to conceal the hiding place, David took a sheaf of bills from beneath a warped plank in the wagon bottom. At the sight of the greenbacks the old man's eyes glittered.

"It's cost me dear," he whined, "to search for my poor little Mattie all these years. I got to be careful of my money, you understand!"

He tucked the bills into his war bag. "Now that we done settled that little matter"—he grinned—"I guess we kin be good friends again, eh?"

David had a sudden impulse to demand his letter back. Blossom was an evil, a suspicious man. But he had already committed himself. To try to get the letter back would incite suspicion.

"Long as we're friends again," the wolfer went on, tying his war bag on the pony, "I'm gonna give you a little advice, pilgrim. Keep an eye peeled and walk careful, less'n you want to go barefoot on top of your head early in life!"

David stared at him uncomprehending. The snow-reddened eyes stared back, small and hard. "I don't follow you," he muttered.

"I mean," Blossom said, "that someone's been sashayin' around stirrin' up the tribes. Last week a pack of Little Man's Cheyennes lifted the hair of three miners that was dug in for the winter on Big Dry Creek. That hard-butt Colonel Garrett, back at Fort Taylor, was real upset. Little Man has been polite as a schoolma'am for a long time. Now all of a sudden his pot comes to a boil!"

David snuffed out the alcohol lamp, returned it to its leather case. "I can't imagine why." He shrugged, aware the old man was watching him. "I certainly didn't have any trouble with Big Hail. Once he understood all I wanted was photographs, we got along fine as frog hair."

Blossom blew his nose between his fingers, climbed on the patient Indian pony. "Big Hail is a little fish and don't signify. Ghost Bull is a big fish, the one that eats the little ones. It was Ghost Bull and Man Afraid of His Horses that massacreed Lootenant Grattan and his men at Frenchy Bordeaux's trading post three, four years back. When Ghost Bull starts raising sand, look *out!*"

Lifting a hand in salute, the wolfer dug moccasined heels into the pony's ribs and clucked to his pack mules. A moment later, the little train disappeared from sight among the snow-laden trees.

A pack of Little Man's Cheyennes lifted the hair of three miners dug in for the winter along Big Dry Creek. Had that, perhaps, been Benjamin Sears' doing? Had the flamboyant youth finally reached the Cheyennes, preached to them, exhorted them already to an act of violence? If so, it was more than David Chantry had yet accomplished. Perhaps Sears had more stuff to him than David had given him credit for.

Then he felt a sudden chill—a coldness not remedied by the hot tea or the bulky bearskin coat. Was Blossom's mention of the incident only a warning, or did it mean the old man was suspicious of David Chantry's activities among the Oglalas?

CHAPTER FIVE

Benjamin Sears and Poor Bird, his nondescript Ree guide and interpreter, had ridden into the Cheyenne camp like two scarecrows, singing hymns. They were so obviously weary, hungry, and half frozen after the journey from Elk City that Little Man decided to give them food and shelter. It was a long-standing Cheyenne tradition.

"They cannot hurt us," Little Man explained to the shaman, Stump Horn. "They are poor creatures. I think they are crazy, too."

Stump Horn was not sure. He waved his feathered rattle at the newcomers to clear the air of evil spirits they might have brought with them.

"Father," he said, "I do not know. Crazy people can make big trouble sometimes."

In spite of his fatigue, Benjie Sears was jubilant. How easy it was, to come into this savage camp and be thus welcomed! While Poor Bird unloaded the pack mules, he stalked among the Cheyennes, Bible clutched in one hand and bony finger upright in warning.

"Hear the word of the Lord! Judgment Day is near! All men— white, red, black, whatever color—better be prepared! It's a good thing the Lord laid a call on me to carry His word to the heathen, else you'd all be condemned to everlasting fire and brimstone!"

The Cheyennes watched him noncommittally, though some giggled. A few had a little English, and there were amused comments behind cupped hands.

"Take a card," Benjie invited.

They stared at the dirty pack he took from his coat. Little Man looked sidewise at Stump Horn, then gingerly extracted a card.

"Ace of diamonds, ain't it?" Benjie demanded.

Little Man nodded.

"Put it back."

Benjie slipped it into the pack, shuffled it expertly, handed the pack to Little Man.

"Look for it!" he commanded. "See if it's in there."

Licking a brown thumb, Little Man searched the deck. The ace of diamonds was absent. Little Man frowned, went through the deck again. Baffled, he looked at Benjamin Sears. "Where?" he gestured.

Benjie whisked the missing card from Little Man's scalp lock.

"Right here," he announced, holding the card aloft. "The Good Lord transmogrified this here ace of diamonds out of the pack right into your left ear!" Raising the Bible aloft, he harangued them. "If the Good Lord can do tricks like that, just imagine what great works He can bring forth when He's *really* set his mind to it!"

The Cheyennes had heard about the white man's gods before, from a traveling French missionary. Father Ribout's story was mildly interesting, but the whole account was so ridiculous—imagine a woman getting a baby without a man to lie with her—that they only laughed. Father Ribout left the camp in discouragement. But the Frenchman had only *talked* about the power of his god. This gaunt man had brought a small sample with him.

Stump Horn was still doubtful. "He is white," he told Little Man, "just like those miners down the river. We are getting too many white men around here. They are bad luck for us—I saw it in a dream!"

Little Man pulled at his lip. Finally he said, "Those miners came into our land without asking. They stay where they are not wanted. But this skinny white man is different. He only wants to rest for a while and get warm and have something to eat. Besides—how did that red card get into my hair?"

Stump Horn grimaced. He gave another wary shake of his rattle toward Benjamin Sears. "I hope he has a better story than that old one about the Jesus who was born with no father!"

It turned out that Sears did indeed have a different story to tell. Sears disclaimed Father Ribout's teachings. With Poor Bird to interpret, he told the Cheyennes they were not to love all men, but only *certain* men. Some white men, Sears said, pained as he was to admit it, were evil. They were trying to dispossess the Cheyennes from their lands along the upper Missouri. When Sears heard about the three miners who had defied Little Man's order to move along, he was excited.

"That's exactly what I'm talking about!" Poor Bird, with only a limited command of English, was hard put to it to keep up with Sears' flow of words. "Those miners are only the beginning! When spring comes, there'll be a lot more of them! They'll come with picks and shovels to dig up the hills, to look for gold in the river! There'll be soldiers from Fort Taylor to stand guard while they dig!" He waved his Bible aloft, eyes hot with emotion. "This book tells all about it, friends! These bad white men, these soldiers, were sent by Beelzebub! They're commanded to do Lucifer's bidding! Act now, right now—do the work of the Lord! Drive out the miners, let the trespassers know the Cheyennes won't allow evil men on this ground where your fathers and grandfathers sleep!"

Little Man rubbed his hairless chin, puffed at his pipe. "Those white men, those miners," he pointed out. "They have a lot of guns, and powder and ball. It will be hard to get rid of them."

With the air of a sorcerer, Benjamin Sears threw open the lid of one of the trunks he had brought on the pack mules. Under a layer of Bibles were rifles: Sharps .52-caliber carbines, shiny with grease, and a great store of cartridges.

"The Lord," he announced, "sends these guns to his good friends the Cheyennes! The Lord says to act now, right now—drive out the miners!" He handed a carbine to Little Man, passing out others to the elders. "There are more guns, plenty more, where these come from!"

The Cheyennes were entranced with the carbines. Quickly they threw down their muzzle-loading muskets. At once they comprehended the workings of the heavy breechblock sliding up and down in grooves behind the chamber, the combined trigger guard and finger lever to eject and reload, the linen-cased cartridges. Some of the new guns had a coffee mill built into the stock. This late in the winter, the Cheyennes had run out of trade coffee, but what a joy it would be, come summer, to grind coffee in that fascinating mill!

"With these guns," Sears preached, "you can destroy the evil white men! You can bring the wrath of the Lord right plumb down on their heads! No one can ever hurt you in this righteous cause!"

Elated, Little Man brandished the new weapon over his head. He shuffled about in the snow, singing:

> "Coffee I grind, coffee I grind!
> With my new gun I grind things!
> I grind up the miners along the river,
> I make them dust, and blow them into the air!"

Others happily bearing the new weapons followed him, chanting in chorus, stamping a broad circle into the snow around a fire. Even sour-faced old Stump Horn joined in, hobbling rheumatically. The snakelike column wound around in the snowy dusk, surrounding the flame so that Benjamin Sears saw only an occasional flicker of smoky orange. He clenched his fists, waved them skyward. "By Jesus Christ, I done it! I got a good brannigan going already! Mr. Kinnear will be proud of me, mebbe give me a bonus!"

Poor Bird stared at him, puzzled. "You say?"

The shabby Ree was not too smart, but his price had been reasonable. Benjie patted his shoulder. "Don't pucker up your brain about it," he counseled. "All I mean is—everything's all right, see?" He remembered a few words of the Cheyenne lingo from the rough dictionary a Council expert had gotten up for him. "*Esh piveh!*" he chortled. "*Esh piveh!*" *It is good. Everything is all right.*

But everything was not all right; the prize was not to be gained so easily. Little Man and his war party went down Big Dry Creek to drive away the miners but lost several braves in the ensuing fight. The miners were well armed, with ample supply of powder and ball. Furthermore, the dugout in the riverbank was deep and capacious, and the occupants had a clear field of fire. Little Man tried first to entice them from their lair with promises of safe conduct to Elk City. The miners, rough characters all, shouted obscenities. Palaver unavailing, the war party finally rushed the dugout after a volley of fire arrows filled the interior with smoke and choking fumes; the three miners were killed and scalped. But Red Hand, Little Man's uncle, died. Gentle Horse, a favorite nephew, was shot through the stomach and perished on a travois while the Cheyennes were returning to their camp. Sears' reputation was considerably dimmed. There were angry words said about him and his Bible book. Stump Horn was particularly eloquent.

"Look!" Benjie snarled, watching Stump Horn pass his lodge and shake his rattle. "The old bastard! He don't like anybody to have bigger medicine than him! I daresay he's cooking up some kind of plot!"

Poor Bird, crouched over the small fire, turned. "You say?"

The camp seemed deserted in the cold. Only a few vaporous tendrils wavered upward from smoke-blackened lodges. A woman emerged, hacked chops from a frozen deer carcass, and hurried again within. Somewhere a wolf howled, a ghostly and mournful lament.

"I say I need a drink," Benjie muttered, searching in the bottom of his trunk.

The Sears family had been big. Even when there was nothing to eat but mush and sorghum molasses and coffee, even when there was no coal in the scuttle, the house had been alive with people. If nothing else, Benjie could always pick a fight with one of his sisters or brothers to enliven a gloomy day. But now—

The next day, he ran out of rum. Leaving Poor Bird snoring, he wrapped himself in a blanket and went into the harsh sunlight. As far as he could see, morning sun glittered on the unbroken expanse of white. He shivered, blew on his chapped knuckles. Stalking across the crust, the powdery fall of new snow creaking and crunching under his boots, he came to a sun-warmed depression in the litter of boulders surrounding the camp. Kneeling, a girl scraped shreds of fat and skin from a deer hide. Startled, she looked up when his shadow fell across her work.

"Don't be scared!" Benjie soothed her. "I ain't going to hurt you! Just wanted someone to talk to."

Averting her eyes, she went on with the methodical scraping. She was a young woman, full of breast, black braids shining in the sunlight. As she stretched forward and back with the clamshell scraper, her lissome form was fetchingly rounded.

"You kind of favor my sister Agnes," Benjie observed.

She did not understand him, but her scraping quickened.

"Or maybe Annie," Benjie mused. "Though of course Annie was real blond. She had that kind of waist, though, like you got, ma'am. Real small, and then kind of—kind of—" He broke off, swallowed.

He was lonely, so lonely. It had been a long time since he had been with a woman. "Kind of swelling out, above and— above and— below."

Of course she did not understand the words, but did she understand his loneliness, his longing? His had been a difficult, a solitary assignment.

He moved closer. It was almost as if another body, one strange to him, was moving to her, pressing against the rounded thigh, while he himself—Benjamin Berrisford Sears—watched disapprovingly. The girl was an Indian, a squaw. Not only that; to have congress with a Cheyenne woman might cause trouble. He already had enough trouble, with old Stump Horn conniving against him. Benjie watched with a strange detachment while he—that other he—bore the woman down against the sun-warm rocky shelf.

She did not resist, only continued to watch him with the strange stare. His hand groped under her skirt, felt the warm softness and fullness of the hips. Even then she did not seem to understand what he was doing; the black eyes looked into his with a blank and hooded aspect.

"I— I— need you," he said thickly. "God damn it, move a little, will you? Do something!"

She lay as passively as she had stared at him, face immobile. Even after he had withdrawn and staggered to his feet, passing a hand over his brow and finding it wet with perspiration, she continued to lie on the shelf of rock, not bothering to pull the deerskin skirt down.

He was shaking. His hand trembled as he reached for the fringed hem and drew it quickly down.

"Don't tell no one about this!" he cautioned. He was suddenly frightened, very frightened. "You won't tell, will you?"

He picked up his Bible, only now remembering he had dropped it in a confusion of white pages when he had taken the Cheyenne woman.

"You won't tell, will you?"

Bible under his arm, he backed away. She did not move; it was almost as if nothing had happened. Damned Indians! How did a man know where he stood with them? Stumbling and falling, Benjie hastened away through the encircling rocks. What a fool he had been!

What a damned, skirt-chasing fool! Briefly he thought of David Chantry, down there on the Tongue. Chantry was quality, Chantry was educated, Chantry was smart. David Chantry would never have gotten mixed up with an Indian woman. Suddenly he wished he could see Chantry again, talk to him, maybe get some good advice.

———◆———

The off back wheel of David Chantry's photographic wagon was broken. Nearing Ghost Bull's camp among the great buttes, he had inadvertently driven over a rocky ledge half submerged in the snow. The straining mules slipped, the wagon slid off the ledge, the wheel catching on a rocky spur at the last moment to prevent the wagon overturning and complete disaster. But the strain had been too much for the hickory spokes. They splintered; now the wagon tipped dismally sidewise, iron-shod wheel turned out at a crazy angle.

"Damn it!" he muttered.

Climbing into the wagon, he picked up bottles and boxes that had fallen. Then, taking up his carbine, he strode to a snowy knoll, looked about. Not three miles away hovered wisps of smoke from Ghost Bull's camp, hidden in a cleft in the great bulk of what was called on his maps Rainy Butte. So near, and then this had to happen! Nig and Pansy looked inquiringly at him. Black Nig made a whuffling noise, warm breath forming clouds of steam.

"I don't know," David said. In his loneliness he had gotten into the habit of talking to the animals as if they were human. "I'm damned if I know! Lordy, lordy, lordy!"

With Blossom's warning about the unfriendliness of Ghost Bull and his people fresh in his mind, he pondered the question of how to approach them. Perhaps he could simply walk unarmed into the camp, carrying a sack of the beads and scraps of bright gingham supplied by the Council. There was risk involved, of course; Ghost Bull's people might shoot him out of hand and pilfer his trinkets. On the other hand, a lone traveler in sacred Oglala lands had to depend on sufferance and goodwill. One man, even with the Spencer carbine the Indians said ". . . loaded in the morning and shot all day, . . ." was hardly a match for a band of hostile savages. So either way there was risk.

He grinned wryly. Not even Blossom the wolfer to help him! But

the grin was bleak; he could feel his loins contract, the muscles at
the back of his neck tighten, a chill invade the pit of his stomach.
Did Wade feel like this when he went into battle? No, Wade
Chantry probably galloped joyously into a fray, anxious to excel.
That was one of the many differences between David Chantry and
his brother.

"You stay here." He spoke conversationally to the mules, the
sound of his own voice breaking some of the tension. "I'm going to
walk down that way for a spell and see what I can see. I'll be back
directly."

Carbine at the trail, shivering in the cold, he crunched along a
frozen rill bearing toward Ghost Bull's camp. The stream was lined
with willows that made a screen he was grateful for. The sun, an orange ball with no warmth, hung low in the west. His shadow
lurched long and black before him as he walked.

Maybe he would find a woman digging for roots under the snow,
perhaps an Oglala child playing hide-and-seek, an old man out to
sniff the fresh air. Then he could explain his purpose, come into the
camp by the good graces of an intermediary. Maybe—

He stopped, stiffened. Somewhere in the jumbled rocks ahead he
saw movement. A bird? Jay, magpie?

Looking, listening, he felt the quickening of pulse, the throb of a
heart so loud it must be heard at the village. But the landscape was
quiet, impersonal. Leafless willow branches stirred; a feathery dusting of snow moved in wind-borne whorls across the frozen crust; the
everlasting buttes towered high, snowy bulk lit with patches of orange from the setting sun.

Carefully he moved on, carbine at the ready, a shell in the chamber. He did not want to appear warlike, yet there was danger. He
had to be prepared.

"*Cola!*" he called out. "*Hau, cola!*" Hello, friend.

Hollow and ghostly, the words echoed back from the buttes. *Hau,
cola! Hau, cola!* There were only the frozen branches of the willows
rubbing each other, the squawk of a faraway crow, murmur of en-
trapped water under the ice of the stream. He trembled, and did not
know whether from fear or the numbing cold.

Moving cautiously, he scanned the rocks, the winter-killed vegetation along the stream. In the tongue of the Oglalas he called out, "I am a friend! I do not mean harm to anyone!"

Well, there was no one; it must have been an overactive imagination! In this weather no Sioux was going to be caught very far from his own fire. Satisfied he had spied out a negotiable trail to Ghost Bull's camp, he started to follow his own tracks back to the wagon. He would unhitch Nig and Pansy, untie Star Boy, and ride to the Oglala camp. The damaged wagon would have to stay where it was. For a moment he was doubtful about leaving unattended all his chemicals, the big Anthony camera, his files of glass plates and prints. But in this winter season, who would bother them?

As he trudged past a thicket of frozen willows, an atavistic prickling of the hairs on the back of his neck warned of danger. He wheeled just in time to be borne down by a painted assailant leaping from the cover of the willows. He dropped the carbine, trying to wrest the strong hands from his throat. Capering figures rushed about him, whooping and shrieking. He had been ambushed, quickly and expertly.

Pulse pounding in his ears as he sought to loosen the garroting hands, he heard Nig and Pansy bray in panic. His bulging eyes fastened on the face above him—a painted face, a cruel and thin-lipped face, black eyes flaming with blood lust.

He tried to shout, to cry out, but no air remained in his tortured chest. The snowy world tipped, whirled, went upside down. As his body, his arms, his legs relaxed in the prelude to death, the final thing he remembered was the necklace of bear claws dangling before his glazed eyes. That, and the painted war club, its span clustered with inset teeth from some animal, that began the lethal swing at his brain. Then consciousness fled from him, like water from a broken clay pot. There was only blackness, a soft deep blackness engulfing him like the muddy waters of the great river at home, at Big Oaks.

———— ◆ ————

For a long time he floated in that endless blackness. Poor David Chantry, dying so young, in Indian country, bones scattered to bleach in the frontier sun! What was worse, his brother would never even know what had become of him. He saw Wade, bemedaled and

beribboned, at some kind of ceremony, wiping his eyes with a handkerchief. David shook his own head in shared grief for the undistin-
guished passing of David Chantry. God had not cared about poor
David. He wept, and was aware of a hand touching his forehead
with a cloth. Who was that? Mother? Black old Aunt Emma?

In the blackness he grimaced. Being dead was not bad—so far, at
any rate. And he had outwitted his bad lungs, perishing instead
from a bash on the head by an Indian club. At least it had been
quick. Better than coughing out his lungs in bloody shreds!

Someone was singing, a weird and plaintive song with a thin
thread of melody. He tried hard to identify the tune, but it hovered
only at the extreme edge of his memory. A slave song? Perhaps. The
blacks at Big Oaks were always singing. The cloth, very gently,
wiped his lips. He hawked, tried to spit, but his mouth was dry. He
sank back almost gratefully into the familiar and clinging blackness.

He did not know how long he floated in that state, like Cleopa-
tra's barge, he thought, drifting down the Nile—or better, the Styx.
But at one time, though there was no real measure of time in his
floating, he saw movement. Squinting his eyes, he made out a jum-
ble of red and blue and ivory. With a start he realized what it was:
the bear-claw necklace. He screamed in terror and anger, but it
darted beyond the ken of his dreaming.

Later, much later, he opened his eyes to what seemed reality. His
head hurt—oh, how it hurt! His skull split with pain. Gingerly he
felt his head, and found plastered there a gigantic poultice. When
his fingers came away they smelled of pine tar and wild herbs. He
stared at his fingers, trying hard to focus his eyes. Were they, after
all, really *his* fingers? They seemed very thin, and bony.

"*Is ta mi na,*" someone said quietly.

He inspected his fingers again, then painfully turned his head. A
man sat in the warm, smoky gloom of the lodge, looking curiously at
him. Around the man's neck was the bear-claw necklace.

"You bastard!" David said in a trembling voice. His voice sounded
thin and faraway, and it hurt his chest to talk. "You hit me with
that damned club! That damned club with all the teeth set into it!"

A moment later, a fat lady bustled over, raised David Chantry in
her arms lightly as if he were a baby, and fed him meat broth from a

chipped enamelware bowl. It tasted good, but after a few mouthfuls he vomited it in her lap.

"Sorry," he muttered. Then, realizing he had been speaking English to these people, he spoke the right Sioux words. "*Hie, hie,*" he said, and signed his gratitude also.

"*Ta me ish i,*" the woman said. *He will live.*

He did live. Crow Dog, one of Ghost Bull's younger and more rash warriors, the man with the bear-claw necklace, had led the party to investigate the queer mule-drawn wagon that came unbidden into their territory. The Army's wagons were mostly blue and this one weathered and dun-colored, but it resembled a vehicle of the hated walk-a-heaps enough for Crow Dog to launch an immediate attack. Just as he was about to dash out David's brains with his war club, one of the war party discovered David's camera and chemicals and prints in the wagon. Thus was David Chantry spared, the downward course of Crow Dog's club being stayed just enough to crack his skull, not smash it completely.

"Then," Crow Dog said uncomfortably, not looking into David's eyes, "we knew you were the picksher man. We heard of you. My father, Ghost Bull, thought it would be nice sometime to have his picksher made, like Big Hail did. He was angry when he found out I hit you in the head with my club. But She Bear knows all about wounds. She fixed your head. She mixed you herb teas to drink. She fed you special hump meat that Bull Head, the shaman, sprinkled healing powders on."

She Bear, sitting across the fire, smiled bashfully at David and shifted her bulk to stir the stew. When David did not speak, could not really think of what to say to a man who only recently split his skull, Crow Dog was further embarrassed.

"I could not help it!" he insisted. "There are a lot of white men in our land who *should* be killed for what they are doing. The soldiers, we do not mind so much. We are both warriors, and we all fight and take our chances. But there are a lot of bad white men who are not soldiers. They write papers and get us to touch the pen over them, and then steal our land. They want too many beaverskins for a pound of tea, and they rape our women, like that ugly white man in Little Man's camp. Do you understand me? You come and go among the Oglalas only because of your pickshers. Any other white man we would drive away." Crow Dog sighed, made a chopping motion with his hand to indicate *finished*. "That was how it was."

"I understand," David said at last.

With the aid of both, he managed to get to his feet. Was there still a real world out there? It had been a long time. He staggered toward the door.

"Is—is my wagon—is it all right? The things in the wagon?"

Snow-covered, the vehicle sat in the middle of the great circle of lodges. The Oglalas had fashioned a kind of skid from a sapling to move it. The broken wheel had been removed and the axle propped on a pile of stones.

"Left Hand Man is fixing the wheel," Crow Dog explained. "A long time ago, he worked for the Army and learned how to fix wagons."

David climbed into the wagon and slumped in the sagging wicker chair. Crow Dog and She Bear peered through the open flap.

"It is all there, just the way we found it," Crow Dog assured him. "No man can touch it, or a devil will get him. That is what my father, Ghost Bull, ordered. All the people are afraid to come near."

With trembling fingers David touched the precious bottles, cradled the Anthony camera in his lap, sorted through the stacks of glass plates, paper prints. Everything was there, just as he had left it. From somewhere he heard the bray of a mule.

"The animals too," Crow Dog added. "The mules and that good pony are down there"—he jerked a brown thumb—"in the corral."

It was only later that David Chantry realized he had not given much thought to his assignment from Horace Kinnear, the important mission entrusted him. Concerned only about his pictures, he had forgotten completely there was a war going on, that men were fighting and dying for the Cause. Crow Dog, seeing his somber face, asked, "Are you sick?"

"No," David said. "Not sick."

So far, he had accomplished little. He had been more interested in the Sioux, their customs and way of life, than in inciting them to rise against blue-coated soldiers in the Territory, *their* territory.

"No," he murmured, "it is just—it is just that I forgot something. Something important."

Crow Dog was mute for a long time, after the fashion of Indians. Then he asked, "Brother, can I do something to help you?"

David shook his head.

"No," he said. "Hie, hie. Thanks. It is something I must take care of myself."

CHAPTER SIX

"Have you got any raisins in that wagon?" Crow Dog wanted to know. He squatted across the fire from David Chantry, watching David fashion an "immobilizer" to hold Ghost Bull's head steady when David took the old man's portrait. In his Biloxi studio he had three of the devices, the best one made in France from shiny metal tubing. Here he was forced to improvise with a rusty pair of mechanic's calipers, which had somehow found their way into the Sioux camp, and whittled scantlings of wood.

"No, friend." David shook his head. The Sioux were fond of sweets but especially loved raisins. At the end of the long winter they always craved sweets. "When I was at Big Hail's camp," he explained, "they ate all my raisins."

Corn Woman, Crow Dog's younger sister, came in to watch. She sat silently across from him, deerskin skirt, heavy with beads, pulled modestly over her knees. For an Oglala woman, she was slight. The dark hair had unexpected bronze tints when the light caught it, and her eyes tended to the green. She was no beauty—not as attractive from the white man's viewpoint as Pretty Nose had been, and with none of Pretty Nose's exultant sexuality—but there was an attractive childlike charm about her. Her eyes were large and liquid, her gaze direct as she watched David's efforts with the immobilizer. When he had been bedfast with his head wound, now healing, Corn Woman had sung to him. She had also cooked for him, and tended to other wants, made strengthening broths while old She Bear mixed potions and poultices.

"Well, I wish I had some raisins," Crow Dog grumbled. "Maybe when we go to the fort sometime, they will give us raisin trees to plant."

Though it was nearing the end of the winter, the weather continued cold. The Sioux had an ingenious device for heating and ventilating their lodges. A rock-lined tunnel led winter air from outside to a place directly below the fire. The cold fresh air, heated by the flames, rose up into the confines of the tipi, smoke escaping through the blackened flaps at the top with their "wings" arranged to catch the wind just so, drawing out the smoke. David had measured inside temperatures with his chemical-mixing thermometer and found it to be nearly seventy degrees around the fire when the outside temperature was below freezing.

"Better yet," Crow Dog mused, still thinking about his beloved raisins, "would be the sweet sap from the *mish ke mai*. Soon it will be rising in the trees. The women catch it in buckets, and we drink all we want."

"You are always talking about sweet things!" Corn Woman teased. "It is always sweet things—candy, raisins, sugar-water from the *mish ke mai*—or is it that girl Red Fan, that you play your flute for?" It was the custom for the young men of the tribe to fashion willow flutes in the spring and play love songs before the lodge of a sweetheart.

Crow Dog scowled at the levity, but eventually grinned. Scratching in the ashes with a stick, he uncovered a baked *pomme blanche* and peeled off the skin. "Red Fan pretends she does not like me." He grinned. "On the outside, she is hard and tough, like the skin of this baked root. But inside—" He bit off a piece, rolling his eyes in ecstasy. "Inside she is very sweet and tender, and pleases me!"

David grinned also. He remembered Wade and himself in their teens, acting the same way about the Biloxi belles.

"I know," he said, "that Red Fan is in love with you. How could she not be, when you are so brave and handsome?"

In the short time he had been in Ghost Bull's camp, he had learned much to further his mission for the Council. Ghost Bull, in spite of his great age, was highly regarded by all Sioux. It was doubtful they would make any move against the white men without the old chief's approval. David had already been granted one audience with him, and now could not wait to get that magnificent face on a photographic plate.

No one knew how old Ghost Bull was. The chief was short and wiry, legs bowed and tendoned under the weight of nearly a century. But it was the face that caught the photographer's eye. Unusual for an Indian, most of the old man's hair was gone, and he wore constantly a cap fashioned of beaver pelt. Under the furry crown, his face reminded David Chantry of a carved head on the handle of his father's best walking stick—all chiseled planes and sharp shadows, eyes narrowed to mystical slits, the nose strong and beaked, lips narrow, tight and firm in spite of age. Ghost Bull's face would not have been out of place in a museum of Assyrian antiquities. David remembered a scrap of poetry:

> The Assyrian came down like the wolf on the fold,
> And his cohorts were gleaming in purple and gold.

Ghost Bull and his Sioux cohorts might be short of purple robes and golden ornament, but if the old man ever decided to have it out with the whites, it would indeed be as the wolf on the fold. There were perhaps twenty thousand Sioux in the Idaho Territory. Even counting soldiers, there could not be over three or four thousand whites. Women and children might make more; the Assyrians would have taken them as slaves after killing all the men. David wondered uneasily what Ghost Bull and his allies would do with white women and children. In spite of his liking and respect for the Sioux, they were still savages; even at intimate moments like this, with Crow Dog and Corn Woman, he was aware that a white man walked a tightrope.

Watching Crow Dog polish the stock of his new Spencer carbine with a rag soaked in bear fat, David asked, "Friend, how do you like that new gun I gave you?"

Crow Dog was a great slayer of bears; that was why he wore his necklace of bear claws. "Hie," he said. "Friend, hie. Some day I will find a way to thank you for this fine gun."

It was a canard, David thought, that Indians did not show emotion. Crow Dog was happy; his lean face split into a grin and he sang softly to himself as he worked the lever and watched the intricate meshing of the sliding parts. The carbine was of a new design. Horace Kinnear's agents had had a hard time obtaining a supply for gifts to the Indians when even the Army of the Potomac was not fully supplied. The weapon was .44 caliber, with a brass frame, lever action, and a fifteen-shot magazine under the barrel for the rim-fire cartridges.

"You can kill a lot of bears with that gun," David suggested slyly. Finishing lashing pads of beaver pelt to the arms of the calipers, David attached the assembly to a whittled stand. The pads would press against the skull and hold Ghost Bull's head steady while David adjusted his focus, took off the lens cap, counted.

"I would rather kill white men!" Crow Dog muttered. "If it was not for that old man, our father Ghost Bull, I could kill a lot of white men with my new gun! I could load this gun and kill fifteen of them one right after the other!"

Corn Woman put a gentle hand on her brother's arm.

"It is not right for you to talk that way," she cautioned. "Our father is very wise. Only he knows what is best to do."

Ghost Bull was not her father, nor the father of Crow Dog. It was customary to speak of the *wakicunza*, the chief, in such terms only as a sign of respect. In fact, Oglalas not at all related often spoke of each other as brother, sister, uncle, or father in a casual way. They seemed to conceive of themselves as one large family.

"I don't care!" Crow Dog grumbled. "He is an old man! His brains are turning into acorn mush!"

Corn Woman was shocked at such language and put her hand over her mouth, but Crow Dog plunged recklessly on.

"Look at us! Once, we were proud people, rich people! All this land—" Crow Dog flung wide his arms. "Once, this land belonged to us—the rivers, the mountains, the trees and rocks and deer and buffalo and all the beavers in the streams! Now we are poor! We don't have anything! The white men come closer and closer around us, like their hide hunters around a herd of buffalo, wanting only to cut out their tongues and skin them and leave the rest for the crows!"

David completed the assembly of the immobilizer by fastening it to a stand made from a slab of rock.

"Do you know *money*?" he asked artfully. He did not know the

Sioux word but used a common sign—passing the right hand over the left palm to simulate the counting of greenbacks.

"Of course I know money," Crow Dog said sullenly, laying aside his new gun. "It is dry stuff, like old leaves. Some of it is little and round, shiny and hard. But it is all money." Moodily he stirred the dying fire. "The Oglalas don't own money. We have to give the traders beaver pelts and things like that to buy powder and ball and knives and hatchets and red cloth."

David knelt beside Corn Woman, holding the immobilizer. "Sister, will you help me?" he asked.

She nodded, uncertain, and he adjusted the pincers-like calipers about her shiny locks. At his touch she trembled like a frightened animal, but when he spoke to her softly and soothingly she relaxed and let him check the fit, adjust the device.

"If you had money," David told Crow Dog, "you could buy a lot of things. You could buy enough red cloth for all the women. You could buy whole sacks of raisins, big sacks like flour comes in."

Crow Dog shrugged. "We don't have money."

David released Corn Woman and sat down cross-legged at the fire, carefully bending the calipers to make a better fit. "I know where there is a lot of money."

Corn Woman was uneasy. "I do not like all this talk about money," she objected. "It is bound to lead to trouble. Money is something of the white man's. It has not got anything to do with the Oglala people!"

Crow Dog was interested. "Where is this money you talk about?"

"The walk-a-heaps," David said, referring to the soldiers at Fort Zachary Taylor, "get paid with money their paymaster brings every moon. He brings it in a wagon from Fort Kearney. There are a few soldiers to guard the paymaster and his money—not more than four or five. It would be easy to get that money. You could shoot all those soldiers and still have bullets in your new gun, friend. Then, when the traders come, you would have plenty of money. Ghost Bull's Oglalas would not be poor any more."

Corn Woman started to protest, but her brother cut her off with a quick gesture. "How much money?"

David flung out both hands, flexed his fingers rapidly; *very many, beyond counting.*

Crow Dog's eyes glittered. He worked the lever of the Spencer. Finally he said, "I will think about it. There are some brave men who would go with me. A lot of them think our father is a fool." He grinned. "Let us say we go to hunt bear! That would be a good thing to do, an exciting thing. We could pull the bear's tail, pull him right out of his cave, show him we are not afraid of his teeth, we are not afraid of his claws! Yes, that would be a good bear hunt!"

David nodded, pleased. "Yes," he said, "that would be a good thing. Then you would be lord of all the bear hunters in the world!"

Crow Dog sprang to his feet. Lean and shining in the ruddy glow of the fire, he drew himself erect and wrapped the red blanket about him with a flourish. *That, too,* David thought. *That fine figure— some day soon I must catch that also in the lens of my Anthony camera.*

When Crow Dog had flung his way out, David and Corn Woman were alone by the fire. It was late afternoon. By rights the wind should have risen, the air grown sharp and cold with the advent of dusk. But all seemed quiet, and it was pleasantly warm in the lodge. The coming of spring was in the air, the Moon When the Buffalo Start to Fill Out.

Corn Woman was displeased. "I do not think you should have talked that way to my brother," she complained, stirring the fire and setting on it an iron pot. During the winter the Oglalas' store of dried meat and vegetables had grown scanty, and there was only a handful to drop into the boiling water. "He is rash," she said. "All the people know that. You know that too, David." She pronounced his name with a lilt that gave him pleasure. "He will only cause trouble. Then my father Ghost Bull will be angry. Bull Head and the old men will be angry, too. There will be a lot of trouble!"

Uncomfortable, he shrugged. "Your brother is just going to hunt bears."

Corn Woman showed an uncharacteristic flash of temper. "You know that is not true! You are telling a lie! A man that lies is no good! My father Ghost Bull never lies! He says a man who lies is weak, and is not a man!"

"Listen!" In anger and confusion he caught her wrist. "Listen to me! You know what Crow Dog says is true! The Sioux were lords of this land, all of it! Now they are poor! The white men are taking everything! It is better to fight them now than let them swallow you up, like a dog does a piece of meat!"

In his frustration he gripped her arm so tightly she winced.

"Maybe we *will* fight!" she cried. "But that is for my father Ghost Bull to decide—he and the elders! It is not for you, a white man, to come to our village and make trouble!"

Her words hurt; perhaps they were true. Still holding her by the wrist, he was fascinated by the cold greenish fire in her eyes. Unafraid, head held high, she gave him look for look. It was a side of her he had never seen, never suspected.

"Yes," he murmured. Almost unconsciously he slipped into English, and realized later it was because he did not want her to know the doubt that gnawed at him. "Yes," he repeated, "you have a good point there, ma'am! I have often raised that very point with myself, and argued it back and forth. First I took one side, then the other. Am I a spy, a traitor, fit for hanging? Or am I a patriot, brave and loyal as ever a man in Wade Chantry's brigade?"

She was puzzled. Not resisting his grasp, she spoke softly. "You say?"

Her flesh was warm and soft. Though slight, Corn Woman was very feminine. What was it papa's niggers used to say, grinning? *The nearer the bone the sweeter the meat.* But that was gross; he didn't mean it that way at all. Corn Woman smelled of aromatic grasses and woodsmoke. Her small breasts were firm and round, like somebody's golden apples in Greek mythology. Yet she was sweet and chaste; thinking of her in a sexual way seemed almost an obscenity—for now.

"I— I say—" he stammered. He broke off, but did not release his grasp on her wrist. Instead he drew her nearer. "I say—"

Again he broke off, not finding the right words in either Sioux or English. *This is Crow Dog's sister,* he told himself, almost savagely. *No one, least of all she herself, has given her young body to you.* He thought of her own words concerning her brother. *You will only cause trouble.*

"You say?" Corn Woman insisted. She came close to him, looking into his eyes.

Growingly fluent in the Sioux tongue, he could still not find the proper words. Again he lapsed into English.

"I think," he murmured, "you are quite the loveliest creature I have seen for a long time. You would do credit to any Biloxi ballroom, and I—"

While he did not hear anyone enter, he was aware of a breath of chill air as the door flap opened. Holding Corn Woman in his arms, he turned to face the unknown intruder, unwilling to deny his love to anyone.

"Hallelujah, brother!" Chilblained, nose and cheeks red and blistered with cold, Benjamin Sears stood like a gaunt bird in the doorway, drawing off a pair of ragged red mittens. "Now, ain't *this* a scene right out of a Frenchy novel!" he chortled.

For a long moment David stood astonished, staring with disbelief at the bogus missionary. Finally he managed to find his voice. "What the hell are *you* doing here?"

Sears smiled, a grimace that stretched the peeling skin tightly over his cheekbones. "Come for a little visit, that's all! Jesus—can't you give a feller a better welcome than that?" He turned, motioned. Following him into the tipi came a tattered and angular Indian with a long nose and a pinched face.

"This here," Benjie explained, "is what you call a Ree kind of Indian. He's my guide and interpreter—feller name of Poor Bird. He ain't much to look at, but he's been real useful in my missionary work among the heathens." Peeling off his rusty black coat, Benjie grinned. "Well, ain't you and your lady friend goin' to ask a man to sit?"

David gestured to Corn Woman. Quickly and quietly she drew a blanket about her slender shoulders and brushed past Benjamin Sears. His gaze followed her from the tipi.

"We're not even supposed to *know* each other!" David said. "Why did you risk coming here?"

Benjie squatted before the fire and held out chapped hands. "Christ!" he mumbled. "Can't you feed a man first?"

Grudgingly David spooned stew into tin bowls for Benjie and the shabby Ree. The Ree bolted his, belched a few times, then settled into somnolence at the edge of the circle of firelight. Sears ate his stew deliberately, washed down with drafts of coffee. Finally he belched also, patted his lean paunch. "God, that tastes good! Poor

Bird and me been living on cheese and crackers the last two days!" He looked toward the door flap. "She boil up that stew?"

"Who?"

Benjie grinned broadly. "Why, that little woman you was bussing when I first come in! That bedmate of yours!"

David was angry. "She cooked the stew, but she's not my bed-mate! She's only the sister of a friend of mine. Corn Woman cooks for me, sews for me, but that doesn't mean anything!"

Benjie shrugged. "All right, all right!" he said hastily. "I didn't mean no harm, Mr. Chantry! She's just a friend, and that's purely all right with me!"

"Now explain!" David insisted. "What are you doing down here on the Powder? You're supposed to be north, with the Cheyennes!"

Benjie stared into the murky depths of his coffee, swished the grounds about. "That's what I wanted to talk to you about." His tone was subdued, melancholy. "Well, I ain't been doing too well. Oh, I preached to the Cheyennes and stirred 'em up a little. Maybe you heard about them three miners Little Man stomped on and hung their hides up to dry along Big Dry Creek?"

"Yes."

"That was my doin'."

David nodded.

"But some of Little Man's folks got scragged in the fighting, after I told 'em they couldn't get hurt in God's sacred cause. Then I—well, I got a little sweet on one good-lookin' gal, and Little Man didn't like it. So I lit a shuck out of there—me and Poor Bird—and went down the line to the other camps, preachin' and stirrin' up as much trouble as I could. They fed me all right, give me a place to sleep, listened to my preachin'. But I never felt they really believed what I was sayin'." Benjie examined his bony knuckles. "Got into some more hot water, too, with another gal—"

Suddenly David remembered Crow Dog's brief mention of the white man who raped a woman in a Cheyenne camp.

"You're a damned fool!" he blurted. "Haven't you got any better sense than that?"

There was a sudden desperate look in Benjie's eyes. "Hell!" he protested. "I get along fine as silk with most folks! Baptists, River Brethren, Quakers, Dutchmen, Holy Rollers, niggers—whatever! But these Indians are hard to understand, Mr. Chantry! They just look at you and *through* you and you don't have the least inkle of what they're thinkin'! And God damn it—I been *lonely!*" He gestured toward the door flap. "I'd give my everlasting soul for a fine little woman like that to be friendly with me! I'm from a big family, see, and while there was a lot of fussing and fighting, I'm still used to being *with* people; cutting up, maybe, playing the fool, joking, or just talking! But out here—" He spread his hands in a discouraged gesture. "I thought it'd be a kind of a lark, something to brag about when I was an old geezer with a long white beard, and children and grandchildren. But I sit all alone in a stinkin' tipi and I can't even say 'howdy' less 'n that shiftless Ree does it for me!"

"You haven't told me yet what you're doing here," David said relentlessly.

"Well," Benjie said, "first I went to Elk City. I had a good reason for goin' there—I picked up a case of Bibles at the Diamond R freight office." Benjie grinned, wryly. "Mostly .44 caliber, they was." Fumbling in a pocket, he brought out a dog-eared newspaper clipping. "By the way, I come across this in Dooley's Hotel. Thought you might be interested."

From an old St. Louis *Missouri Democrat* David read the item:

Reports reaching St. Louis this week indicate that General Jackson is planning a sweep northward soon, possibly through the Shenandoah Valley. Documents found on a captured rebel officer speak of Chantry's Ninth Brigade of cavalry spearheading the attack. In anticipation of a flanking move toward Washington itself, the capital has been strongly reinforced.

"Your brother, ain't he?" Benjie asked. "Seems to me Mr. Kinnear said he was." His tone was respectful. "Got a brother that's breveted brigadier already! That's some punkins!"

David slipped the clipping into the beaded pouch at his waist. His civilian clothes were completely gone; he wore only Sioux garb, except for a flat-crowned felt hat the worse for wear.

"I appreciate it," he said, and did. "But you've got to get out of here quick, Benjie."

Sears got up, anxiously paced back and forth like a lean, dark bird. "I know I ain't welcome as the flowers in May nor nothing like that, but there ain't no call for you to treat me like a polecat neither! Here I been marooned among the Indians and all I wanted was to talk to you, get some advice! Christ, Mr. Chantry, you're *educated!* And you speak the lingo, I heard you! You—you know how to make friends with these people, and I don't!" He twined big-knuckled fingers together. "You got to help me!"

David felt a twinge of compassion. Benjie was certainly necessary to the Cause; the Cheyennes had to be brought into the picture, and soon. Spring was on the way. Perhaps he *could* help Benjie, make his efforts more successful, less clumsy and dangerous. Sighing, he motioned Benjie to sit beside him at the fire.

"I was put out at you—yes! You know damned well you could compromise me, you, and the whole damned Council undertaking out here! No one, so far at least, knows there's any connection between us, and that's the way it's got to stay, don't you see? Colonel Garrett at Fort Taylor isn't a fool! If he gets wind of this he'll put two and two together. You've got to get out of here as soon as you can—tomorrow morning—get back to your Cheyennes!"

Benjie groaned, rocked back and forth on his haunches.

"I can't! I'm purely exhausted! And I'm scared, too!"

David put a hand on his shoulder. "After a good night's sleep you'll feel better, believe me. I'll see you get food and fresh animals. Benjie, the South needs you, the Council needs you. Time is running out."

Benjie shook his head, ran a hand through the mop of uncut hair. "I ain't doing any good, I tell you! Better for me to cut back to Elk City and ride a freight wagon to Omaha! The Council can send someone else out!"

"Listen!" David took Benjie's arm in his fingers and squeezed it so hard Benjie winced. "Listen to me! There are men right now in Virginia, in Tennessee, in Pennsylvania, fighting and dying, wounded, freezing to death, widows and orphans weeping at home in both the North *and* the South. God damn it, *you* ought to know—your brothers were killed, weren't they? Benjie, we've got to stop that war! Don't make any difference how it's done, but the best way is for General Lee to win—fast!"

"I *want* for him to win," Benjie said soberly.

"Then, stop this whining about going home! In the morning you're setting out for the north country again, to do your part. We—the Council, the South—*need* the Cheyennes! Now, listen. . . ."

While the dusk grew closer about Ghost Bull's village in the buttes, David talked earnestly to Benjamin Sears. Though David was not an expert on the Cheyennes, they were close enough to the Oglala Sioux to resemble them in many respects.

"Try to learn the language," he counseled. "Work at it! The hand talk—the *wibluta*—is easier, though. Get started on that. Watch their hands, their fingers, as they talk, because they frequently speak and sign at the same time." He showed Benjie a few of the gestures that were the common language of the Cheyennes and the Rees, the Sioux and the Assiniboines and the Absaroka, the tribe the white men called the Crows.

"I guess maybe I could learn that," Benjie muttered, fingers awkwardly following David's own. "I can do card tricks, and that's bound to help. Already some of 'em seem to understand me when I make motions about Hell and Heaven and everlasting fire and brimstone and all that claptrap." He grinned, showed David his tattered Bible. "I don't *believe* none of this stuff in here, but I know it by heart, I surely do!"

"And women," David added as an afterthought.

Benjie looked uncomfortable.

"Don't tamper with their women unless someone invites you! Maybe one of the elders will offer you a niece as a gesture of friendship. Maybe a woman will just come to you and want to share your bed. No one will think anything about it. They're not harlots, understand—it's just that lying together isn't made much of among Indians. But don't ever *take* a woman—do you understand what I mean?"

Benjie nodded, essayed a smile. "I know what you mean, all right, and I'll try! I'll try hard, Mr. Chantry, believe me! I was downhearted when I first come here, but maybe I can cut her now. Leastways I'll try, and I'm beholden to you. I never had much education, myself, except for a few weeks at the Blood of the Lamb Seminary and Christian Agricultural College. But I admire you, the way you say words! The way you talked about the war and all, that was fine! I'm everlastingly obliged."

The shabby Ree guide and interpreter awoke, yawned, scratched himself.

"There's a woman called She Bear," David concluded. "She's old but spry, and a good cook. I'll send for her. She'll fix you a place to sleep, make you breakfast in the morning, pack a lunch for you and Poor Bird."

When they were gone, Benjamin Sears still insisting on his gratitude, David sat staring into the embers of the fire. Damned fool, Sears! He had risked both their necks by coming to the Oglala camp. But Benjie was so forlorn, so friendless, that it was hard to stay mad at him. David was glad he had finally befriended him. And that talk about the war! The eloquence Benjie so admired must have been nothing more than David Chantry's own efforts to convince himself of the rightness of his conduct, the denial of a solemn oath. Had he succeeded? He didn't know. Wade Chantry, at least, knew his own mind. But Wade's problems were simpler; all Wade had to do was shoot and saber down anything in blue.

Even with the fire smoldering out, it was warm in the lodge. He stepped outside. The sky was dark, without a shred of moon; stars blazed like small suns. He heard water dripping, and realized there was a thaw. A soft wind blew from the south, caressed his cheek. The Sioux, he remembered, believed the south wind was unlucky, brought sickness and death and misfortune. The south wind was greatly feared.

He did not realize the significance of the omen, the south wind, until next morning, when Benjie and his ragged Ree guide were preparing to leave. Corn Woman stood near, watching, while David helped Benjie adjust a pack on a fresh pony.

"Wisht I had me a fine little gal like that!" the irrepressible Benjie teased. "No offense, though, Mr. Chantry! Guess I'll just have to look me one up when I get the chancet! Nothing hasty, like you told me—just wait for a nice little squaw to notice my great natural beauty, and chase *me!*"

"Now you've got it," David agreed. "Remember, they have their own customs, different from ours. When they do something that seems strange or peculiar, never laugh—that can make them very angry!"

Benjie threw a long leg over his pony. "I ain't aiming to make them mad at me no more, Mr. Chantry, that's a fact! I'll do exactly like you say." His lips, however, twisted in a grin. "Sometimes it ain't easy. They do some real funny things!"

"Like what?" David asked, hoping to explain to Benjie the peculiarities of the Sioux philosophy.

"Oh, they believe in evil spirits and monsters and devil animals and all kinds of truck like that! It's a pure marvel how a big strong buck can get scared as a young 'un in a dark room at night!"

"They think," David said, "that there are both good and bad influences all around them, and that sometimes those influences take strange physical shapes, that's all."

"The whole camp," Benjie reminisced, "got spooked one day, and no one wouldn't hardly come out of his tipi. During the night a big grizzly or something prowled around the camp and made some giant prints, almost like someone had took a dinner plate and pressed it down in the snow. I'll swear if they didn't tell me it was a devil bird of some kind, and might snatch someone up and fly up in a tree and eat 'em! Little Man hisself said he'd seen one once; it was bigger than a horse and walked on its hind feet and had feathers all over it, like a rooster! Now, you ever hear of such foolishness? And yet these was growed men!"

David shrugged, amused at the thought of a horse-sized rooster. "Well," he said, "you'd better be getting on your way."

Benjie nodded, waved farewell. In a few moments he and his nondescript Ree and the pack animals passed from view beyond the dripping, snow-laden trees. It was not until then that the import of Benjie's remarks struck home, with the chilling impact of an iron lance. Suddenly David remembered Cassie Garrett speaking of Chris Rowley, the night he and Cassie stood together on the colonel's porch. *He's one of Owen's civilian scouts. The surgeon had to take off the front parts of both feet.* There was more, he remembered. *He sort of hobbles on the stumps, but Owen depends on him a lot.* Was that—could that have been—Chris Rowley, nosing around Little Man's camp, suspicious of Benjamin Sears' missionary efforts among the Cheyennes? Were the strange, saucer-shaped prints those of Rowley's maimed feet?

Corn Woman looked at him solicitously, took his hands in hers. "You are cold," she said.

"Yes," he agreed, "I am cold."

Fear chilled his veins, tightened his muscles, invaded his stomach in a cold wash of near nausea. Even in the warm south wind he was cold.

CHAPTER SEVEN

Ghost Bull's camp in the shadow of Rainy Butte lay sodden and cheerless in the unseasonable spring thaw. For days, the warm south wind had blown, and the camp was a sea of mud with only token patches of snow. Rills of clear snow water ran everywhere, and there were emerging stands of green grass. But this kind of spring in winter was, the Oglalas knew, often treacherous. The winter god could strike hard when people forgot his great powers.

There was illness in the camp. Babies and some of the old men and women died of a fever, racked with ague and coughing. Bull Head, the shaman, burned sacred grasses and chanted in vain against the sickness. David Chantry did not see a great deal of Corn Woman; she was too busy hurrying about the camp, nursing the ill, comforting the dying, speaking words of solace to the bereaved. In the press of his own personal affairs he could not think much about Corn Woman. He was busy planning further mischief—and taking Ghost Bull's portrait.

Naked from the waist up, the old man sat like a graven statue in the gloom of the big lodge. Around his legs was wrapped his best red blanket, and on his arms were shiny coils of brass. In his fur cap was stuck a single modest eagle feather, though Ghost Bull was entitled to an array of plumes attesting to many coups. Around his neck, on a necklace of blue beads, hung the eagle leg-bone whistle, sign of his status as head of the Scalp-Shirt Men, the hereditary chiefs of the tribe.

"Ai—ee—ee!" Ghost Bull objected as David adjusted the immobilizer clamps around his skull. "That thing bites like a fox!"

David apologized. The light in the tipi was dim, and the portrait would require a lengthy exposure with the old man absolutely motionless. "Father," he explained, "it has got to be this way to get a good picture."

"Well, then—" Ghost Bull stiffened again into monolithic silence.

David squinted at the ground-glass focusing screen. Not much light, certainly; how long an exposure? Twenty seconds? Thirty?

"Be quick!" Ghost Bull grumbled. "I am getting a headache!"

Hurrying out to his wagon, David sensitized a plate, slipped it into the holder, and hastened back. Emissaries from other tribes, he saw, had come to talk to Ghost Bull. Tall, handsome men, they sat their mud-splashed ponies with an injured air as they watched the white interloper take precedence over them.

With a last look at his subject, David pulled the black cloth over his head and gave a minuscule adjustment to the brass focusing knob. The old man sat proudly, one brown arm draped over his warrior's drum—a circle of willow wood over which was stretched rawhide, the whole ornamented with feathers and a painted design. Ghost Bull's eyes stared into the distance. There was somber strength in the hooked nose, the jut of his chin.

"Now!" David said.

He snatched off the lens cap. *One. . . . Two. . . . Three. . . .*

Somewhere, water dripped.

Four. . . . Five. . . . Six. . . . Seven. . . .

This could be the finest thing he had ever done! *Lordy, lordy!* he thought. *Don't let him move!*

Eighteen. . . . Nineteen. . . . Twenty. . . .

A fly, swooping about the lodge, caromed against Ghost Bull's nose and buzzed into the smoke flaps above. The old man did not move. The hooded eyes stared far into the future.

Twenty-nine. . . . Thirty.

David clapped the lens cap on and drew out the plate holder.

"We are finished?" Ghost Bull asked.

David nodded, releasing the old man's skull from the immobilizer clamps.

"Picksher?"

"Only a few minutes," David promised.

When he emerged from the wagon with the finished plate, the Indian emissaries were noticeably restless. One man waved a feathered lance at him in annoyance, but David was too elated to pay any attention.

"Father, look!" He held the plate by the edges before Ghost Bull's old eyes. "*Sha, sha!*" The Sioux word *sha* meant *red; sha sha,* or the reddest of reds, meant *beautiful.* The Sioux loved the color red, and the reddest of reds was undoubtedly beautiful.

The picture was a classic portrait study, as good as ever Julian Vannerson or even Mr. Brady could have done. But Ghost Bull's face fell; his brow furrowed. For a long time he stared at the portrait. Finally he asked, "This is what I look like?"

"Yes, father," David said. "The magic box tells the truth." He gestured with his thumb, the Sioux way of indicating "speak truth." The portrait did indeed speak truth; the power and kingly bearing of Ghost Bull glowed from the still-wet plate. But the old man had something else on his mind. "I do not think I look that old!" he grumbled. "And that camera box makes my eye look crooked!"

There was indeed a cast in one of the old man's eyes, but it only served to intensify the distant and reflective quality of his gaze. David had caught it well on the plate, but Ghost Bull viewed it as detracting from his image. Great a chief as he was, the old man had his quirks. He was very vain, wearing the fur hat day and night to cover his thin locks.

"Put it away," Ghost Bull said crossly. "Maybe I will look at it again sometime and like it better."

David started to leave, but the chief summoned him back with a curt wave of his eagle-feather fan.

"Sit, and we talk."

"There are men outside," David told him. "Men on horses. They come to see you. Maybe—"

Ghost Bull stared coldly at him.

David squatted meekly at his feet.

"They can wait," the old man said.

For a long time the chief sat in silence, puffing at his pipe. Once, it went out. Ghost Bull reached casually into the fire, plucked out a coal between leathery fingers, and stuffed it into the carved soapstone bowl. David remembered hearing from Big Hail that there was a secret society among the Oglalas, men whose medicine was so great they could handle live coals, even walk on them, eat them.

"Crow Dog has gone hunting," the chief finally said.

David remained silent, observant of etiquette.

Ghost Bull exhausted the charge of willow bark in his pipe. Knocking out the dottle on a slab of stone near the fire, he loaded the pipe again and lit it.

"Hunting is bad in winter," the old man went on. "No one hunts in winter. Summer is the time for hunting. In winter the animals stay close to the ground. They are in their burrows, or in caves sleeping. Sometimes they go right out of our mountains, down into the flatlands."

David nodded in agreement.

"The young men are very foolish," Ghost Bull complained. "All they want to do is fight! Well, there is a time to fight, but there is a time to talk. I hear the white men are planning a big talk with us when the weather gets warm. That is what I hear." He puffed again, watching a smoke ring waver upward. "Sometimes fighting is good. Sometimes talking is good. If talk does not get what we want, then we can fight. But that is hard to explain to the young men." He stared at David Chantry. "Do you understand me?"

"Yes, father," David said. He made the sign for *understand*, which was the same as *know*: closed fist held to the left breast, then sweeping the palm outward, opening it at the same time. *Something closed, mysterious, then opened to the light of day.* It was a graceful, eloquent gesture that always delighted him. Now, however, he was apprehensive. How much did Ghost Bull know of his talks with Crow Dog?

"A chief," Ghost Bull grumbled, "has got to think of all the people: the old people, the sick people, the children. A chief cannot just think about the young men who talk loud and always want to shoot someone." He jabbed the stem of the pipe at David Chantry. "You are a white man! Talk to me like a white man! Tell me what the white man wants."

Carefully David chose his words. "Father, the Oglalas are different from the Miniconjou. The Brulés are different from the Sans Arcs. Yet they are all Sioux. It is the same with white men. Some are from the North, some are from the South. Some are good, some bad. Some wear blue, like the soldiers at Fort Taylor. Others wear gray clothes. They have a different flag from the striped one that flies over the post. So it is hard to say what the white men think, because some think different things."

They sat thus for a long time, Ghost Bull puffing at his pipe, David staring into the fire. When a proper lapse had been observed, David spoke again.

"Back there, where the sun comes from"—he gestured—"back there, a long way away, men in blue uniforms are fighting men in gray uniforms. The blue men want to beat the gray men, take away their lands, make them bend their necks. Out here it is the same. The blue men want to beat the Sioux, take away their lands, make them bend their necks. They want to herd the Sioux onto little pieces of poor land, like animals in cages."

Ghost Bull watched impassively. A vagrant shaft of sun struck through the open smoke flaps, bathed the chief in luminance.

"The Sioux are my friends," David went on. "The Sioux cannot live in cages, I know that. So I think it is better to fight now, when there are not so many blue men."

The sun glow grew, brightened; the slanting shaft lit the interior of the lodge. Motes of dust danced in the beam. Ghost Bull rubbed his nose with the stem of the pipe.

"You are a gray man," he observed.

David nodded. "I am a gray man." There was no use attempting concealment before the majestic gaze.

Someone scratched at the door flap.

"Come!" Ghost Bull called.

Bull Head, the shaman, entered. "Father," he said, "the Miniconjou friends and the Sans Arc friends are waiting. They say it is important."

Ghost Bull nodded. To David Chantry he said, "I will think about what you told me. Gray is not a pretty color. The Sioux like bright colors, like blue. But a gray horse can be a very good horse." His face twisted in a grimace. "*Ai—ee—ee!*" he complained. "It is hard to be a chief!"

David withdrew, standing respectfully aside as the emissaries of the Miniconjou and Sans Arcs stalked past to enter the great lodge. It was a tricky game he was playing; he felt apprehensive, yet elated.

Corn Woman awaited him in her brother's lodge, where she "did for him," as they said in Biloxi. Very casually she slept on a pile of robes at the far circumference of the lodge. She cooked for him, mended his clothes, and in her quiet way was watchful of his needs. After the night she had been so angry with him, their relationship had settled into that of brother and sister. David was comfortable with the relationship. At his least gesture she would probably come to sleep with him, share his robes near the fire. But the thought repelled him. Corn Woman was honest, direct and childlike, far removed from the physicality of Pretty Nose. Lying with Corn Woman would profane their relationship. So they lived chastely together, waiting for Crow Dog to return.

Quilling a shirt, she sat in her accustomed corner, singing to herself. He suspected the shirt was a present for him, David Chantry. It was custom for the Sioux women to soften porcupine quills in hot water, then draw the quills through their teeth to flatten them. After that, the quills were dyed in various colors, dried, and sewed with sinew to the garment. Some of the old women had teeth worn down to the gumline by years of quilling clothing for their menfolk, but Corn Woman's teeth were bright and even.

"There is no word from my brother?" she asked.

He shook his head.

Corn Woman sighed, her eyes misted. "*Wakan*," she murmured. "*Wakan, wakan.*"

It was a Sioux portmanteau word, carrying many meanings. *Wakan* meant anything mysterious, unknown, in the hands of the gods. *Wakan tanka* was the name for the chief god of Sioux theology, the Great Spirit, Father of All. *Wakan ishi* meant evil spirits, mischief-makers like the god Iktomi, who played bad tricks on people. *Shonka wakan* was the Sioux name for horse: literally, "God's dog." In this case it simply meant, "No one knows where my brother is. I hope the gods take good care of him, bring him back safely."

"*Wakan*," David agreed, not without a twinge of conscience. Crow Dog and his band should by now be approaching the rising moraine where David had seen the paymaster's wagon and its escort. Feeling uncomfortable, he opened his violin case and took out the instrument, plucking the strings and twisting the pegs until it was in fair tune. Corn Woman liked for him to play the violin, listening intently and trying to hum the melody.

Entranced, she crept near him. Bowing idly, he remembered an old song the blacks had used to sing at Big Oaks:

> "Possum put on an overcoat,
> Raccoon put on gown,
> Rabbit put on ruffled shirt,
> All buttoned up and down.
> Wait, Billy, wait, wait, I say,
> And I will marry you bime by."

The first measures were lively; then the melody slowed, slipped into a minor key, ended on a plaintive lingering strain. Though Corn Woman spoke no English, she seemed affected by the song and laid her sleek head on his knee. He felt a surge of affection, warmed and fulfilled by the childish gesture. *And I will marry you bime by.* Gently he touched the shining white part in her hair. There was another song jailers and prisoners both had sung at the state penitentiary in Columbus. *When this cruel war is over.* He whispered the words in English. *When this cruel war is over. When you are grown. When you are a woman.*

He was eating the stew she prepared when he heard the commotion outside. It was a very good stew, rabbit stew thick with slivers of dried *pomme blanche.* He did not notice the noise until Corn Woman frowned and raised a slender forefinger.

"Listen!"

He listened. Voices were raised in anger against a background of subdued murmuring. Then he heard a shot, a flat crack that must be a pistol, rather than a larger weapon.

Springing to his feet, he brushed aside the door flap and ran out in the gloom of late afternoon. In the failing light a group of Ghost Bull's braves surrounded a ragged figure, an angry white man who mouthed obscenities and writhed as he tried to break free from their grasp.

"God damn it!" he snarled. "Give me back my pistol! I ain't done nothing!"

David spoke to Long Walker, the young man who pinioned Blossom's arms.

"How did he come here? What has he done?"

Long Walker made a gesture of anger and contempt. "This old man is on our land! Ghost Bull told him not to come near our camp any more. No one likes him. He kills wolves that belong to us, the Oglalas!"

Blossom sneered. "Thick as thieves with 'em, ain't you, Chantry?" he snarled. "Regular runagate, I'd say!" He spat a brown gout into the snow.

"What are you going to do with him?" David asked.

Long Walker gestured toward Blossom's pack mules. "Take his animals, his things—his guns and food—then drive him away from our camp."

"But he'll die!"

Long Walker shrugged, grinned.

David turned to Blossom. In English he asked, "What were you doing, prowling around Ghost Bull's camp?"

Blossom twisted free from Long Walker's grasp. "That's what I was trying to tell 'em!" he squalled. "I was just passin' through, on my way to my diggin's up the river! That's where I spend my summers, when I ain't wolfin'! I didn't mean no harm! I run off the trail to get around some swampy ground, and mebbe I come too near the old grouch's camp— I ain't saying I didn't! But I didn't mean no offense!"

David's first impulse had been to turn on his heel and walk away. Blossom was an unsavory character; he had cheated David Chantry, taken advantage of him, threatened his life. But Blossom was, after all, a white man.

"I know him," he said to Long Walker. "I think he did not mean to come this close to our father's camp. Maybe it is better to let him go away in peace." He almost regretted his statement. If he were consistent, he should let Long Walker and his braves have their way with the old rascal. When Colonel Garrett learned of the killing of another white man, it would only exacerbate the tension between the Sioux and the whites, and so help the Cause. But somehow or other he could not let it happen so. "He was only on his way to his mine up the river," he said finally. "He digs for gold there."

Long Walker looked doubtful. He glanced at the mules, the loaded packs. Oglala supplies were running short; besides, they liked mule meat.

"I will take him into my lodge and explain he should never again come near," David suggested. "That is a better way than to kill him and have the soldiers come against us now, in this winter season."

Long Walker was undecided. But David Chantry, the picksher man, had come to be an important person in Ghost Bull's camp. Long Walker frowned, sighed, shifted his feet, avoiding David's eyes. Finally he nodded and signed quickly, making the sign for *uncertain*, bringing the closed right hand near his mouth, then jabbing a forefinger at David Chantry. The meaning was eloquent. *I am not sure about this, but the responsibility is yours—I wash my hands of it.* Watching with narrowed eyes, Blossom nodded with satisfaction.

"Guess I got to thank you, pilgrim, savin' my hide from the damned brutes!" he said to David. "Much obliged!"

After seeing to his animals, Blossom went with David Chantry to the tipi, their moccasins wet and making sucking noises as they walked.

"Early thaw," Blossom grunted. "Bad sign!"

David held back the door flap for the wolfer to enter. For a moment the old man stood within the doorway, eyes adjusting to the gloom. David, impatient to change his footgear, pushed against him, but Blossom stood rigid, transfixed.

"What's the matter?" David asked.

The old man made a hoarse sound. He pointed.

"What's the matter?" David demanded. Shouldering the wolfer aside, he strode within.

Corn Woman knelt before the fire. She had just placed a bundle of twigs on the flame; her face was clearly illuminated by the flaring up of the dry branches.

"It's her!"

"Her? Who?" David looked from one to the other. Corn Woman regarded Blossom without comprehension. The wolfer stared back at her, a light kindling in his bloodshot eyes. He took a step forward, holding out his arms.

"Mattie!" he cried. "It's your pa! Don't you know me? Christ, I found you at last!"

The March weather was bad in Washington. For the past six days, it had rained heavily. Rock Creek was filled from bank to bank with a yellow torrent threatening the foundations of Horace Kinnear's summerhouse. Even as the Council convened, they could hear the rush of waters through the heavy drapes; on the roof, the impact of the drops kept up a steady drumming. Most of the members of the Council arrived in sodden garments, grumbling about the weather. But Horace Kinnear was cheerful. After the others had made detailed reports, he went quickly to the matter of the treaty convocation on the Powder.

"As you know," he said, "the plans of the Indian Office to meet with the Sioux and the Cheyennes to arrange a treaty are now fact, rather than rumor. It is their intention to hold the meetings in June. The seasonal rise on the river will make transportation easier—the steamboats can navigate much farther up the Missouri and the Yellowstone—and a June date will enable them to talk treaty before the Indians go on their summer hunt. Our people in the Indian Office are working to delay the treaty talks, perhaps squelch them altogether, though that is unlikely. In the field, also, our people are active." He consulted a memorandum at his elbow. "Benjamin Sears, our representative on the upper Missouri, among the Cheyennes, was successful in fomenting a fracas there. Through his efforts a raid was mounted on a party of white miners by Little Man and his band. David Chantry has also been successful. Ghost Bull's warriors were encouraged to attack the paymaster's wagon en route to Fort Taylor, and carried off several thousand dollars in gold. There is every likelihood that Colonel Garrett at Fort Taylor will be obliged to punish the Indians, and that will certainly put a spoke in the wheel of any treaty negotiations! Ghost Bull is a powerful leader among the Sioux. Without him, it is unlikely the treaty talks will succeed."

"Chantry?" The man with the wen unfolded a dog-eared copy of the Washington *Daily Chronicle*. "Didn't I see—" He spread the damp paper on the table. "Yes, here it is." He read the brief dispatch. The youngest general officer in the rebel army had been killed; Chantry's brigade was without a leader. Wade Chantry had been killed at Culpeper, near the junction of the Rapidan and Rappahannock rivers, in a skirmish with Federal cavalry. "Wasn't that our Chantry's brother?"

Major Ashmore, the Confederate officer who posed as a dealer in livestock while in the capital, confirmed the relationship. "Although," he said soberly, "I am very sorry to hear of it. Wade Chantry was a fine man, a gallant officer." He shook his head, stared down at the ash of his cigar. "Such a waste! Good men on both sides dying by the thousands!"

"That is so," Horace Kinnear agreed. "And that is the chiefest of reasons why the efforts of the Council *must* be successful! We owe it to our country, though it is a pity we must work in secret and risk condemnation as traitors to accomplish our ends."

A few members of the Council had lately faltered in their dedication, Kinnear knew. Quickly he turned to the next item, a surprise he hoped would rally flagging spirits.

"The Indian Office," he reported, "has gone so far with the treaty preparations as to come out with a list of proposed commissioners to meet with the Indians." Putting on his steel-rimmed spectacles, he read a lengthy document outlining plans for the talks and ending with a list of candidates to represent the government. "James Tate—you all know him—Robert Clarkson, from the Merchant's Bank; Henry Dockstader, Patent Office; William Bunting, pastor of the Georgia Avenue Episcopal Church; Isham Jones of the Christian Commission—" He paused, looked benignly around. "And Mr. Horace Kinnear, publisher of the *Illustrated Weekly News.*"

There was commotion, general astonishment. Mr. Gosling, the wholesale grocer, was incredulous. "You, Horace? However, in Heaven's name, did you—"

"It was not in Heaven's name," Kinnear said, smiling. "It was obviously brought about by other forces. That is to say—what better choice for a seat on the Treaty Commission than myself; a prominent citizen of the capital, publisher of the leading weekly journal of the area with a readership of some thirty thousand, and—" He polished his spectacles and blinked amiably. "And sponsor of a project to photograph the ways and customs of our Indian brothers, lest in their latter days this rich culture be lost!"

There was chuckling at the irony of it, applause. Mr. Dillard-Hume, the British ambassador's secretary, was encouraged.

"As you know, sir," he said, "Her Majesty's government has been equivocal about our continued interest in the affairs of the Council. But I am sure this development will reassure them." The B. & O. Railroad official was likewise enthusiastic. Major Ashmore proposed three cheers for Horace Kinnear, and they all joined in. Afterward, when the business of the Council had been completed, they partook of a bountiful buffet. It had been, Horace Kinnear reflected, a fine day in spite of the rain.

CHAPTER EIGHT

For a moment, the tableau was frozen into immobility; Blossom the wolfer, arms outstretched to the Indian girl he believed his daughter; David Chantry standing in the doorway, astonished; Corn Woman kneeling before the buffalo-chip fire, face lit by the flames, eyes startled.

"It's Mattie!" Blossom cried again. Still holding out his arms, he advanced toward her. But Corn Woman was frightened by the bearded stranger. Running to David Chantry, she clung to him; one hand made a quick gesture. *This man—who?*

"It's me, it's only me!" Blossom insisted. He thrust out horny palms in supplication. "She don't know me, don't even know her own pa! Livin' with savages all this time kind of addled her brains!"

"Wait a minute!" David fended off the wolfer's attempted embrace. "What in hell are you talking about? This isn't Mattie! This isn't your daughter! This is Corn Woman!"

Blossom scowled. "Look at them eyes! Ever see a Sioux with green eyes? And her hair! It ain't coal-black, like an Oglala woman. It's just kind of dark!"

Corn Woman clung to David. "I am afraid," she whispered. "What does this man want?"

Gently he disengaged her. "There is no need to be afraid," he said. "Go sit down—there." He nodded toward the corner where she had sat working on his new quilled shirt. "This man thinks you are his daughter."

The fright grew; she clung to him more tightly. "His daughter? *His* daughter?"

Blossom's lips set in a hard line. "You take your hands off'n her and let her come to me!"

"She won't come to you," David explained. "She's afraid of you. No wonder—barging in here like a catamount and claiming this Sioux girl as your flesh and blood!"

Blossom watched Corn Woman as she slipped past him, trembling, to sit in the gloom at the edge of the fire. "I tell you she's Mattie!" he squalled. "That there is my little Mattie, stole from me by the Sioux along the Niobrara back in '50, when she was just a tyke! Don't I know my own child?"

Blossom wore a razor-sharp Green River skinning knife in a scabbard at his belt. A gnarled hand fumbled at the thong-wrapped haft; his eyes narrowed to slits. Taking a step forward, he stared at David Chantry. "What in perdition is goin' on here? Are you tryin' to keep her from me? By God, I allus suspected you of *somethin'*, Chantry! What's your game now?"

"Don't threaten me, you old bastard!" David snapped. "Ghost Bull and his Oglalas don't like you for sour apples, and you know it! One hostile move and they'd roast your gizzard on a forked stick!" He poured scarce coffee from the battered pot and handed a tin cup to the wolfer. "Sit down, and we'll talk."

Warily Blossom took the cup, squatted, watching David under the thatch of brow. "Don't mind if I do swaller a little refreshment before I take her home," he growled. "Just don't try none of your tricks on me, Chantry! I know your kind! You're thick as thieves with these rascals!"

"Listen," David said. "Listen to me! This girl is named Corn Woman. Her brother is Crow Dog, a young man who is going to be a Scalp-Shirt Man someday. How can she be your daughter, and a full-blooded Oglala into the bargain?"

Corn Woman watched intently, whites of her eyes showing in the firelight, not understanding the English in which they spoke.

"Blood allus tells!" Blossom insisted. "Look there!" He pointed, and Corn Woman shrank back into the shadows. "Look at her nose!" He tweaked his own. "Long—long and narrow, like mine! That ain't no Sioux nose!" Coming to his knees, he held out his arms in a pleading gesture. "Mattie, little Mattie—come to me! It's your pa! I ain't goin' to hurt you!" In his passion he spilled the precious coffee; a measure rolled into the embers of the fire, where it hissed and bubbled. "God damn it!" he cried, exasperated at her refusal to embrace him. "Come *here*, girl!"

David grabbed the fringed hem of the wolfer's coat and dragged him away from Corn Woman. "Let her *alone*, will you, you crazy old coot!"

The wolfer's hand clawed at the sheath and came away holding the ancient Green River knife, sharpened so many times it was by now only a stiletto. Fire winked on the polished blade. Blossom raised it high but David caught his wrist and stayed the downward plunge of the weapon. The attack was vicious, unsuspected, and he had been caught unaware. Together they rolled into the ashes of the fire, fighting for control of the weapon.

Corn Woman screamed—it was odd, he did not recall a Sioux female ever making such a noise—and ran to him. Snatching up a brand, she jabbed at Blossom's whiskered face. Trying to shield his eyes from the live coal the wolfer dropped his knife and rolled away. His whiskers were singed, and the tipi smelled of burned hair.

"I don't know what you done to my little gal," he wheezed, "but I'll get you for this if it's the last thing I do on this here earth!" Gasping, he stumbled to his feet, patting out sparks that glowed in the buckskin jacket. "Damned fancy Dan! Think you're the genuine fair-haired article, don't you? Well, I'll soon enough fix your clock, Mr. David Chantry!"

Corn Woman clung to David, fearful. "It is all right," he soothed. "He will not harm you." Through their clothing, he could feel the softness of budding breasts, the frantic pace of her young heart.

"Speak the lingo pretty good by now, don't you?" Blossom jeered. "By God, you're in with the Sioux thick as clabber, and that ain't natural!" Suddenly his tone changed; he became wheedling, crafty. "Say, now—I just thought! Let me talk to old Ghost Bull about this! Maybe I can straighten out things with him!"

David shook his head. Other considerations aside, Ghost Bull had been very cross since Crow Dog and his party had left without ceremony, and without the chief's permission.

"I think you'd better leave camp quick as you can in the morning. I'll see you get your animals and all your truck back. But don't linger—do you hear me?"

The wolfer rubbed his nose with a greasy thumb; his small eyes sparkled malevolently. "I'll go," he muttered. "I'll go, all right, without my little gal that rightly belongs to me! But I'll be back with folks that can back up my claim—with guns, that is. Guns! You understand me?"

"I understand you," David said, an arm around the girl's trembling shoulders.

Blossom made a last effort. "I— I—" He turned his whiskered face away. "Guess you savvy the lingo better 'n me now, Chantry. Tell her something for me, will you?"

David didn't answer.

"Tell her—" The old man's voice broke. "Tell her I still love her. Tell her I ain't going to abandon her here in a lousy Indian camp! Tell her back there—" He flung out a skinny arm. "There's houses, and proper schools and pretty dresses. I saved all my life, and I got money now. I kin buy her whatever she wants. We kin live in Omaha or Chicago or New York City or wherever she fancies! Tell her that, will you, Chantry?"

David shook his head, touched by the old man's genuine grief. "It wouldn't make any difference. She's not Mattie Blossom. She's Corn Woman. Her life is here." He went to the doorway and called out. A moment later, She Bear, whose own lodge was nearby, came.

"This woman," David explained, "will give you food and a bed for the night." He spoke rapidly to She Bear; she nodded and held the flap aside for the wolfer.

"I'm sorry," David said again.

Blossom picked up the knife, slipped it into the scabbard.

"I ain't never liked you," he muttered, "but you and me, we're blood enemies now! I guess you know that!"

"Nevertheless," David said as the door flap dropped, "I hope you find Mattie someday! The *real* Mattie Blossom!"

In the new silence of the lodge, Corn Woman clung to him. Perhaps she was still frightened, but there seemed to him a growing sexuality in her manner. Uncomfortably he squirmed, tried to disengage her arms from about his neck. "I thank you," he murmured, "for helping when the wolf killer tried to cut me with his knife."

She whispered in his ear.

"Eh?" he asked.

Her voice was so soft and hushed that he still did not understand. When he had finally freed himself, she stood before him, eyes downcast, and signed the words *I love you.* Slender wrists crossed before her, she pressed them to her young breast. *I love you. I press you to my heart—thus.* She did not make any further effort to touch him, only stood in that modest supplicating posture, eyes downcast, body submissive.

He was perplexed and angry at the same time. Arms hung helplessly at his sides, and he chewed at the fringe of beard surrounding his mouth. He could not frame his thoughts into any coherent structure, but she was Crow Dog's sister, and only a child at that. There were various ceremonies and social arrangements *de rigueur* with the Indians, even if he wanted to, which he really didn't, he told himself, because she was only a child, perhaps not even sixteen yet, and after all—

When she raised her eyes after a long time, there was pain in them; they shone with unshed tears. Quietly she walked to the perimeter of the lodge and lay down among the robes, turning her back. Though he had never heard an Indian woman weep, from the way her slender shoulders shook, Corn Woman was undoubtedly weeping.

That night, he lay for a long time before sleeping. Blossom and he had never really got along. Now the wolfer was his sworn enemy. Had Blossom divined his true mission? Benjie Sears, also; did Chris Rowley, the maimed scout, suspect Benjie—and through Benjamin Sears *him*, David Chantry? The game was getting dangerous.

In the still watches of the night, an idea came to him. Cassie Garrett had mentioned a display of his photographic works, a kind of salon display, the way Mr. Brady did in his Pennsylvania Avenue studios before the War. What better cover for his activities than to ride boldly into Elk City with his best prints, hang them in the scruffy "lobby" of Dooley's Hotel, maybe even charge admission? He could take along the Anthony camera, too, and make camera portraits for a nominal fee; that would also tend to allay suspicion. Besides, he needed a fresh supply of collodion and the necessary excitants—bromides and iodides of potassium. The chemicals should be waiting in Elk City, shipped in on the Diamond R bull trains. Diamond R service, if scanty, was reliable. While the Sioux might steal

white men's horses, they had no interest in Diamond R's oxen; the
buffalo better served their needs. So he would ride to Elk City, taking one of the mules as a pack animal to carry his impedimenta.
Most of the snow was gone, the remainder lying in patches in hol-
lows and on the northern slopes. While the going might be muddy
and some of the streams starting to rise with melted snow water, the
journey should take no more than two days—three at the most.

That night, he was shaken by fits of coughing. In the morning he
was dismayed to find his shirt flecked with spots of blood. The lungs
again; his anger at Blossom the night before must have started them
to bleed! Certainly their struggle through the fire had been no pre-
scription for a man with weak lungs. He swore, viciously. Corn
Woman, coming in with a strip of hump hacked from the quarter on
the meat rack outside, averted her eyes as she passed.

"I am going to Elk City," he said. "I will be gone for—" Two
weeks? How did you say "two weeks"? He extemporized, holding
thumb and forefinger together to signify the present stage of the
moon, then making a wiping motion with his hand. *Until the
moon is gone.*

She seemed to understand, but said nothing.

Uncomfortable, he went outside to breathe deep of the morning
air, feeling the south wind lave his bare chest, play through the gin-
ger beard he now sported. Soon he would have to hack it off. Indians did not like hairy men; their own slight beards, they plucked
out with clamshell tweezers. Bull Head, the shaman, was casting
handfuls of ground white sage over the fresh tracks of several horses.

"The wolf killer has gone, then?" David asked.

The old man shook his rattle at the line of hoofprints straggling
away from the camp and into the rocky shale. "That man is bad," he
grunted. "Very bad!"

"Yes," David agreed. "He is evil."

"He wanted to talk to my father Ghost Bull, but I made him go
away. Ghost Bull does not want to talk to anyone these days. My father Ghost Bull is struggling with a strong devil. I want to help
him but he sits in his lodge and will not talk to anyone. He is
worried."

David changed the subject. "Now I go to Elk City, to get things I
need to make more pickshers. I will be back in—" He repeated the

gesture. *Two weeks.* Bull Head nodded, touched his right ear with a finger, indicating understanding. He gave David Chantry a pinch of sacred powder from his medicine bag for good luck, sprinkling it over David's unshorn locks.

Inside the lodge, stewed meat awaited him for breakfast, along with a cup of boiled-down box-elder sap to stick his finger in and lick. It was very sweet, and tasted good after the rich buffalo meat. He had not known there was any left after the long winter. Corn Woman must have brought it from a secret hiding place as a present. But when he tried to talk to her, she again averted her face, sitting quietly near the fire, packing pemmican in a pair of new moccasins she had just finished. The meat would serve him well on the trail.

When he left, she had disappeared. David searched for her, following the small footprints into the thickets near the camp. Calling her name in vain, he did not find her. Dispirited, he rode away.

The next day, halfway to Elk City, he reined up sharp at the sight of a war party riding toward him. Kneeing Star Boy into a willow thicket, he pulled hard at Nig's lead rope. They concealed themselves, not sure of the intentions of the advancing warriors. Through his field glasses he watched, seeing the tails of their mounts tied up and full of feathers, in war style. Absaroka? This far south? And this early in the season? The Sioux fought ceremonially with the Absaroka each summer; it was an ancient and honored custom. But these were not Absaroka. With relief he recognized Crow Dog on his painted horse, Little Wolf, Smoke, Bobtail Fox, others. At the same time, they saw him and came riding hard, whooping, waving pennoned lances and firing into the air. Crow Dog reined up so hard, the wiry spring-legged pony almost sat on its haunches.

"Brother!" Crow Dog jumped down, grinning. He slapped his bare chest hard and gestured toward the iron-bound box strapped to the back of a lead horse. *"Onhey!"* he shouted. It was the Sioux war whoop; *I have overcome!* He pulled the box from its lashings while the rest gathered around, grinning broadly. Crow Dog threw back the mangled lid and buried his arms in gold coin, greenbacks, what must be dust, carefully weighed out in identical bags. *"Onhey!"* he exulted. "Brother, did you ever see so much money?"

David nodded. "You have done well." He looked about. "I do not see Crane," he remarked. "And where is Two Knife?"

Crow Dog shrugged. "They have gone up the Star Way to the sky. I tell you, friend, those soldiers fought hard! But we killed them, and took their box!"

The party was out of food, and David shared tea and pemmican with them.

"What is the matter, friend?" Crow Dog asked, squatting beside him at the small fire.

David sipped tea. "Nothing. Nothing is the matter."

"Did I not do well? Did I not shoot those soldiers, take their money?"

"Yes."

"Then, why do you have a long face?"

David threw out the grounds, wiped the cup with the hem of his shirt. "A bad spirit is on me," he explained.

With the Sioux respect for a man plagued by bad spirits, Crow Dog nodded and fell silent. Later the band rode away toward Ghost Bull's camp, laughing and joking among themselves.

In their abandon they had recklessly scattered greenbacks. David picked one up. The bill had been stepped on by a pony; it was smeared with mud and torn almost in half. He stared at it, then dropped it again into the mud. Whistling to his mount, he got on Star Boy. Old Nig shambled obediently behind with the camera, immobilizer, blankets, rifle. As David rode, the south wind blew relentlessly after him.

———————◆———————

In this early spring, Fort Taylor was a mudhole, but there were patches of new-sprouted grass that mitigated the scene. The few cottonwoods remaining after so many had been cut and sawn for lumber began to show a haze of green. Cassie Garrett, too, began to feel the juices of spring rising within her.

Owen, as usual, was working late in the office. At dusk a smelly-whiskered old man had knocked at the commandant's door and demanded to talk to the colonel. Without so much as an "I'm sorry" Owen rushed away to post headquarters with the old relic, leaving a hot dinner untouched. Now Cassie told Private Dobbs to put away the supper things. "For I know," she said angrily, "that the colonel will not be back until very late!"

The old man's loyalties were mixed. "Yes, ma'am," he said. "I hate to see good cooking go to waste, but then the colonel is awful busy these days."

"I know all about it," Cassie said tartly, and she did. Since Chris Rowley and his Absaroka scouts brought in Mr. Benjamin Sears, the bogus missionary, the whole post buzzed with rumor. Sears, so it was said, had been caught with contraband rifles. In addition, it was rumored that incriminating code messages had been found in a shipment of Bibles sent him by Diamond R freight. So far, the youth had remained tight-lipped and silent.

"Sears," Owen said, "is the key to all this trouble we've been having with the Indians. Oh, he's not the big mucketymuck, I'm sure of that! He's working for someone else. I think he stirred up Little Man to bushwhack those miners on Big Dry Creek last winter. Sears may even have had something to do with the attack on the pay wagon! If anyone can get it out of him, Chris can! He knows a lot of Indian tricks!"

Ordinarily Cassie did not care to discuss military matters with her husband; such things bored her. But the look in Owen's eyes when he spoke of Sears and Chris Rowley made her feel cold and somewhat faint.

"You—you wouldn't torture the man? Isn't that against regulations?" Army Regulations, she knew, were sacred to Owen Garrett.

He grinned, fondled his mustache. "Of course I wouldn't!"

She was relieved, but then he went on. "What Rowley does, of course, is something else."

"What do you mean?"

"Why, I can't be expected to be everywhere at once, can I? I'll just have to trust Chris to use good judgment." Turning on his heel, Owen left, whistling. The state of the Powder River Sioux had recently been the subject of acrimonious correspondence from the War Department in Washington. Now, for the first time, Owen seemed to "have a handle" on it, as he said. But—torture? Cassie shuddered, and wished she had not asked.

At nine o'clock she undressed and went to bed. For a long time she lay on the coverlet in only her shift, listening to the night sounds. Tattoo sounded, then taps. Still Owen did not return. Somewhere a bird called, a plaintive, lonesome sound. Another answered; soon the two were engaging in a duet of liquid sound, rippling and breaking into joyous cadenzas. Somewhere, she thought, somewhere one loving thing had found another, and they were making music together. A long time ago she thought she and Owen would be like that, happy and joyous in each other's company. But since he was wounded at Ball's Bluff, Owen had been moody and sullen; something had gone out of their marriage. Now they were strangers, except for the brief intervals when he would speak, almost in a monologue, about his great responsibilities as commandant at Fort Taylor. *Damn it,* she thought in the warm, humid darkness, *I do not want a colonel in bed with me—I want Owen Garrett the man, the one who used to dance the mazurka so well, and sent me flowers and cologne!*

Perhaps she slept—she was not sure—but a little after midnight, according to the ormolu clock on the bureau, he came in and lit a candle.

"Cassie?"

She roused from her melancholy reverie.

"Cassie?"

"I'm here," she said curtly. "Wherever else do you think I'd be this time of night?"

He was too pleased with himself to take offense.

"Got a new lead on this trouble with the Sioux," he said, pulling off his boots. In spite of the fact that she didn't like him smoking in the house, he sat in his undershirt on a chair near her bed and lit a cheroot, puffing quickly. "Old Blossom put me wise to a few things. Oh, I guess I'd suspected all along, but he really put the capper on it!"

She rolled over, the shift pulling high about her thighs. For a moment she lay like that, thinking the rays of the candle lit the contours of her body rather well. But Owen did not respond, except to chew on the cheroot and repeat, "Yes, sir—he surely did!"

"All right," she said finally. "But come to bed, Owen—do! It's after midnight! You know you need your sleep."

Rising, he paced about the room, puffing at the cigar. The lean body in undershirt and drawers cast sprawling shadows on the wall.

"Yes, sir," he exulted, gnawing the cigar, "this is a big thing! A *very* big thing! May go all the way back to New York or Washington! Someone high up doesn't want us to make peace with the damned Sioux! *Someone* back there, someone with plenty of money and influence, is busy at treason. That's what it is, Cass! Treason!" In the candlelight his dark eyes glittered. "Do you know what this means? If I manage to break this cabal, if I can somehow manage to sweat the truth out of Sears and—" He broke off. "Sears and—"

"For Heaven's sake, Owen!" Balked, impatient, Cassie sat up in bed. "Whatever are you talking about?"

He grinned in a mysterious fashion and unbuttoned his undershirt. "Nothing. I was just talking." As always, he threw the undershirt in a pile on the floor. "All I meant was—if I get to the root of this trouble, I stand to win my silver eagles." Pulling off his drawers, he sat for a moment, naked, on the edge of the bed. Around the tattered stub of cigar he demanded, "Now, wouldn't that be nice, Cassie? Mrs. Full Colonel Owen Garrett? I'm only thirty-eight, you know!"

"Owen," she pleaded, "come to bed! It's late!"

"After the eagles," he said pleasurably, "comes the star. The star, Cassie!"

At last she was out of patience. "I don't care about eagles or stars or anything else! Owen, I've been lonesome all day, with you gone since reveille! Then you come home for supper and rush right out again! Now that you're finally home all you can do is talk about eagles and stars. Damn eagles! Damn stars!"

He turned, looking at her as if at a stranger.

"Come to bed, please!" she begged.

He shook his head. "Sometimes, Cassie, I'm damned if I know what gets into you! It's that Sadler blood, I guess. All the Sadlers were kind of flighty!"

That, of course, led to an argument. She could not stand attacks on her relatives. Owen eased himself into bed, deliberately showing her his back.

"Owen!" She rose on her elbow, prepared to make up. But he only grunted and pulled the sheet tighter about his naked shoulders.

Sadly Cassie lay back on her pillow, staring at the lighter blackness marking the open window. Again the two birds sang their melody. She wept, though very softly so that Owen would not hear.

CHAPTER NINE

"Pictures?" Mr. Dooley wanted to know. "Hang pictures in my hotel? What kind of pictures?"

"My photographic studies of the Oglala Sioux," David explained. "The Powder River Sioux—the way they live and hunt and talk and pray and have babies; their way of life."

The proprietor was doubtful. "Ain't no one around here wants to know anything about the Sioux except how to keep 'em from murdering innocent miners and settlers in the Territory!"

David was prepared. "Look at it this way," he urged. "If you're going to fight someone, it's well to know as much about your enemy as you can find out, isn't it? I think a lot of people will want to study these pictures, especially people from Fort Taylor, like Colonel Garrett and Chris Rowley."

Dooley was at last convinced. He liked David, and the clinching argument had been David's offer of a handsome photographic portrait of Mr. Dooley himself, no charge. Dooley helped move aside a sprung sofa and rickety chairs from the lobby to make room for the exhibition.

"Ain't a professor, are you?" he asked, watching David paint a muslin banner to be draped across the front of the hotel.

"A professor? No. Why do you ask?"

"Well, a feller come through here last summer selling Magic Electric Tractors, where you hold these rods in your hands and someone cranks a handle and shocks all the rotten juices out of your system. Cures the clap, fevers, ague, bad smells, anything. Professor Healey, he was, and it helped sales, I can tell you. People respects a professor."

"I did go to college," David admitted, "but nothing much ever came of it."

Dooley held one end of the banner while David drove nails. Dusting his hands, he gave Dooley back the borrowed hammer and the nails. "There!" he said with satisfaction. "That ought to drum up customers!"

Though it was raining and the road before the hotel a morass of wheel-tracked mud, he waded across River Street to inspect the banner from that vantage point.

GRAND EXHIBITION OF AUTHENTIC PHOTOGRAPHIC STUDIES TAKEN BY MR. DAVID CHANTRY IN THE HOSTILE SIOUX CAMPS AT RISK OF LIFE AND LIMB! ADMISSION FREE! YOUR OWN PORTRAIT TAKEN BY MR. CHANTRY HIMSELF FOR ONLY FIVE DOLLARS! THIS LIMITED ENGAGEMENT OF THE WORLD-RENOWNED PHOTOGRAPHIC ARTIST TUESDAY THROUGH THURSDAY ONLY!

He had taken some liberties with his reputation; he was hardly world-renowned. Also, his lettering had never been good, and the rain was already streaking some of the words. But the general effect was pleasing; he nodded with satisfaction.

At the Diamond R freight station, at the end of River Street, he found a wooden box awaiting him, dispatched from a fictitious address on Connecticut Avenue in Washington, D.C. Starting to pry open the box, he noticed a splintered board and the marks of a claw hammer.

"Has anyone been at this box?" he demanded.

The Diamond R clerk, a gray-haired man with sateen sleeve guards, looked up from a sheaf of manifests.

"This box seems to have been tampered with," David pointed out.

The man shook his head. "We do the best we can, but a thousand miles in a bull train can be hard on delicate items." He peered over the counter. "Looks to me like normal wear and tear. If you want, you can make out a damage claim, though Diamond R ain't paid too many of *them!*"

Carefully David pried off the rest of the boards, took the bottles from their sawdust nests. Everything appeared to be in order, but he was still uneasy. If someone had been sniffing about his freight shipment, the unknown investigator was an expert.

On his way back to the hotel, he bought a copy of the Elk City *Gazette*. It offered little news that was not months old. Lincoln had relieved McClellan of his command. Bragg and Kirby Smith had driven north into Kentucky but were forced to retreat, according to a St. Louis item, before they had done much damage. Search as he would, David was disappointed to find no mention of Chantry's brigade. He was about to fold the paper and put it into his coat for later reading when another item caught his eye. Old Lincoln, it was rumored, intended to issue some sort of paper freeing the slaves. David smiled tolerantly. He could not imagine what the Big Oaks niggers would do if they were freed; starve to death, most likely.

Back at the hotel, he dug out the wax-sealed cork of a bottle of potassium-iodide crystals and carefully extracted a roll of tissue-thin paper. By the light of the lamp, he worked for an hour decoding the latest communication from the Council:

CARE IN OPERATIONS IS OF UTMOST IMPORTANCE. REPEAT UT-MOST. SOME SUSPICION HAS ALREADY FALLEN ON OUR OPERA-TIONS IN THE EAST AND MUST NOT JEOPARDIZE YOUR WORK IN THE IDAHO TERRITORY. COVER AS PHOTOGRAPHER IS EXCELLENT BUT FEEL YOU MAY BE NEGLECTING PRIMARY MISSION.

He frowned. What did they mean by that? He had inserted in his last coded report some details of Sioux customs, language, and other items he thought would interest Horace Kinnear and the Council, but he was hardly neglecting his duty to incite trouble among the Sioux. Annoyed, he read on:

TREATY TALKS BETWEEN FEDERAL OFFICIALS AND SIOUX NOW DEFINITELY PLANNED AT FORT TAYLOR MIDDLE OF JUNE. WILL ADVISE EXACT DATE LATER. COUNCIL PLACES ITS RELIANCE IN YOU AND BENJAMIN SEARS TO PREVENT OR DISRUPT SUCH TALKS.

That was more than three months away. He hoped to accomplish much during that time, and wondered how Benjamin Sears was making out now with his Cheyennes. Eyes weary and smarting after a long day, he read on:

LATEST INFORMATION INDICATES GENERAL LEE PLANS A MAJOR FLANKING MOVEMENT THROUGH THE SHENANDOAH VALLEY THIS SUMMER. YOUR SUCCESSFUL EFFORTS CAN GREATLY IMPROVE CHANCES FOR AN EARLY CONFEDERATE VICTORY. MAY STARS AND BARS SOON FLY OVER THE CAPITAL!

Of course the dispatch was unsigned, but David recognized Horace Kinnear's florid prose. Now he felt better about the lack of information in the *Gazette* about Chantry's brigade. If General Lee was actually planning a northward move through the Shenandoah, the details would be well guarded and not likely to be reported in the public press. Wade Chantry's brigade would of course lead the way. Probably Wade and his dashing cavalry were already conducting secret maneuvers leading to the invasion of the rich Shenandoah, so near Washington the Yanks would be petrified with fear.

"Go, Wade!" he murmured. "Go, boy! Good hunting!"

He wished he could be with Wade instead of mired in the Idaho Territory two thousand miles west of the fighting, the *real* fighting. Settling back in the rocker and closing his eyes, he could see Wade in his mind's eye, long hair streaming as he jumped his charger over Federal cannon to saber the panic-stricken gunners. If only David Chantry himself were there, yelling a wild battle cry beside Wade, the way they used to pursue scurrying rabbits at Big Oaks! Going to the front window, he looked moodily out at the rain-streaked night. Already the ice was breaking up on the Yellowstone. Soon the steamboats would be churning foamily up the rolling torrent, the *soo—hah—soo—hah* of their engines announcing their arrival long before they rounded a bend, just as they did on the Mississippi.

Suddenly he felt a great wash of loneliness. The street scene turned strange and foreboding. A bar of light from a saloon illuminated the rain-pocked mud of River Street, men crowded into gaming houses and saloons, a teamster with a load of lager barrels from the new brewery cursed his mules in an effort to pull the wagon from the quagmire. Elk City, Idaho Territory, so far from home, from Biloxi, from Big Oaks! Sighing, David went to bed, and restless sleep.

‎◆‎

By most standards, David Chantry's photographic exhibition was a success. The leading citizens of Elk City came, judging it to be a kind of cultural event, which Elk City greatly lacked. Many of the officers from Fort Taylor attended also, bringing their wives, who sipped tea and ate oatmeal cookies baked by Mrs. Dooley. A few of the more uncouth types—miners, freighters, and some enlisted yellowlegs—came to jeer at the idea of photographs of Indians, murdering Sioux at that. Mr. Dooley, wearing the only boiled dickey in the Idaho Territory, dissuaded them with a bung starter. In two days David made over a hundred dollars from portrait sittings. He did not, however, see either Colonel or Mrs. Garrett among the attendees, and was disappointed.

"I dunno," Mr. Dooley said, helping on the final day to take down David's pictures and roll up the banner. "They say Garrett's real busy gettin' ready for some kind of a confab with the Sioux soon. Probably ain't got time to stop by with the missus." He clucked appreciatively. "That Mrs. Garrett—she's sure a looker!"

"Well," David said, "they were friends, and I'd hoped they would come. Maybe I'll ride out to the post before I leave, and pay my respects."

Holding a picture of Bull Head, the Oglala medicine man, at arm's length, Dooley stared at it. "Damn if that old buck ain't the spittin' image of my pa! Give him a woolly beard and a gold watch chain across his middle and I'd be skeered he'd tan my hide right now, the way he used to, back when I was a kid in Moline, Iowa!" He turned to David. "But they're savages all the same! A man can't forget that or he's apt to lose his hair mighty quick!" He looked at David over steel-rimmed spectacles. "How in tarnation do *you* manage to get along so well with 'em?"

David pulled a leather strap tight around the case for the Anthony camera. "They're people, like anyone else. Good and bad both. But treat them fair, and they'll treat you fair."

Dooley pursed his lips, shook his bald head. "I dunno. Them miners up on Big Dry Creek wasn't doin' Little Man no harm, was they? But he sure'n hell massacreed 'em." He bit off the tip of a wheeler, scratched a sulfur match on the seat of his pants. "'Course Chris Rowley and his Absaroka scouts caught the rascal that was stirrin' up them Cheyennes. Maybe that'll put the quietus on hostilities till a proper treaty gets signed in June, the way the talk goes."

Trying to keep his hand steady, David tucked the end of the strap under. "They— they caught someone?"

Dooley exhaled a smoke ring, helped David carry his gear down the hall to the ground-floor room he had rented. "Yep—that Sears feller, that so-called missionary that come through here preachin' hellfire two, three months ago. Old Dobbs, at the post, told me. Rowley picked Sears up at Castle Butte and brung him in last week. They think he's a spy for the rebels. More'n likely they'll string him up, soon's they sweat the truth out of him."

Breathing hard with the effort of carrying the boxes, David sat on the edge of his bed while Dooley lit the lamp. "Truth?" he asked. "What do you mean?"

"Sears had accomplices, so the story runs," Dooley said. "Garrett suspicions they're all part of a plot, working for higher-ups back East somewheres." At the door he paused.

"Winded, are ye, boy? Just from luggin' a few boxes? I thought you looked kind of peaked. Mrs. Dooley's got some yarb tea that's quite a revivifier. Why don't I get her to bile up a pot and—"

"No." David shook his head. "I mean— no, thanks." Aware Dooley was staring at him, he added, "It's my lungs, you see. Weak lungs—a tendency toward consumption. For a while I thought the air out here would help, but now I'm not so sure."

"All right," Dooley said, "but you be careful now, you hear? A man with weak lungs oughtn't to be traipsing around in wet weather like this."

When the proprietor left, David bolted the door and poured himself three fingers of Racehorse whiskey. Sears caught! Benjamin Sears, Benjamin Berrisford Sears, foolish Benjie, in custody at Fort Taylor! *Soon's they sweat the truth out of him,* Dooley had said. His hands shook as he gulped down the fiery liquor. How much had Benjie told them—told the maimed Chris Rowley, Colonel Owen Garrett? Had Benjie implicated him—David Chantry? Benjie was a weak character, and never should have been sent out on such an assignment by the Council. Had Benjie confessed, implicated David Chantry too—the parole breaker?

It was raining again, a soft spring downpour. Fingers of rain stroked the roof, the tin-roofed lean-to addition Dooley had built in anticipation of increased business when the ice went out of the river and gold seekers came up on the boats. He poured himself more whiskey and tried to think, to plan. If he *was* suspected, Owen Garrett would certainly not let him ride out of town unmolested. On the other hand, the wily colonel might just do that, sending the ubiquitous Rowley and his Absaroka scouts to trail him in the hope of finding him *in flagrante delicto* or whatever the lawyers called it. Both prospects were frightening.

In spite of its raw, frontier quality, Elk City went to bed fairly early. It was after midnight, and the streets quiet, when he heard the faint tap at his door. He rose, went to the door, laid his ear against it, apprehensive.

Again the faint tap sounded. "I don't want any herb tea, Mrs. Dooley," he protested. "I'm in bed!"

"David?"

It was a feminine voice.

"David?" The tap sounded again. "David, are you there?"

Picking up the lamp, he unbolted the door. In the golden rays of the lamp stood Cassie Garrett.

"Cassie!" he blurted. "Whatever are you doing here?"

She pushed past him, leaving behind a fragrance. "Close the door!" she said in a tight voice. "Please, David—quickly!"

He closed and barred the door. "Cassie," he whispered, "you shouldn't have come here like this, and at such a time of night!"

"I had to," she said. "Listen!" She sat on the edge of his bed, face pale and blue eyes frightened. "I had to come, David! There is something I must tell you!"

"But Owen—"

"Damn Owen!" she snapped. Taking off her hat, with its rain-wet plumes, she laid it on the bed beside her, shrugged her way out of the long coat, and let it slide to the floor. "You needn't worry," she said, appearing to regain some of her composure. "Owen thinks I'm at Madge Vail's house for the night. Madge is going to have a baby and I told Owen I'd stay with her the night."

"But how did you get here?"

Some color returned to her cheeks. "Dobbs brought me in the buckboard. There's nothing that old man wants more than to make corporal before he retires, and I promised him if he'd keep his mouth shut I'd intercede with Owen to get him his stripes." She nodded toward the stables in the rear of the hotel. "He hitched the buckboard back there and sneaked in the rear entrance to see if there was anyone around. Then he came out and got me, and I hurried in. Don't worry—no one knows I'm here, David."

Uncomfortable, he said, "Well, God knows I've missed you, Cassie." He tried to smile. "If the commanding officer and his lady had attended my Grand Exhibition it would have put a kind of cachet on my efforts that would have been most appreciated."

She touched his sleeve. "David, do you remember that time in Columbus, in the stables, when we—"

"I don't want to talk about that, Cassie," he said abruptly. "That's all past and gone now, and doesn't signify. We were very foolish, both you and I." He moved away, made a pretense of adjusting the flame of the lamp. "You said you had something to tell me."

Affronted, she sat in the rocker, slender hands gripping the carved arms. "I don't know that it's past and gone at all, David Chantry! Not with me, anyway! Otherwise, would I have come here at night, in a gentleman's room, risking gossip and divorce and everything else? Would I have told my husband a lie, just to get away and exchange pleasantries with you?"

He sighed. "Cassie, what is it you have to tell me? It's awfully late and people might—"

"All right." She stopped her quick rocking. "All right, then! This is the way it is! Have you heard that Chris Rowley and his scouts picked up a supposed missionary named Sears, Benjamin Sears, and have him in the stockade on charges of being some kind of spy for the South?"

"I have heard that," he said.

"Well, Owen is bound and determined there is some sort of southern plot to stir up the Sioux and draw soldiers away from the eastern theater."

He sat on the bed opposite her, crossing one moccasined foot over the other. "I have heard that also."

"You're so smart," she said, with an edge to her voice. "I guess you've heard everything, David Chantry! But there's one thing I'll bet you *don't* know!"

"Cassie," he said wearily, "it's late, and I'm too tired to play games! Early in the morning, I've got to pack my animals and ride all the way back to Ghost Bull's camp in the buttes. What is it I don't know?"

Quickly she came to sit beside him on the bed. "You don't always need to try to get away from me!" she protested. "David, I've missed you so! Why do you treat me so coldly?"

"I'm not being cold," he protested. "I like you very much, Cassie. But this is an impossible situation, you must realize that. Why did you come here?"

"Owen," she said, "suspects you, too, David."

His foot stopped its restless twitching. "How do you know?"

"The wife of the commanding officer gets to know a lot of things. Owen talks at times, says little things, sometimes talks in his sleep." She giggled. "The post wives gossip; Dobbs tells me the latest rumors. Mrs. Moffett—the stockade sergeant's wife—does our laundry and keeps me informed." She leaned forward, touched his cheek. "David, I know it isn't true, of course. You took the loyalty oath, received your parole, and you're too much of a gentleman ever to go back on your solemn word."

He was glad she could not see the agony in his face. She went quickly on, for which he was grateful.

"I know you're just taking photographs for Mr. Kinnear and the *Illustrated Weekly News*, as you told me. But Owen doesn't like you, and I don't think he ever did. Owen is a *very* suspicious man, suspicious of everything and everybody." She gave a nervous little laugh. "Of me, especially! But he's bound and determined you're a spy like poor Mr. Sears, sent out here to make trouble." Her voice became confidential. She moved closer to him on the bed; his rigid thigh touched the softness of her own. "Why it's so dangerous, David, is that I really think Owen is jealous of *you*, and that can be a very dangerous thing for both of us. That's why he hopes to make you a scapegoat."

"Jealous?"

"In Columbus," Cassie recalled, "he was watching us—you and

me—all the time. Then, the night you came to supper with us, he
had to leave to go to headquarters—you remember that, surely."

"I remember."

"I'm convinced he set Chris Rowley to watch us while he was
gone. Owen never trusted me, David. If he had, perhaps things
would have been different. But his insane jealousy is why I never
could love him, *really* love him as a wife should." She started to cry.

"Cassie," he protested, "you mustn't talk that way! And you must
leave—now! Your coming here is dangerous for us both, regardless of
what Owen thinks about me being a spy or some such nonsense!"

She clung to him, still weeping, murmuring.

With the drumming of the rain on the roof, he did not understand her words. "What?"

"You didn't even thank me!" she sobbed.

"Thank you?"

"For coming! For risking my reputation to warn you!"

"I thank you," he said contritely. "Now you must go."

Instead, she threw her arms about him, toppled him to the bed,
pinned him there. Cassie looked hungrily into his face, her eyes
haunted by shadows. "David," she begged, "help me, do! I've been
so lonely! You can't imagine how dreary life has been for me in this
wasteland!"

Her scent smothered him. For a moment he struggled. She
weighed him down, pressing her lips wetly against his. He was help-
less; for weeks, now, he had been without a woman. The juices of
manhood rose within him in spite of a resolution to deny them.

"Cassie!" he groaned. "For God's sake—"

In tinny clamor, rain pelted the roof. Cassie reached out to dim
the lamp.

"Cassie!" he protested, weakly. "My God, Cassie, if someone finds
us this way—" Against his will he let himself be gathered up in a
wave of passion. "Cassie, you damned little fool!"

But he was glad she'd come. He forgot Owen Garrett, Chris
Rowley, Benjie Sears, his present peril. Cassie was the whole world
—the whole world was Cassie Garrett.

"Ah, Cassie!" His voice was thick and tremulous. "Cassie, Cassie,
Cassie!"

Afterward they lay for precious moments, bodies warm and flushed under the sleazy blanket. It was late, very late. Detachedly he wondered what time it was.

Finally, Cassie raised herself on an elbow. "I'll have to go," she said. "Dobbs will be impatient." A wan moon shone through a scud of clouds; the rain had ceased. In the pale light he watched her, silvery and lissome, putting on her clothes. Tucking her skirt under her chin, she put on her stockings. He reached out and pinched the soft flesh of her thigh. All of woman was in that thigh; female flesh, soft and yielding to the proper touch, yet somehow resilient and firm.

Cassie smiled down at him, touched his cheek. "I'll have to leave now."

He lay sated and relaxed, aware of danger but not caring. "I'm sorry," he murmured.

"Sorry?"

"Sorry you have to go. Sorry this has to end."

Going to the door, she opened it cautiously, peeked up and down the hall. "No," she decided, "there's no one there." Quickly she crossed to the bed, laid her cheek against his. "Do you love me?"

The question had not occurred to him, at least not in the way she meant it. He had enjoyed her, yes, and she was beautiful.

"Well?" Her voice had an edge of impatience.

She was good in bed, no doubt of that. But—love? "Yes," he said finally. After all, his whole career in the Idaho Territory was a lie. What matter one more falsehood, if it gave her pleasure? She had been very kind to him in Columbus, more than kind, and now out here. "Yes, Cassie," he said. "I love you."

So quickly it astonished him, she kissed his cheek and was gone. The door clicked to. A bar of moonlight fell across his face, putting him in a dreamy and contemplative mood. It was a long time before his senses sharpened and focused enough so that he remembered danger. Rolling out of bed, he hurried to the window. The stables were deserted. The moon shone lonesomely on the upraised handle of a pump, rusting wagon parts, a mound of hay under a wet canvas. Satisfied, he burrowed again into bed and slept better than he had for some nights. He did not even cough.

Early in the morning, Dooley himself saw David Chantry off. "You're allus welcome here," the proprietor said. "That show of yours drew quite a bit of trade to my bar. When you comin' back this way?"

David climbed on Star Boy, took a last look at the lashings on his mule. "I don't know, Mr. Dooley. My schedule is uncertain. Maybe in the summer."

Dooley shook hands. His wife had baked a dried-peach pie for David, which he carried, carefully wrapped and packed, in the raw-hide Sioux bag dangling from the cantle.

"Be careful!" Dooley urged. "Don't do nothin' to cross them there savages! Photographs or no photographs, they'll lift your hair quicker 'n an alligator can chew a puppy!"

The Idaho Territory, it was said, had every kind of weather there was. All a man had to do was wait, and the Territory would oblige him. Now the rain had stopped. The sun hid its face, the air was cold and metallic with a smell of snow to come. David raised his hand in farewell and cantered from the stable yard.

Passing the window of his late lodgings, he saw something that turned his veins to marble, his heart to ice. Below the window, in the mud, were strange prints—strange round prints, clearly limned. Drawing rein, he paused for a moment beside his curtained window. *Chris was a soldier,* Cassie had said that night on the porch when David visited her and Owen Garrett. *Till he got frozen, up in the Badlands. The surgeon had to take off the front parts of both feet.* Chris Rowley, Colonel Owen Garrett's chief scout. *He sort of hobbles on the stumps, but Owen depends on him a lot.* There was more. Cassie had said something else. *I'm convinced he set Chris to watch us while he was gone.*

Abruptly he dug moccasined heels into Star Boy's ribs, clucked at the mule. Aware Mr. Dooley was watching him, he set Star Boy quickly on the trail back to the buttes, and Ghost Bull's camp. It seemed like a refuge, a refuge he must quickly reach. Frequently he turned in the saddle to see if anyone was following him, but he detected no one.

CHAPTER TEN

Unknowing, he rode home to tragedy.

Certainly there was nothing in the air to presage what had happened. After the momentary threat of snow, the weather had again turned mild. Early spring came to the Territory. Cottonwood buds swelled with the promise of new life, the meadows were unexpectedly deep in yellow daisies, mauve hyacinth blossoms, the brilliant carmine of clustering vetch; the white of mariposa lilies dotted the scene. Frogs croaked in the marshes, and torrents of birdsong competed with the lugubrious sound. Soon the Sioux would be thinking about going out on their pastime of fighting the Absaroka, stealing Absaroka horses, counting coup on the ancient enemies.

David was in no great hurry. He rode slumped in the saddle, listening to the sounds of spring, letting his body shift languidly to the amble of trailwise Star Boy. From time to time the pony nickered, seeming also to enjoy the spring season. *Home,* David thought. *Going home.* Going home again to see Corn Woman, Crow Dog, Ghost Bull, Bull Head the shaman, She Bear, the rest of his good friends. Of course, there would probably be some explaining to do about his part in urging Crow Dog to raid the paymaster's wagon, but that should not be hard. The Sioux were poor; the white men had robbed them for generations. Plundering the paymaster's wagon was only simple justice. Refusing to bother his head further, he rode on, singing softly, lulled by the drowsy hum of bees. *Swing low—* How did that nigger song go? *Comin' for to carry me home.*

Though the song was an old slave spiritual, sung for generations at Big Oaks, it was not really Big Oaks David Chantry was thinking about at all. He was thinking of Ghost Bull's camp in the buttes. Could that be home, *really* home, now? He shook his head, feeling disloyal to his heritage. Digging heels into Star Boy's ribs, he clucked to old Nig. "Hurry along!" he admonished them, cocking an eye at a rain-bellied cloud on the southern horizon. "There may be weather making up over there!"

Nearing camp, splashing with his little train through the flood-waters of Mizpah Creek, a sixth sense warned him he was being watched. On the far bank he stopped, listened. Nig shook his sweating hide; Star Boy neighed. "Be quiet," David said, and listened again. With the rushing of the swollen waters he could hear nothing, so they trotted quickly on.

He *had* been watched. From the cover of a willow thicket, an Oglala youth in a red blanket rode out to block his way. It was Limber Lance, a young man whom David knew and liked. Limber Lance would soon be admitted to the prestigious Fox Society. He was very conscious of his responsibilities as sentry in the northern approaches of Ghost Bull's camp.

"Stop!" he commanded.

David stopped. "I am glad to see you, friend," he said mildly.

"Who are you?" Limber Lance demanded.

David grinned. "You know who I am, friend. And please put down that gun. It might go off and hurt someone."

Limber Lance was embarrassed. "All right," he agreed. "You can go on to my father's camp."

David paused for a while to chat. "Is my father well?" he asked.

Limber Lance extended a forefinger toward David. *My father's path is smooth and straight. He is well. Ghost Bull is well.*

"My friend Crow Dog? My friend She Bear? My friend Corn Woman?"

Limber Lance did not speak. A look of sadness spread over his mobile young face. Suddenly he spread his scarlet blanket over his face and wheeled his mount into the screen of willows. David called after him.

"Friend, what is the matter?"

Limber Lance did not reply.

"Friend," David insisted, "what is wrong?"

Through the budding willows, he could see a splash of red. Limber Lance had returned to his duty post, but it was obvious the young man did not want to talk any more. When a man had a bad spirit come on him suddenly, as appeared to be the case with Limber Lance, it was good manners to let him alone.

"Get along there!" David ordered, jerking at old Nig's lead rope. Riding into Ghost Bull's great camp, he was puzzled and apprehensive.

Though the low scud of cloud had grown until it filled the southern sky, the camp still lay in sunshine. A kind of dispirit, however, seemed to have come upon it. Few children played in the meadow, no men sat on thresholds pulling out chin hair and painting themselves. Even the ponies in the brush corrals seemed quiet and subdued, with little of the prancing, kicking, and biting normal to their high spirits. One woman, carrying a leather bucket of water, saw David approach and deliberately turned her head away, weeping. What had happened?

Dismounting before the tipi he and Corn Woman and Crow Dog shared, he threw aside the flap and stepped within. He was at last home, but what evil spirit had fallen on his home since his departure?

Inside it was dark and cold. No fire was laid, and the only illumination was from sunlight filtering through the translucent skins. In the center of the lodge, Corn Woman lay on a slatted mat of willow rods stitched together with sinew. She was naked, except for a remnant of sleazy trade calico covering her slender body. As David stared, she cried out for water.

"What is wrong?" David demanded, and rushed to kneel beside She Bear, who held a gourd dipper to the girl's thirsty lips.

The old woman turned a stricken face to him. Her eyes were red and puffy. "Our daughter is sick. She is very sick. I think she is going to die."

In David's haste, he had not noticed Bull Head, the shaman, grinding colored rocks to powder with a pestle and mixing in handfuls of sacred seeds, dusty yellow pollen. Crow Dog, too, crouched in the shadows.

"Tell me!" David begged. "What sickness is this? How did it happen? How long has she lain like this, brother, not knowing anyone?"

Crow Dog's face was smeared with ashes. He did not answer, only rocked back and forth on his haunches, eyes closed and head bowed in sorrow. Bull Head continued to chant and mix his sorcerer's powders.

"Why is there not a fire in here?" David demanded.

She Bear filled the gourd again and tried to give Corn Woman water, but the girl's eyes were glassy, her lips set. The liquid spilled out, lacing its way down between the young breasts.

"She is hot," She Bear told David. "Here—feel." Gently she placed his hand on the girl's brow. "She has a fever. All the time, she is hot and cries out for water, but her throat is swollen almost shut and she cannot take any."

Crow Dog spoke, but his eyes seemed to stare through David, unseeing. "When you went away, she was sad to see you go. She was sad she had been angry with you. She was sad she did not say good-by to you. But then, when it was time for you to come back, she was happy. She sang. She put on her best clothes."

"I am sorry," David murmured. "It was the spring. I did not hurry." He leaned over the prostrate form until his bearded cheek touched hers. "I am here," he whispered. "I have come back. Do not be sick any more."

Feverishly she tossed. Her eyes rolled till the whites showed but she did not know him, something that pierced his heart.

"I will try one more thing," Bull Head announced. "This is the strongest medicine I have. No Sioux has anything more powerful. This medicine is *wakan!* It was handed down to me from my ancestors, all the way to the greatest of great-grandfathers, and they were all famous shamans. It cannot fail."

Creakingly the old man got to his feet, carrying a china saucer filled with medicine dust. He wore his best vest with the fur side out, the exclusive prerogative of the medicine man. Around his head was a ceremonial band of black otter fur with a buffalo horn attached to each ear. His face was painted blue. A white moon was on his forehead and a star across the bridge of his nose. Shuffling around David and the sick girl, he threw his sacred dust high into the air, shaking his rattle. In a high-pitched falsetto timed to his shuffling he chanted a prayer:

"Father of all, father of all!
    Hear me sing, watch me dance!
    I sing, I dance, I throw sacred powders into the air.
    With my magic I drive out devils, bad spirits!"

Faster and faster he shuffled; his chanting became higher in pitch, a shrill keening; his face took on an appearance of rapture. Beads of sweat broke out on his forehead, and he shook them off:

"Faster and faster I dance!
    The devils are afraid, the devils leave!
    Faster and faster my daughter gets better.
    Waugh! Waugh! Waugh!"

In a frenzy, the old man capered about the tipi, perspiring, moccasins wet with the sweat running down his thin legs. Suddenly, so quickly it startled David, he came to a halt and shouted unknown and unintelligible words, face upturned toward the smoke flaps and the Father of All. With a final gesture, he cast the remainder of the sacred medicine into the air. The lodge filled with the dust, and an acrid stench came to David's nostrils.

For a long moment, Bull Head stood in a trance, head upraised toward the gods. Then he opened his eyes and shook his head as if to clear it. On trembling legs, he tottered to a robe and sat down, taking off the buffalo-horn headgear.

"That is all," he wheezed. "That is all I can do! I have no more medicine."

"It was a good prayer," David said. "Hie, hie. Surely the Father of All heard you. Surely he will help Corn Woman."

The shaman wiped his leathery cheeks and brow. "We will see."

There were medicines in David's photographic wagon. Council experts had devised for him a selection of common remedies packed in a wooden chest. When he left the tipi, he saw many of the people ringing the lodge, united in their common concern for the beloved Corn Woman. Men squatted silently on the new grass, smoking. The women covered their faces, the children were wide-eyed and solemn.

Nothing in his medicine chest seemed to fit the situation. While

David was examining vials and bottles and paper twists of powders, trying to correlate them with the numbers in the pamphlet, he heard a commotion. He peered out. Some of the people surrounding the tipi were standing. Some cried out in grief. She Bear ran from the lodge and gestured to him to hurry. "She is dying!" she said, holding the door flap wide for him. "It is her time! Her time has come!"

Crow Dog held his sister in his arms. Corn Woman's eyes were open, shining with some mysterious ecstasy. Her breath came quick and shallow, the young breasts heaved in an effort to draw air into dying lungs. When she saw David Chantry, there was at last recognition in her eyes. She watched him fondly as he knelt beside the pallet of willow rods.

"I am here," he said. "I will stay here with you. I will not leave you again."

Corn Woman attempted a smile. One hand rose, then fell back. Trembling, the hand wavered upward again. With a great effort she signed, "I am glad"—the small heart, made with thumb and forefinger curling over the breast; *sunshine,* hand palm down over the heart, then sweeping outward. *Sunshine in my heart.*

Crow Dog gestured, and David took her in his arms. Corn Woman's lips were blue. Her eyes finally grew vacant, but with some remnant of consciousness she moved her lips. David bent closer to hear. She seemed to be trying to sing, a curious melody that waned and wavered but continued. David could not make out the words, nor the tune. Her lips seemed numbed, the words thick and slurred.

"What is it?" he asked. "What is that she is singing?"

Crow Dog's face was stained with tears. "Maybe it is her death song. We all have a death song. Warriors sing the death song when they know they are going to die in battle, when there is no hope. Maybe women sing, too."

Outside, the sun still shone, painting the skins of the lodge with shadows. The new grass was a soft green, birds sang in leafing trees, the enervating south wind had changed to a brisk northerly breeze. But, in the darkened tipi, a young woman was dying in the spring of her life. David held her tighter and tighter in his arms, as if to deny death's hold. Finally life passed from her. Her body became heavy and lifeless in his arms. Later he remembered thinking how odd it was; something left the body, but she lay heavier in his arms.

"She is dead!" Bull Head mourned. "My medicine did no good!"

Gently David laid her down. The face, contorted before with pain and suffering, was now relaxed, smooth and untroubled in appearance. His eyes filled with tears. *You would be a credit to any Biloxi ballroom,* he remembered. Now she would be a credit to the gods.

"I loved her," he said in the unaccustomed English. "In a very strange way, perhaps—but I loved her."

"Singing, she died," Bull Head chanted. He sat cross-legged near the dead fire, wrinkled face upturned, eyes closed. "Now Corn Woman is singing her way up to the moon, to the stars, to the Father of All. Father, receive her with kindness! She has not lived in this world long enough to know sin!"

As a special gesture of affection and respect, the Oglalas placed Corn Woman, wrapped in a blanket, on a high scaffold near the camp, a funeral rite usually reserved for warriors and important men. With her they placed her cooking pans, her sewing awl, and fine clothing for use in the spirit world. As was the custom, many of the women gashed themselves on the forearms in sign of mourning. She Bear chopped off her little finger with a hatchet in her special grief. Thus the Oglalas gave her body back to the elements, to the four winds, the rains, the winged things of the air.

The spring rain began again as the funeral procession, men with faces painted black and women with brows smeared with ashes, straggled back to the camp. David, wet and bedraggled, sat with Crow Dog in the tipi, now empty and sterile without Corn Woman.

"This is a bad time for me," Crow Dog muttered, stirring the remnants of the fire. "My sister dies. Ghost Bull is angry with me because I robbed that paymaster and killed some soldiers. He took all the money I brought back in the chest. I do not know what he wants to do with it. He and the old men are having a meeting." He glanced at David. "I did not tell him anything about you, friend, but he knows you are to blame, too. He is angry with me and with you. But we will have to wait and see what they are going to do with us."

David Chantry had never really loved a woman. Of course, he had *had* women; but that was different. There had been Clarissa Soames, at a Christmas party once at Big Oaks. Then there was Betsy— Betsy— what was her name? He had forgotten, except that she was a brainless flibbertigibbet of a girl who thought she loved him. A girl named Sarah in Atlanta, and others. Cassie Garrett, too, though that was in a special category. No, he had really never known the tender passion, or whatever it was called; the real thing. Yet now, for a departed Oglala girl, he felt a wrenching sadness. Was it—had it been—love? If it was, then it had been a sweet and chaste love, a spiritual thing, free from the carnality of other conquests. If Corn Woman had lived—

As if divining his thoughts, Crow Dog spoke.

"We grew together, she and I, from the time we were small. I don't remember not being with her. They traded for her with the Assiniboines, but that was a long time ago, longer than my memory runs, anyway. But it was told to me. They gave seven good ponies for her, and a lot of red blankets."

David roused sharply from his reverie. "Who? Traded who for her?"

Crow Dog blew at the fire and tossed on a handful of twigs. Most of the wood was wet from the rains. "My father Ghost Bull traded the ponies and blankets with the Assiniboines for her, for my sister."

"She is not your sister?"

Crow Dog shook his head, surprised. "I called her that, as we do. But she was more than a sister. More than blood was between us." He held index fingers close together. *The same path.* "Our spirits always walked together, hand in hand. That means more than being blood sister and brother."

Something stirred in David. "From the Assiniboines? Then, you do not know where Corn Woman really came from?"

Crow Dog shrugged. "What does it matter?" He cupped his hands before the smoking embers. "She was a pretty child, always. Even that bad old man—the wolf killer—wanted her for himself. When he came back—"

David's heart missed a beat. "Friend," he said, "I know the wolf killer was here and tried to take Corn Woman away with him. I know that. I was here then, and I made him go away from our camp. But he came back?"

Crow Dog nodded. "After you rode away to Elk City, he sneaked back. We did not know he was here. Corn Woman was at the river, getting water in a bucket. He grabbed her and tried to take her away. She fought him, and screamed. The people came to her, and the wolf killer ran away. We looked for him to kill him, but could not find him. But he did not go far. At night he would creep out of the trees in the moonlight and call to Corn Woman, like a bad spirit, beg her to come with him. Once, I heard him and ran out with my new gun, but he was gone. Friend, that old man was like the ghost lights that shine at night over the swamps along the river! Some people finally believed the old man was really a spirit, a devil, because we could not catch him. I tell you, friend, my sister was frightened! She could not eat much, she could not sleep."

In a corner of David's mind ran the queer little melody Corn Woman had sung on her deathbed.

"Then what happened?" he asked.

"Bull Head made special charms and amulets from feathers and deer guts and gunpowder and hung them around the camp on bushes. After that, the wolf killer went away. Anyway, we did not see him or hear him any more. But Corn Woman was still frightened. She thought the old man would come back and get her. She did not eat much, and sometimes she was sick."

Rabbit, David thought. *Something about a rabbit.* What was it?

"She got worse," Crow Dog went on. "She Bear cooked for her, Bull Head prayed over her, made medicine—good charms to help her —but she did not get better. Finally—yesterday—she had to lie down, she was so sick. And then you came."

David put his head in his hands, closed his eyes. *Rabbit. Run, Rabbit, Run.* Was that it, the childish melody he played on his violin that first night in the wagon? What was it the wolfer said? *There was a song—my daughter used to sing it before she—* He felt a chill course along his spine, into his shoulders, his arms, his chest.

"No one knows where the Assiniboines got her? I mean—was she born an Assiniboine? Would they have traded off one of their own children?"

Crow Dog shrugged. "That was a long time ago. Maybe Ghost

Bull knows. Maybe some of the old men remember. But it does not make any difference now, friend. She is dead."

Blossom—Blossom, the wolfer! The tallow balls laced with strychnine. *Wolf hardly swallers it till he goes crazy for water! Staggers around whooping and hollering, finally lays on his back, griped at the stomach and pawing in the air!*

"Where are you going?" Crow Dog asked.

David went to the doorway, flung aside the flap. A carcass hung on the meat rack. The nights were cold; meat still kept, hung thus and shaded during the day. Pulling off the cloth, he examined the meat. Bending closer, he sniffed at it, ran his fingers over bones, sinew, fat, flesh.

"Friend," Crow Dog asked, "what are you doing?"

David looked at his fingers. They were greasy, slightly sticky, a slight yellowish cast to them.

"Did you eat of this meat?" he asked.

Crow Dog shook his head. "My father Ghost Bull is angry with me. I took a vow to eat no meat until he gives me leave."

"Did She Bear eat of this meat?"

Crow Dog's brows rose in surprise. "She cooked some of it for my sister, but She Bear has plenty of her own meat!"

David dug with his knife in the carcass. It was laced with congealed sheep tallow. He had eaten mutton before, and knew the smell.

"Listen to me," he said. "Listen, friend! Now I know how our sister Corn Woman died!"

Puzzled, Crow Dog stared at him.

"A long time ago, on the Niobrara, the wolf killer's daughter—little Mattie—was stolen by Indians. He believed Corn Woman was his lost daughter. Maybe she was, but that is not important now. When he could not get Corn Woman to come away with him, back to the big cities where the white men live, to come with him and live her life like a white woman, he was very angry. So he decided to poison her, poison her with the poison he puts in his wolf baits." He showed Crow Dog smears of the deadly mutton fat on the blade of his knife. "Maybe she did not get enough to kill her the first time, but each day she got a little more. Finally. . . ."

In late afternoon, the sun slanting low over the trees to the west, they stood together, neither speaking. A deputation of Brûlé Sioux rode by on their way to palaver with Ghost Bull and the elders of the tribe. They were tall, broad-shouldered men, taller than the Oglalas. They rode their ponies majestically, with great dignity, like King Arthur's knights of old.

"So that is how it was," Crow Dog muttered. His face retained its composure, but his fists clenched at his sides. "So the old man killed her, killed my sister as he killed wolves!"

David felt tired. He was drained, exhausted, and leaned heavily against the tripod. His fevered brain did not want to function properly. There were so many things to consider now: Corn Woman dead, Chris Rowley's misshapen prints beneath his window in Elk City, the bumbling Benjie Sears and the danger he had brought. There was his wagon—now repaired—filled with glass plates and chemicals. Wade Chantry was somewhere in the Shenandoah, the Brûlés had come to confer, deciding whether it would be peace or war when summer came.

"Friend," Crow Dog said, "I go to kill that man! I will kill the wolf killer, make him suffer in dying the way his wolves suffered, the way my sister Corn Woman suffered! I will make him eat his own poison, and laugh at him when he is in agony!"

David blinked, rubbed his forehead. "Where will you find him?"

Crow Dog pointed south. "That way, along the river. He has a place there where he goes to dig in the ground each spring, when wolf pelts are not good any more. He digs up—" Crow Dog made the sign for gold; first *money*, thumb and forefinger touching each other in a small circle, then pointing to the yellow flowers at their feet. *Money—yellow.*

David remembered Blossom talking about his diggings on the upper Powder. "Gold," he murmured.

"Yes," Crow Dog said. "Gold! And if we do not find him there, we will look everywhere until we find him! He cannot run anyplace where I will not come after him! I will make him eat his own wolf bait, and laugh when he cries out for water, begs us to kill him!"

We, Crow Dog had said. *You and I.* "I don't know," David said. "Friend, I don't know what to do!" The Council had assigned him a mission, an important mission. His place was in the Oglala camp, doing his utmost to urge the Sioux to a summer war with the whites.

The presence of the Brûlé emissaries, even now tying their horses before Ghost Bull's lodge, only emphasized that commitment.

Crow Dog stared. "How can you think of anything else? You loved my sister! I saw it! I saw it in your eyes when she sewed shirts for you, made moccasins, cooked! And she loved you too. Friend, how can you think of anything more important than to look for the wolf killer!"

David's bowels twisted in indecision. Sweat broke out on his brow, he clenched his hands till the nails cut into his palms. Wade was fighting in the Shenandoah, risking his life. Could he—David Chantry—do any less than stay here in the Oglala camp, play the dangerous game, risk hanging on a gallows at Fort Zachary Taylor to insure better odds for Wade Chantry and the flower of the South?

"She loved you!" Crow Dog insisted. "She followed you always with her eyes! When you were gone, she was unhappy! When you came back, it was like the sun rose again, a new day began! Friend, how can you think not to avenge her death?"

The Brûlé emissaries entered Ghost Bull's lodge. Children played in the twilight. It was almost The Moon When Geese Lay Eggs.

Crow Dog took the knife from the sheath at his waist, squatted, began to hone it on a ledge of rock. "It is not far," he urged. "We can get there in one day. Then you can come back here in a hurry and make more trouble."

David looked sharply at him, but Crow Dog only spat on the razor-sharp blade and rubbed it again across the stone.

"Well, friend?"

The sun had almost set. Cooking fires glowed through the translucent skins of the lodges; they resembled nothing so much as giant candles lit against the coming of the night. Smoke drifted up, overlay the camp in a fragrant pall. From the corral came a pony's whinny.

In sudden resolve David snatched at the tripod, overturning it so that the tainted meat, dangling from a rawhide cord, fell to the ground. "I will go," he said between set teeth, "but we will play the hand game to see who gets to kill him—you or I!"

Together he and Crow Dog hauled the deer carcass to a fire smoldering in the middle of the great circle of lodges, and piled on fresh wood. The fuel was wet, and smoked, but the flesh quickly caught, popping and crackling.

The next morning, as they were riding up the valley of the Powder, bound for Blossom's gold mine, Star Boy suddenly whinnied, an indication the pony had scented a strange horse. Cautious, David raised his hand. Crow Dog reined up also, searching the willows ahead.

"There is someone up there!" David muttered.

Tying their ponies, they dismounted and made a cautious reconnaissance. Crawling on hands and knees, they prowled along the river bottom, now loud and brawling with the spring freshet. Mud-spattered and winded, David finally stood up, looking about. He signed to Crow Dog; index and middle finger spread and pointing forward to indicate *see*, then the whole hand swept out and turned over to show emptiness—the negative sign. *I don't see anyone.*

Crow Dog grunted assent. They returned to the patient ponies. Riding on, they were still careful, though Star Boy did not whinny any more. Perhaps there was no one. On the other hand, maybe it was a change of wind; an enemy could still be watching them. Perhaps there were Absarokas about—the "horse stealers," ancient enemies of the Sioux.

After a while their tension relaxed. It was a fine day. Crow Dog, chewing a blade of grass, slumped in the saddle as the sun warmed his bare back. At noon they dismounted and ate a mouthful of dried meat and parched corn, washed down with river water from cupped hands. Watching Star Boy dance restlessly, roll his eyes and prick up the small ears, David felt a return of his uneasiness. He levered a shell into the chamber of his carbine, staring about.

"Friend!" he called to Crow Dog. "There is something wrong here!"

That was when he saw the clay-smeared topknot of an Absaroka brave rise from behind a tangle of driftwood near the river. The black eyes stared balefully down the barrel of the rifle.

"Friend!" David shouted, "the horse stealers are here!"

Throwing himself flat on the ground, he rolled into the willows and loosed a shot at the Absaroka. Crow Dog shouted a defiant battle cry and ran at the ancient enemy, holding the treasured fifteen-shot carbine to his shoulder and firing. But the willows were swarm-

ing with Absaroka warriors. One dashed from the reeds and shot
Crow Dog through the chest. As he toppled, another Absaroka
speared him, almost casually, with a ribboned lance. Others leaped
on David, wrested the weapon from him, and took him prisoner.
They bound him, prodding him to where Chris Rowley squatted in
the shade of a lone cottonwood, well away from the scene of battle.
The scout's voice was calm, matter-of-fact.

"Any more, I'm too old for that sort of gravy-stirring." He
grinned. He nodded to one of the Absarokas, and the man untied
David's hands. Ringed by hostile faces, there was no place David
could go anyway. He almost wept with rage and frustration.

"Didn't want to try to peel you out of Ghost Bull's camp," Rowley
went on. "Relations with the Sioux are mighty touchy these days,
Mr. Chantry. I guess you know that. But when you and that Oglala
buck rode out from camp, you come right into our parlor! Now I got
to tell you, sir: you're under arrest on charges of breaking your parole and working as an agent for Jeff Davis and—oh, a lot of things!"

CHAPTER ELEVEN

The spring rise on the upper Missouri and the Yellowstone came early, far earlier than the oldest settler could remember. Winter snows melted in the unseasonable warmth; the Idaho Territory turned into a gigantic morass. Torrents of muddy water raced down the mountains, filling each rill and brook and stream to its banks. The Missouri deepened, spilling into new channels, creating bays and lakes and estuaries where none had before existed. The vanguard of the river boats—such vessels as the *Eclipse* and the *F. Y. Batchelor*—fought their way up the brown torrent, and pilots found themselves confounded by a whole new river geography. Familiar landmarks were gone. The river perversely turned old dog-leg channels into straight runs. Previously straight stretches disappeared, to be replaced by a meandering route that caused consternation, profanity, and bottom-scraping. Fortunately the river still rose. When a vessel grounded, all that was necessary was to wait for a few hours until rising waters lifted the boat free. Then it could proceed with its cargo of whiskey, flour, tobacco, kitchenware, calico, nails, canned goods, bucksaws, harness, and all the items Elk City and other river landings had run low on during the winter. Because of the freight rates, the goods were expensive: a can of Blue Hen tomatoes sold for a dollar. But there was gold in the Territory, and no one complained much at the prices. Daily the meandering streams disclosed "color," and lucky prospectors occasionally stumbled across gold nuggets big as walnuts. Good times were coming to the Territory.

Colonel Garrett sat in his office at post headquarters reading a copy of the Chicago *Times* only two weeks old. Hooker had been before Chancellorsville, but Lee outflanked him and rolled up his right wing with Jackson's corps; old "Fighting Joe" had been forced back across the Rappahannock. Flushed with success, it was probable Lee would soon strike into Pennsylvania through the rich Shenandoah Valley. Angrily Garrett chewed on the stub of a cigar. Why couldn't *he* be with Hooker or Pope or Sedgwick instead of banished to this frontier outpost? It was a damned shame! The war—the real war—was going on two thousand miles away while he vegetated at soggy Fort Taylor, Idaho Territory!

"Sir?"

He looked up. Old Moffett, the stockade sergeant, emptied a sack on his desk. "This is all we could find on the prisoner."

Folding his newspaper, the colonel searched through the contents of David Chantry's war bag; dried pemmican cakes, new moccasins, a little tobacco, a pair of worn and battered field glasses in a flannel sack, a dog-eared clipping from a newspaper concerning the possibility of Chantry's Ninth Brigade of cavalry spearheading a new attack toward the nation's capital.

"Chantry," Garrett muttered. "That was the rascal's brother!"

"Sir?"

The colonel waved him away. "Nothing; just talking to myself." Suddenly he called after the sergeant. "Ah— just a minute!"

Moffett returned, to stand rigid at attention.

"Where's Chris Rowley?"

"In stockade, sir, questioning that preacher feller—Sears, or whatever his name is."

"Has Chris had any luck?"

"No, sir, not yet. Leastways, not much. Sears is hard to get any sense out of. All he does is spout Scripture."

"Thank you, Moffett. I'll be out directly."

The stockade was a rectangular enclosure of cottonwood logs set on end in the ground, upper ends sharpened to discourage escape. Along one side were a series of lean-tos housing malcontents and drunks—the dregs sent out to man Fort Taylor, I.T., while the Army was at Malvern Hill and Fair Oaks, along the Chickahominy and the Rapidan. Garrett flicked a finger at the sentry presenting arms and walked gingerly through the muddy stockade yard to the large hut containing cells reserved for those guilty of thieving, sodomy, murder, and other serious transgressions. Sergeant Moffett followed, nervous at the colonel's unaccustomed visit to his stockade.

"That will be all, Sergeant," Garrett said.

"Sir?"

"I want to talk to Chris Rowley—alone."

Inside the tin-roofed building Benjamin Sears sat on a stool in an anteroom off the corridor leading to the individual cells. Cuffed and in leg irons, he clutched a Bible to his chest. The black parson's coat was rent and frayed, his boots split, hair long uncut and unkempt hung over one bruised eye while the other was heavy with melancholy. Chris Rowley lounged at a desk made from wooden crates, puffing at his pipe. When the colonel entered, the scout got to his maimed feet, propping himself upright with one hand.

"Any luck, Chris?"

The bearded scout knocked the dottle from his pipe and shook his head. "I cuffed him around a little bit but it didn't do no good."

"That's right," Benjie agreed hoarsely. "Hell, I had nine brothers, most of 'em older 'n me! They used to beat the whey out of me!"

"Colonel," Rowley said, "plain beatin' don't do no good. If you'd let me—"

"There's time for that," Garrett said. He took out a fresh cheroot, bit off the end, lit it. "Have you told Sears we brought in Chantry?"

Benjie blinked. "I don't know no Chantry. Chantry who?"

While Chris Rowley sat on a nail keg in the corner of the room, Garrett paced up and down, hands clasped behind his back, puffing the stogie.

"Benjie, what we don't get from you we'll get from David Chantry, and vice versa. We'll play one of you against the other, and in that way get a full confession from both of you. But first . . . I want you to understand the seriousness of your situation! You are charged with treason against the United States of America. We already have evidence you distributed contraband arms and ammunition among the Cheyennes, and that's against the law. Further, your man Poor Bird confessed you incited Little Man and his band to attack and kill three peaceable miners near his camp. Further, we have found more guns and ammunition in packing cases, addressed to you here in Elk City, disguised as shipments of Bibles. Certain coded messages found in the pages of one Bible are even now being examined by a Pinkerton man sent out from the War Department. A preliminary decoding indicates they are instructions for you to work further mischief among our Indians here in the Territory."

"I ain't talkin'!" Benjie said defiantly. "That's my right! I know my Bible, but I know some law, too! I don't have to talk!"

The colonel shook his head in admonition. "Benjie, we know enough right now to hang you out of hand! What we *don't* know is who put you and David Chantry up to this dirty business."

Benjie shook his head. "I don't know no David Chantry, I tell you."

Garrett took the cigar from his lips and pressed it hard into Benjie's cheek. Sears muffled a cry, drew away. His face paled, and the room smelled of burned flesh.

"You damned well know David Chantry!" Garrett growled, resuming his cigar. "You met him at Ghost Bull's camp, probably to compare notes on your progress—he with the Oglala Sioux, you with the Cheyennes." He shook Benjie by the shoulder. "Isn't that right?"

With difficulty because of his manacled hands, Benjie opened the pages of his Bible. The red weal on his cheek glowed. He began to read. "Lord, how they are increased that trouble me! Many are they that rise up against me. Many there be which say of my soul, there is no help for him in God. Selah. But thou, O Lord—"

With an oath, Garrett struck the Bible from Benjie's hand. It dropped to the floor in a flutter of white pages.

"I used to think," Benjamin Sears said, "that them there words was all a passel of nonsense. I used to giggle in church, and play tricks on the parson. When I got to be a young man, I did considerable whoring and spoke blasphemies. But since I been in jail here, charged with all these crimes, I found some sustenance in the Bible. Ain't it queer?"

Garrett hit him in the face. Benjie reeled, almost fell from the stool, but did not raise his manacled hands to protect himself.

"Don't do you no good, does it?" he murmured through bruised lips. "I don't know no David Chantry, and I never done nothin' against no law! I'm just a pore country preacher, that's all, sent out here to minister to the Indians."

The colonel chewed hard on the tattered stub of his cigar. His face flushed. "I guess you're right, Chris," he admitted. "Maybe it takes something a little more sophisticated, you might say, to get the truth from this lying bastard!"

"I don't even *need* the Book." Benjie went on with a recitation of the Third Psalm. "But thou, O Lord, art a shield for me; my glory, and the lifter up of mine head!"

In response to a nod from Garrett, Chris Rowley got up, drawing a skinning knife from the sheath at his belt.

"I cried unto the Lord with my voice," Benjie recited, "and he heard me out of his holy hill. Selah."

As the colonel left the building, walking quickly, he heard a sudden cry of pain. Then the quavering voice took up again.

"I— I will not be afraid of ten thousands of people, that have set themselves against me round about. Arise, O Lord; save me—"

The words were bitten off in a sudden shriek. The colonel walked faster and faster until he reached his quarters. Even from the porch of the shabby house, he seemed to hear echoes of the Psalm. Hand on the knob, he paused, shook his head. He felt guilty but consoled himself with the thought that nothing he had done matched for shame the black deeds of those who sought to tear down the flag, *his* flag, and destroy the Union.

The Indian woman had gone to visit relatives. Private Dobbs brought his supper on a tray: hot roast beef and gravy, a fresh-baked loaf of bread, some boiled greens, coffee.

"Where is Mrs. Garrett?" the colonel asked.

Dobbs nodded toward the bedroom. "Said she had a headache, Colonel. I fixed her some tea, but that's all she wanted."

Weary, he read a sheaf of correspondence brought up on the *F. Y. Batchelor*. His eyes burned, and his chin sagged on his chest. Awaking with a start, he unbuttoned his collar and went into the bedroom, carrying the lamp.

"Cassie?"

She rolled over, shielding her eyes with an arm.

"Sorry," he said, setting the lamp on the bureau. "Were you asleep?"

"I was."

He sat on the edge of the bed to remove his boots, moving carefully so as not to disturb her. He had enough on his mind without a quarrel.

For a long time they lay side by side, neither touching. The rushing of the river was loud. Tattoo sounded, then taps; the post was asleep. Owen felt suddenly, desperately lonely. Twisting, he managed to get his arm under her head, with little co-operation from Cassie. They lay that way for a while longer. At the far edge of the parade ground a coyote howled; a sentry challenged a straggler from the gin mills in town; through the half-open window came the moist, earthy smell of spring.

"Cassie?"

She didn't answer.

He pulled her to him, cupping her breast. "Cassie?"

She recoiled from the touch of his hand.

"God damn it, Cassie!" he protested, "what's wrong?"

"I was thinking," she said. "Just . . . thinking."

"That's the trouble with you!" he grumbled. "Thinking! You think too damn much! When you're in bed with your husband, Cassie, you ought not to think. Just . . . react! That is, if you love me."

She faltered. "Yes . . . I guess. I mean . . . I want to love you."

"Then, show me!"

She tolerated his hand, and after a while her body lost some of its chill. Owen heard with pleasure her deepened breathing, and became ecstatic when her body trembled at his groping. Suddenly she rolled away and sat on the edge of the bed, naked back turned. Bewildered, he rose on an elbow. "What is it now?" he asked in exasperation. When she was silent, he became angry. "Thinking again?"

Her voice was faraway, ruminative. "Yes."

"About what, damn it all!"

She turned toward him. In the darkness her eyes were luminous. "I want you to let me talk to David Chantry."

He was suspicious. "Chantry? You know that's against regulations! He's a prisoner, charged with a capital crime!"

"I know that," she said. "But at Fort Taylor *you're* the regulations! You can arrange it!"

Balked in his ardor, he was impatient. But remembering how stubborn and intransigent she could be, he spoke cautiously. "Why do you want to talk to Chantry?"

"I don't know. We were . . . friends, once."

Malicious, he grinned. "Yes, I know that. But your friend got his pretty neck in a noose, now, didn't he? Breaking parole is one of the least things he's got to answer for!"

She gathered a lock of the long blond hair and pensively brushed it against her cheek. "I'm not convinced he's *really* guilty of anything! Surely a trial is required to establish guilt."

"We've got him," Owen said curtly. "We've got him dead to rights. Now, come to bed!"

"Owen!" she protested.

He paused, hand on the softness of her upper arm.

"I'm serious! I *do* want to talk to him! The stockade is not a pleasant place—I've heard tales from Mrs. Moffett when she comes to clean. And I know the prisoners get really awful food; weevily beef and hard bread and coffee that's mostly chicory. I want to go down tomorrow and take David one good meal; some of the bread I baked today, and that new butter off the *F. Y. Batchelor,* and a jug of milk. I know the prisoners don't get things like that in your old stockade." When he hesitated, she added, "Isn't there a question of simple humanity, Owen? After all, no matter what David Chantry has done— if he's done anything, that is—he is a gentleman, and has been a guest in our house."

A wild idea burgeoned in his mind, but it was so extreme, so unlikely, that he immediately banished it. Surely not! No, in spite of everything— surely not! Nevertheless, he would drop a word of caution to Sergeant Moffett, and to Chris Rowley. Loins tingling, desire trembling in every limb, he grabbed her and rolled over in the bed with an almost animal growl. "All right!" he conceded. "All *right,* Cassie! God, you make things difficult for a man!"

Afterward, they lay for a long time together before either slept. Owen finally said, "Good night," and turned on his side, burying his face in the pillow. He still was not satisfied, but did not want to risk provoking Cassie.

———◆◆———

That night, Benjamin Sears hanged himself in his cell. Private Dobbs, relishing the incident, told Cassie about it when he brought in breakfast. Owen had long since departed to post headquarters.

"Moffett said Sears never let on. Sears thanked Moffett nice as pie when he brought his grub that evening. Later, Moffett heard the prisoner singing hymns, figgered everything was all right. This morning, early, they found Sears hanging. He'd used his belt, you see, and just hooked it over a top bar and stepped off the stool!" The old man set oatmeal, milk, and a rasher of bacon before her. "Sears' eyes were all bulged out, they said and—"

"That will be all, Dobbs," Cassie said sharply.

"Ma'am?"

She shoved the platter of bacon away. "I can't eat this. I'm really not hungry."

Later, she sent Dobbs out to prune the winter-killed branches of the trees she had planted around the porch. Then she packed a basket with the food she was going to take to David Chantry in the stockade: prime slices of last night's beef roast, a jar of her own applesauce rich with cinnamon and spices, a crusty loaf of bread, milk in a stone jug, springerles—the German Christmas cookies—long delayed in transit from her grandmother in Buffalo, New York.

Basket over her arm, she paused on the steps.

"I'm going down to post headquarters, Dobbs. I will be back for dinner." She cast a critical eye at his pruning. "Cut just above where it branches," she instructed. "Then the new shoot will come out in the right place."

As she crossed the parade ground, she saw the F. Y. Batchelor at the landing, taking on a deckload of cordwood for the fast, downriver passage. The sternwheeler would be leaving the next morning. Cassie closed her eyes, imagining herself departing this barren frontier post. Fort Union, Yankton, Sioux City, Omaha, Kansas City, St. Louis. St. Louis! Her pulse quickened. On their way out to Fort Taylor she and Owen had stopped there. Fellow officers entertained them lavishly. There were levees and afternoon teas and giddy evenings of champagne and dancing. St. Louis was full of German people, and they loved to dance the polka.

At the stockade the sentry was doubtful, but Sergeant Moffett had apparently been expecting her. He came bustling to the gate to escort her.

"Colonel told me you was coming, ma'am," he confirmed. "How be you this fine morning?"

Perhaps this time spring had come to stay. The cottonwoods were a haze of green, squadrons of clouds drifted across the cerulean sky, birds built nests in the crevices between the sharpened ends of the stockade logs. But a pall lay over the stockade. No spring day, she thought, could ever sweeten that dreadful place.

"I— I understand," she remarked, more to make conversation than anything else, "that one— one of the prisoners hanged himself last night."

Sergeant Moffett took her basket and opened the door. "That's right, ma'am. But Sears was a troubled man, surely was. When a feller like that decides to put an end onto it, there ain't much can be done. Anyways, he's out of his torment now."

Chris Rowley lounged in a corner of the stockade office. When he saw her, he took off his black slouch hat and bowed. "Ma'am."

"Now, I hope you won't be offended," Moffett said, placing the basket on the desk, "but there's always regulations, you see. I got to look through this basket to see if you're carrying any saws or files to help prisoners escape." He grinned at her, but she did not smile back, only fussed nervously with her reticule.

"Loaf of bread," Moffett said. "Jam in this jar?"

"Applesauce."

"Beef—that don't look like the pickled stuff *we* get! Ma'am, what's in this tin can?"

"Cookies. Springerles, they're called."

She had lined the bottom of the basket with a sheet of newspaper. Moffett peeled it back and stared for a moment. Then he took out the long carving knife. It was the biggest, sharpest one she had been able to find in the kitchen.

"To— to cut the bread," she stammered.

He hefted the knife, held it to the light, ran a thumb along the blade.

"How else," she demanded, "is he to cut the bread? It's in the loaf, as you can plainly see!"

Moffett kept looking at the swordlike knife. He seemed ill at ease, and she hoped she appeared that way, too. Finally he said, "I can't allow that in the prisoner's cell, ma'am! That's an actual weapon, long and sharp as it is! Chantry might threaten me to give up my keys. Or he might stab hisself with it—no telling. Anyway"— carefully he laid the knife aside—"I guess he can just tear chunks off that loaf."

He started to put the food back into the basket, but in annoyance she took them away from him and carefully repacked them.

"Now, please, may I go in?"

So far she had succeeded in her plan, but she had not counted on Chris Rowley. Stumping on maimed feet, he accompanied her to the cell, unlocking it with a key from a ring. "More regulations, ma'am," he apologized. "Ten minutes is all that's allowed. I got to stay right out here in the corridor and keep an eye on you both."

"Very well," she said stiffly, and went into David Chantry's cell, hearing the lock click to as the door closed. Chris Rowley put the keys back in his pocket and leaned against the log wall, eyes hidden in shadow under the brim of his hat.

"Mr. Chantry," she said. "David! How are you?"

He was thinner than she remembered. The fine blond hair was tangled and matted, and there were circles under his eyes. They had dressed him in prison garb: a blue flannel shirt with a straggling P painted on the back, nondescript woollen trousers. He still wore his Indian moccasins. A burr-laden blanket was pulled around his shoulders against the dampness of the cell.

"Mrs.— Mrs. Garrett!" he stammered.

"Yes," she said coolly, "it is I." She placed the basket on the table between them. "And I have brought you some good food. I understand the meals in the stockade are not exactly gourmet fare."

She wanted to touch him, put her arms around him, kiss the pale cheeks, but she was aware of Chris Rowley in the corridor, arms crossed, puffing at his pipe. Disregarding the question in David's eyes, she went on with manufactured conversation, pulling up a chair herself and quickly positioning the other opposite her. "Sit down," she invited, "and we shall talk." She was careful to keep her back to Rowley and the corridor, and had worn on her errand the shortest dress that would satisfy propriety. They sat together, knees almost touching, while she prattled on.

"I understand one of the prisoners killed himself last night, a man named Sears. It was very unfortunate."

He was watching her intently, the question still in his eyes. "I did not know him," he said.

"Well, I am sorry to see *you* in these dreadful circumstances," she went on. "I know there are serious charges against you, but I refuse to believe them. How can they ever accuse you of such things? You signed an oath to the Republic, I know that, and I know further that you are too much of a gentleman ever to deny a solemn oath."

He smiled. "Ma'am, I am indebted for your good opinion!"

"You must tell me," she went on, crossing her legs and giving the slightest upward hitch to the hem of her skirt, "how your Indian photographs are coming! That is— I mean— how they *were* coming before this unhappy affair."

Suddenly, so suddenly it startled her, he started to cough. For a moment she was alarmed at the intensity of the paroxysm, the way it seemed to shake his body, rack his chest. When he saw her concern, he tried hard to stifle the cough, but was finally forced to reach in a pocket and bring out a crumpled handkerchief to dab at his lips.

"I'm sorry," he said, quickly stuffing the cloth back into a pocket. "It's the lungs again, you see. As you might recall from Columbus, I had a tendency to consumption. Out here in the Territory I thought they were doing some better, but in this cell they have betrayed me again. It's probably the cold and the damp." He watched her as she pulled the skirt an inch higher. "Mrs. Garrett," he said, "I'm glad you mentioned the pictures. I hesitate to ask it, but I must. All my pictures—glass plates as well as paper prints—are in the wagon back at Ghost Bull's camp among the buttes. I was taken so suddenly I had no way to see they were properly taken care of. They are precious to me, and I should not want to see them lost or destroyed. Can you—will you—talk to your husband about them, see if in some way they can be recovered?"

"Have you talked to the colonel about them?" she asked. "Surely he—"

He looked down; his eyes blinked in surprise at the derringer pistol under her garter, the little pistol Owen had given her when they first came out to the Territory.

"Surely," she said quickly, "he would see to it that your work is not lost!"

David Chantry started to cough again, but suppressed it with an almost superhuman effort. He half rose, pulling his chair closer. His hand quickly moved toward her knee, but she shook her head, only the slightest of motions, and frowned in warning.

"I have brought up the matter," he said, "but I do not think the colonel was very sympathetic. As you will recall, that night at dinner at your home he was not in favor of, or impressed by, photographs." He glanced casually over her shoulder at Chris Rowley. "They are my work," he went on. "My lifework, perhaps, if I should not be able to refute these silly charges made against me."

Rowley fidgeted, took a watch from a vest pocket.

"I will talk to the colonel," Cassie promised. "Don't worry, David! I'm quite sure some arrangement can be made to recover your pictures—your wagon too, and all your chemicals and things."

"Ma'am," Rowley called, "it's been a good ten minutes!"

"All right, I'm coming." She held her skirt in place with one hand, clearly exposing the pistol, and placed the other on David's blond head. "Now," she said, "if you will, David, let us pray for your quick deliverance."

In response to the gentle pressure he knelt before her, hands clasped before him, head bowed over her knees.

"Father," she prayed, lifting her head, eyes closed, "this is a time of travail for Thy child David Chantry. He is in the presence of his enemies, and is sorely pressed. He—"

At the feel of his hand on her naked thigh she trembled; her voice broke. A wave of passion rose in her and she fought to steady her voice.

"His head is bowed down in grief and pain, and—"

His hand pressed tenderly against the soft flesh of her inner thigh; his lips brushed her naked knee.

"—he comes to You now asking for succor in this great trial."

She was torn by conflicting emotions: one Cassie Garrett luxuriated in the touch of his hand, the other screamed, *Hurry, David! Hurry!*

"Father, we ask Thy blessing on this Thy servant—"

The pistol was slowly removed. For a moment it caught on the frilly garter. She felt her heart sag with a suspended beat. Then it lurched, regaining its frantic pace.

"And we ask Thee to watch over him and sustain him in the—in the difficult days—"

The pistol was gone.

"—in the difficult days ahead. Amen."

David raised his head. There was joy in his eyes, triumph. "Amen!" he said. "Ma'am, amen to that!"

Nervous and trembling she rose, holding for support to the back of her chair, feeling the long skirt slide down again into its proper folds. "Now," she said in a faint voice, "I must go."

Taking her elbow, he followed her to the cell door. Chris Rowley stumped forward to open it.

"I thank you for everything," David said. "You have been most kind, ma'am." He bowed, and kissed her hand.

As the iron door clanged shut he grasped the bars tightly. His knuckles were white as they grasped the chill iron.

"Mrs. Garrett," he begged, "*please* remember my pictures! No matter—" For a moment he broke off; she feared he was about to have another spasm of coughing. But instead he seemed to be thinking. When he spoke, he chose his words carefully. "Ma'am, whatever happens, or whatever has happened— yes, indeed, whatever *does* come to pass, I hope you will find a way to preserve those pictures. The Sioux are a race whose time is passing. I want people to know them as I did, if only through the photographs. I cannot tell you how important that is to me! I would give my eternal soul to know that the pictures were saved!"

She was crying, and did not know it until she felt the spring breeze chilling her wet cheeks as she left the stockade.

CHAPTER TWELVE

During the long hours of the night, David Chantry sat in his cell and pondered his situation. He had failed, failed miserably. He had failed Horace Kinnear and the Council. He had failed his brother, Brigadier Wade Chantry. Worst of all, he had failed the Cause, the Stars and Bars, the sore-pressed Confederate States of America.

The night was quiet. In the anteroom his jailer dozed; he could hear regular breathing, interrupted by a gasp or snort as the soldier woke from uneasy sleep. In the dim light from the kerosene lamp in the anteroom, David examined the little derringer pistol Cassie had smuggled to him in her garter. But there were many obstacles: the locked door of his cell, the jailer, and outside probably more guards, along with the high stockade and locked outer gate with its sentry. The pistol was small but deadly, apparently .44 caliber. For the second time, he broke the action, made sure of the two metal-cased cartridges in the over-and-under barrels of the weapon. Two bullets only; not very many for a desperate situation. Really, only one bullet if he decided to make a break for freedom. The second bullet he would put in his own head if they seemed about to recapture him. He would never be taken— not alive, anyway.

The night wore on. Except for the heavy tick of the wall clock in the anteroom, the post was silent. He could imagine the dozing jailer, feet on the desk, head sunk on chest. If he could overpower the jailer, he might have the beginnings of a chance. But the stockade wall was a good twelve feet high; no way to climb over it. He would have to go out the gate.

Striking four, the brazen gong of the anteroom clock startled him.

He heard the jailer snort, then cough, and the scraping-back of a chair as the man picked up the lamp to walk down the corridor on a routine inspection. There were four cells. Benjie Sears had occupied one, at the far end. For the moment, the middle two were empty. David blinked as the jailer raised the lamp, peered in.

"You all right, reb?"

"I'm perfectly well," David assured him. "Go back to sleep and don't bother yourself about me."

"Smart, ain't you?" the soldier grumbled. He tried the door, shaking it. When he had assured himself it was secure, he scratched his groin pleasurably and shuffled back to the anteroom. Moments later, David heard him resume his snoring.

Why had Cassie risked bringing him the pistol? He did not love Cassie Garrett, and in spite of his words to her that night in Dooley's Hotel she must know that also. Surely, suspicion must sooner or later fall on her; she had been his only visitor. In the darkness he shook his head, sighed. Women were strange creatures.

He recalled dismally the dictionary of the Sioux sign language he had contemplated writing. Fascinated by the grace and fluidity of the *wibluta*, he had wanted to compile a dictionary. No scholar, so far as he knew, had yet done so. In fact, he had a few scribbled pages completed. Now what would happen to the dictionary?

For a while he dozed, sitting on the cot with his back painfully against the log outer walls. Striking five, the clock awakened him. Again the jailer came to make his rounds. "If I was you," he advised, "I'd get me some sleep. They say Chris Rowley's goin' to innergrate you this mornin', and he's a rough one."

"Innergrate?"

"That's what I said, didn't I? It means question you."

"Oh," David said. "Well— thanks. I'll try."

Somewhere, a long way off, across the parade ground, a cock crowed. David moved to the barred window and looked out. It seemed still full dark, although in the east there was a grayness to herald the coming of another day. Through the open window, the air was fresh and loamy-smelling, laced with river damp—the air of freedom.

Suddenly he had an idea. Why not? Since Benjie Sears' tragic death the jailers were under special charge to be vigilant. They had taken David's belt, but there were other ways. Carefully tearing his prison shirt with the grain, trying to do it as soundlessly as possible, he manufactured long strips of cotton cloth and braided them into a rope. Pulling his cot next to the bars of his cell, he stood on it to fasten the makeshift rope as high as possible. Looping a crude noose, he finished it off with a square knot so that it fit comfortably around his neck but could not strangle him. Dying was no part of his present plans.

Before he stepped into space he felt again in his pocket for the comforting outline of the derringer. The time must be nearly six. Through the window he saw streamers of rose and saffron. As he watched, the streamers were lit gradually from beneath by the first rays of the sun. He wondered, just before he stepped off the cot, if he would ever see another May dawn.

"Aaaagh!" he cried as the rope took the weight of his body. The feeling was uncomfortable but he could breathe, though with difficulty. "Aaaagh!" he gurgled. For good measure he kicked the cell door; it responded with a satisfactory clanking. "Aaaagh!" he appealed. "Aaaagh!"

He heard a chair overturn, a scuffle of boots on planks. Staggering shadows painted the walls as the jailer clumped down the corridor.

"Good Godamighty!" Setting the lamp on the floor, the jailer fumbled at his ring of keys. "Hang on there, reb— I'm a-comin'!" Finding the key, he turned it in the lock. Rushing forward, he grabbed David around the legs to lift the weight of his body from the noose. Drawing a penknife from his pocket, the soldier opened it with his teeth, holding David aloft with the other arm, and slashed the makeshift rope. David, by design, fell heavily on him and knocked the man sprawling. As the soldier lay beneath him, dazed, David drew the derringer and shoved it in the jailer's ribs. "One move," he cautioned, "and I'll blow your guts all over this cell!"

The man's mouth opened. He seemed about to yell, but David pushed harder and snarled a warning. The jailer's face blanched. He chewed his lip in perplexity, finally spoke.

"I ain't no hero!" he grumbled. "What in hell you want me to do?"

David rose, backed away, holding the derringer pointed at the man's head. Picking up the lamp, he nodded toward the anteroom. "Walk ahead of me and keep your hands up!"

In the anteroom, the rosy light of dawn suffused dirty windows. The jailer's pistol lay on the desk. David dropped the derringer in his pocket, picked up the pistol. It was a late-model Remington, .44 caliber. Probably in accord with stockade regulations, the weapon was fully loaded, a percussion cap on each of the six nipples in back of the cylinder. The hammer would have to be eared back for each shot, and that made it awkward. But there were six shots. That was an advantage—five for anyone who now stood in his way, and the sixth—

He was not prepared for the outside door to open, but it was a bit of luck. Old Moffett, the stockade sergeant, stood silhouetted, in the doorway, carrying a tin cup of coffee.

"Close the door quietly behind you," David commanded. "Then walk over to that corner"—he gestured—"and no tricks, old man! Keep your hands high!"

Indecision twisted Sergeant Moffett's face. After all, it was his own jail. But when David raised the revolver and squinted along the barrel, Moffett gingerly closed the door and padded across the floor in carpet slippers.

"Prosser, you damned idiot!" he said bitterly to the jailer, eyes never leaving David, coffee cup obediently on high. "What the hell's going on here?"

Prosser was aggrieved, put-upon. "Sergeant, the prisoner done tried to hang hisself! When I heard him gagging and choking, I run to cut him down, but he jumped me with a little derringer, then took *my* gun!"

Though the sun was rising, it was chilly in the anteroom. David, clad only in cotton pants and Indian moccasins, shivered, and not entirely from the cold. Again he felt the reckless elation that sometimes gripped him with the threat of danger.

"Take off your shirt and give it to me," he ordered Prosser.

The man looked sullen, glanced at his superior.

"Do what he says!" Moffett growled.

David put on the sweat-smelling woollen shirt, letting the long tails hang out. When he left the anteroom, the tails would cover the revolver in his waistband.

"Take cuffs and leg irons from your cabinet over there," he instructed Moffett, "and chain Prosser to the bars of the cell around the corner. Stuff your red bandanna into his mouth, and wrap your belt good and tight around his face so he can't make any outcry."

Moffett put down the coffee cup, reluctantly complied. "You'll never get away with this!" he muttered. To Private Prosser he said, "I'm sorry, Luke. Open your trap wider, damn it all!" He gave a final tug at the gag and glared at David Chantry. "What in hell you propose to do with *me* now?"

The stockade sergeant had been kind to David. "I'll tell you," he said. "You and I are going to walk out that stockade gate as nice as you please." He peered through the dirty window. "When we come up on that sentry at the gate, tell him Colonel Garrett wants the prisoner brought to headquarters for questioning and that's where you're taking me." He held out one wrist. "Take another pair of those cuffs and hook our hands together so it'll look legitimate. And give me the key. If you co-operate, nothing will happen to you."

Moffett hesitated. "Suppose I yell bloody murder, right now, and call for help?"

"Then," David said evenly, "we'd both be dead, that's all. I'd shoot you and kill myself. I'll not be taken alive. I hope you believe that, and someday sit under your own fig tree, as it says in the Bible, and enjoy your retirement."

Moffett handed him the key to the manacles. "I did plan it that way," he said. To Private Prosser, making ineffectual mewling noises, he added, "Stop your squalling, damn it! If you wasn't such a tarnation fool, none of this would have happened!"

David opened the door and they stepped into the growing dawn. The air of freedom was sweet in his nostrils. In the stockade yard, some of the lesser prisoners—thieves and malcontents and drunks— were standing in line with tin plates, awaiting mess. The guard at the high gate straightened from his slouch and tried to appear alert.

"Remember," David muttered. "I'll blow your head off if there's any hitch!"

"Gilmore," Moffett told the guard in a weary voice, "unlock the gate. I'm taking this here prisoner over to headquarters. Colonel wants to question him this morning."

"Yes, sir." Gilmore leaned his bayoneted Springfield against the wall, took out a massive brass key, twisted it in the lock, pulled loose a chain. Together David and Sergeant Moffett strolled through the gate. A moment later, there was again the rattle of chain, a heavy click as the lock tumblers went home.

"Now what you goin' to do?" Moffett demanded.

In the shadows under the stockade wall, David studied the scene. Across the parade ground lay the headquarters building, and beyond it the commandant's house. To the left stretched a line of leafing willows and box elder marking the bank of the Yellowstone. At the end of the line of trees lay Elk City itself, a pall of smoke marking the imminent departure of one of the sternwheelers.

"What you doin'?" Moffett protested as David hurried him deep into the tangle of willows.

"Shut up!" David snarled. Quickly he unlocked the bracelet from his wrist and snapped it to a slender sapling. "Turn around," he ordered.

Uneasy, Moffett turned. Pulling the revolver from his waistband, David struck him behind the ear, trying not to hit too hard. How do you club a man into unconsciousness, yet not hurt him? With a sigh Moffett collapsed, sliding down the sapling into a crumpled heap. That would, David thought, keep him quiet for a while. Even if he came to, Moffett was a considerable earshot from the post.

Now that he had escaped, what was he to do, where was he to go? In an agony of indecision, he stumbled through the willows, parting the thick screen of willow and box elder to look up and down the river. The Yellowstone surged relentlessly past, tawny, crested with foam, carrying with it slabs of water-carved ice. There was no way to cross except the cable ferry at Elk City. A man would be foolish to try to swim the icy torrent. On the other hand, across the river was the land of the Tongue and the Powder, Mizpah Creek, the Wolf Mountains the Sioux called the *Chetish*, the endless ranges of buttes where lay the winter camp of Ghost Bull. That was where he had to go. Blossom the wolfer was there, too, thinking himself secure in his mine diggings.

Sharp and clear above the rushing of the floodwaters, he heard a bugle from the post. He did not know all the routine calls but supposed it was sick call or something like that. When the bugle was almost immediately drowned out by the wild clanging of a bell, he knew something had gone wrong. Perhaps Private Prosser had spread the alarm. Maybe the sentry at the stockade gate had grown suspicious. Old Moffett himself might have come to, freed himself, run to headquarters with the news David Chantry had escaped. Heart pounding, he drew the Remington from his waistband. *Calm,* he told himself. *Be calm! Don't panic!*

Somewhere a gunshot sounded. There were shouts, another bugle call, which cracked on a high note. Listening, David heard a voice that carried clearly in spite of the noise of the river. "Where? Which way?"

The voices grew louder. Though his view of the post was blocked by the willows, he knew they were coming toward him. Escape up the river was patently impossible. He leaped into the greenery, stumbling, falling, sliding in marshy ooze where he came too near the bank.

Elk City residents did not rise quite as soon as the soldiers at the post, and for that he was grateful. Like an animal, he dodged behind the rabbit warren of storefronts, lean-tos, shacks, even tents, habitable now in this mild weather; he was unobserved, so far as he could tell. Emerging from the back door of the Yellowstone Dining Hall, a cook threw a pail of slops into the river from a rickety staircase. A spotted dog, observing David's flight, barked and ran up to gambol alongside him, thinking it a game. Steamy smells came from a laundry; in a splintered packing case, a drunk slept off last night's popskull. Behind the brewery David paused, out of breath, to crouch behind a row of empty barrels. His hiding place smelled of sour beer.

Downstream, the sun thrust its way through the trees bordering the river, casting a ladder of light across the maelstrom of the Yellowstone. River mists thinned, drifting away in torn shreds as he watched. His throat felt dry, and he swallowed painfully. He must not linger here, waiting for capture. He would have to move soon— but where?

In River Street there sounded the pounding of hoofs, a shouted command. An excited soldier ran past his lair, piece at a high port and whooping with the elation of the hunt. The chase made him think of Big Oak's hounds on a coon scent. At the river's edge the soldier paused, peered up and down the river, called back to someone on a rooftop.

A plume of steam wavered upward from the sternwheeler—*F. Y. Batchelor*, David read in gold letters on her bow—and he jumped at the long, wavering blasts of her whistle. They were casting off for the downriver run.

Now there were soldiers prowling about the beer barrels, calling back and forth to each other, enjoying the hunt, which was a respite from a humdrum barracks life. He was sweating heavily: moisture beaded his forehead and dripped into his eyes; his grasp on the revolver was wet and clammy. Craning his neck, he saw more men on the roofs overlooking the river. The rising sun glanced off the lenses of a pair of field glasses. From up there, they had an excellent view. If they looked down, toward the piled barrels, they would see him at once.

The *F. Y. Batchelor* whistled again. Two men cranked a windlass to lift her gangplank and stow it along the gunwales. On the bank, between David and the departing sternwheeler, stood ricks of cordwood waiting for the next boat up. If he could reach the stacks of wood. . . .

He was not thinking clearly, logically. All he knew was that he could no longer remain in the shelter of the stinking barrels. Blindly he stood up and ran toward the bank. Behind him sounded a chorus of yelps, shouts, cries of glee. One shot sent up a gout of mud at his feet and stung his heel. Another whistled over his head. As he plunged into the shelter of the cordwood, another shot exploded into the high-piled billets, showering him with splinters. Cowering, lungs laboring, he put a hand to his face; it came away smeared with blood. A splinter must have entered his eye too. He could not see well.

Prosser's revolver still clutched in his hand, he stumbled through the ricks of wood. Through a break in their serried ranks, he saw the sternwheeler backing into the river, maneuvering into the swift current to head downstream. Her paddles churned yellow foam; a familiar smell of hot oil and smoke came to him. For a moment, she paused in delicate balance, thrashing wheel and river current equal and opposed.

Now there was no chance of escape. They had him surrounded, like a coon in a tree. But he would not be caught. He would not be taken! The Sioux were free yet, free people. He could not be otherwise. Tossing his revolver into the glutinous mud, he splashed into the river. The bottom was clinging muck. He stumbled and fell, staggered to his feet. Icy water drove the hysteria from him as he struck out toward the departing sternwheeler, now slowly drifting downstream.

They were still shooting at him from the bank, from the rooftops of Elk City. Spouts of water pocked the surface around his body. A strong swimmer since childhood, he drove his cupped hands hard into the yellow torrent, rolling to and fro, remembering to breathe properly, suck in air when the left arm extended, burying his face and stroking again with the other arm.

Something hit him heavily in the back as if he had been struck with a floating timber, but it hardly diminished his powerful swimming. Thoughts reeled and spun in his fevered brain: Big Hail, Pretty Nose, Cassie Garrett's garter with its deadly freight, Corn Woman and her green-speckled eyes, Blossom the wolfer who killed his own daughter.

The engineer on the *F. Y. Batchelor* hooked her up again. Her bows came around, she steadied in her marks. Against the splashing of the great wheel, the hiss of foam, he could hear again, as a child, the long "soooo—haaah—sooo—haaah" of the engines. He could imagine the great walking beam tipping up and down, up and down, the way it had on the Mississippi of his youth.

"Wait!" he called. "Wait for me!"

He was reaching out for something, he did not know what. Perhaps it was to childhood, to the time he and Wade used to run with his father's niggers, to the time when they stood together knee-deep in cool, dark waters, watching the boats, dreaming the long dreams of youth.

"Wait for me!" he insisted. Liquid bubbled in his throat and made breathing difficult.

On the weather deck of the *F. Y. Batchelor,* by the gallows frame of the walking beam, someone stood. High above the churning wheel, the solitary figure watched, waited, finally waved.

"Wade!" he screamed. "Wait for me!"

It was Wade Chantry, Brigadier Wade Chantry, no doubt of that. Wade was smiling, beckoning him. David did not know how his brother had got there, all the way from the Shenandoah Valley, but he was happy to see Wade again. Now he was under the churning wheel. Torrents of muddy water fell on him, cooling and refreshing him. With a final thrust, he pulled himself forward and into the wheel, feeling his body rising up, up, and up, miraculously light, carried high into a sunlit place of peace and contentment.

CHAPTER THIRTEEN

In midmorning, Cassie was in the parlor, knitting, when Owen clumped in. His boots were caked with mud, his coat torn and a button missing, chin dark with unshaven beard. Propping his carbine in the corner, he slumped into the chair opposite her, triumph in his bloodshot eyes.

"Got the bastard," he announced. He was out of breath. "Your precious friend David Chantry!"

She had known it must be so. The knitting was badly done, with many stitches dropped. She had sat there, next to the window, knitting with cold and trembling fingers, not even watching her work, ever since Owen first heard the alarm bell and dashed half clothed from the house.

"I think I got him myself," Owen went on. "Of course, with so many shooting at him, it's hard to tell. But I *think* I got him. I was on the roof of Riker's Mercantile, and I propped my carbine on the ledge and—"

"Stop it!" Cassie cried.

"After that, he kind of thrashed around in the river. He was swimming toward the *F. Y. Batchelor,* and I don't know what was on his mind, because he swam right into the paddles! The blades just picked him up, like a doll, and flung him into the air!"

"Owen, for God's sake!"

His lips twisted in a smile. "He got caught there, in the wheel, and it dragged him up and down, up and down, until—"

Weeping, she put her hands over her ears. "I won't hear any more! I won't!"

Owen rummaged in a drawer and found a cigar. Biting off the end, he lit it, puffing a series of rings that wavered and twisted in the morning sun filtering through the curtains. "Had quite a personal interest in David Chantry, didn't you, Cassie?" He sat down again, crossed his booted legs, loosened his collar. "But I guess we took care of *that*, all right!" He rocked comfortably, the chair creaking, as he followed upward the course of a fresh smoke ring. "Ah, Cassie, I suppose a lot of it was my fault! When a man has a valuable possession, he should take care of it! I guess I was too busy with other things." He leaned forward, laying his hand on her arm. "But things will be different now! As soon as this damned treaty meeting with the Indians is over—"

"I'm *not* your possession!" She snatched away her arm. "I never *was* your possession, as you call it! And now I never *will* be!"

He regarded her tolerantly through the haze of smoke.

"Let's not retreat into pique, my dear! I suspect you dallied a little with the young man; flirted, let's say. But I can't actually accuse you of anything that would make me love you less. I'm willing to let bygones be bygones, Cassie." Ash fell unnoticed onto his coat. "Though I must say, I regret David Chantry's passing."

She stared, eyes bright with unshed tears.

"I mean," he explained, "that with both Sears and Chantry dead, there's no chance now to find out who the higher-ups were in this damnable plot to incite the Sioux."

Staring bleakly out the window, she said nothing. It was May, and David Chantry was dead; dead on a May morning.

"Now, come on!" Owen wheedled. He tried to draw her to him but she resisted. "All right," he sighed. "I guess I can wait a while. After all, death is a great shock to a woman. I'm used to it, I suppose —hardened, you might say, as a soldier. But women are the font of life. They bring it forth, and death is—well, almost a denial of womanhood, isn't it?" He brightened. "Tell you what, Cass; we'll have a baby! How about it? When I've got my eagles they promised me a cushy staff job at the War Department—"

"I'm *going* to have a baby," she said, face stony.

He took the cigar from his mouth.

"I'm going to have a baby," she repeated.

The rocking stopped; his body seemed suddenly frozen into immobility.

"By David Chantry," she told him. "I hope it is a boy! I hope he will be blond, like David, with blue eyes! I hope he will be beautiful, like David, and I hope he will love me, for there is no love in you for me, nor ever was, Owen."

Stunned, he rose, disbelieving. He pushed away the rocker and it fell on its side. "You're joking—having me on." It was half question, half statement. "You *are*, aren't you, Cass?"

Her hands gripped the arms of the chair. Her voice was steady; David Chantry's death had given her strength. "I am not joking, Owen. I am well started on my pregnancy, and certainly not by *you*."

Owen's face was ashen. He groped at his unshaven chin, his lips, pulled at his ear as if begging it to deny her words. "Cassie," he said. "Cassie, I—"

"It should not be so very strange," Cassie went on. "You never loved me, Owen. I was a possession, like your damned guns and horses. Your gold oak leaves were more important than I was. Your silver leaves were more precious still. When you get the eagles, you will not even see me any more. Your eyes will be fixed on a star, a silver star for each shoulder. You do not need or want a wife. All you need is a mechanical French doll to cling to your arm at official functions, smile, nod brightly. That is all I ever was, and I am tired of the role!"

His face suffused with color. "Cassie, really— I— I—" He rose to pace the floor. "I have never seen you like this!"

"You have never seen me at all," she said in a tight voice. "Not the real, the actual, Cassie. The one that was lonely, the one that cried out for love, the one that wept every night, softly so as not to disturb you. You have never known *that* Cassie. You never *wanted* to know her! So she turned elsewhere for love. Do you know, Owen, David Chantry and I lay together in the stable at the big old house on Third Street in Columbus when you were commanding troops at the penitentiary there? We—"

He struck her hard across the face. Her fingers rose to touch the place, but she did not flinch.

"And in Dooley's Hotel that night—"

He stared in wordless horror.

"I think you had Chris Rowley follow me there; I am not sure. But we lay there in each other's arms for a long time. Since I have known that love, I am stronger now; stronger than you."

Furious, he raised clenched fists as if to strike her again. Suddenly his face blanched. "My God!" he muttered.

She picked up her knitting, arranged it carefully on her lap.

"Moffett," Owen said in a strangled voice, "told me Chantry had a gun—a derringer pistol."

"Yes," she said. "That is right."

He rushed into the bedroom. Throwing open the drawers of the bureau, he scattered her things on the floor—camisoles, stockings, nightgowns. "The gun! That little pistol I gave you once!"

She bent over her knitting. "It's gone, isn't it?"

He emerged from the bedroom, wild-eyed.

"I took it to David when I brought him dinner that day," she explained. "It was in my garter. He took it from my garter with his own hand, while Chris Rowley watched us." She knitted faster. "His—his touch was very gentle. I am sorry I shall never feel that touch again, Owen."

Distraught, he stalked the room, groaning with the burden of her words. Finally he slumped in the rocker, head sunk on chest. "That was a crime, Cassie!" he said in a hoarse voice. "You committed a great crime! I cannot in good conscience save you!"

The knitting needles clacked industriously. "I think you will save me," she said coolly.

"I will see to a divorce also!" he threatened. "I have very good grounds, have I not? You admitted to everything!"

Private Dobbs came from the kitchen, knocked at the bead-curtained passageway. His face was uneasy. "Ma'am? Sir?"

Owen turned. "What is it, damn you?"

"Dinner, that's all, Colonel! Just . . . dinner is served!"

Owen watched the old man back confusedly away, then turned again to Cassie.

Anticipating him, she said, "There will be no divorce, either, Owen. You must realize that!"

His face was baffled.

"Because," she said, laying down her knitting, "that would be a great scandal. A southern spy cuckolding you? Now, what would they make of that in the War Department? Can you imagine what the generals would say? Where would the silver eagles be then? No, Owen. You are hoist on your own petard, or whatever it is they say. I don't know, really, what a petard is, but you are hoist high and dry. There will be no more talk about a derringer. There will be no divorce." For a moment, her voice faltered. "My baby will need a good home, an education, all the advantages, so we shall go on being a happily married couple. I promise I will be a great credit to you in your career, Owen, though I will not love you any more. Perhaps the baby will take after me more than it will you, but such things can be explained." She stood up, taking his hand. It lay lifeless in hers. "Now," she said brightly, "shall we go to dinner? Dobbs baked a dried-apple pie especially for you—you know how you love dried-apple pie! And I *must* speak to you about his corporal's stripes! It would be only right to promote Dobbs, I think, before he retires."

◆

Though the Indian office tried hard to arrange treaty talks with the Sioux for June of 1863, it was impossible. For hundreds of years, according to the Sioux calendar painted on thin-scraped deerhide, the Sioux had gone forth to fight their hereditary enemies, the Absaroka—the Crows, white men called them—each summer. They were not willing to give up the ancient pastime. The Cheyennes had other business also, and refused to come in to Fort Zachary Taylor. Both tribes relished their summer freedom too much to waste it on palaver with the white men.

In consequence it was nearly September when the tribal chiefs, rich in ceremonial finery, arrived at the post where the treaty commissioners awaited their coming. Ghost Bull attended, High Bear, Two Moons, Little Wolf, White Hawk, Old Smoke, Bobtail Horse, and many others of the tribal hierarchy, along with swarms of retainers and hundreds of favorite war ponies. Colonel Garrett arranged to put up dozens of Sibley tents for the Indians, conical shelters erected on a tripod holding a single pole. The tents made a pretty sight against the emerald turf of the parade ground, greened by the heavy spring rains. The Indians, strolling about in paint and finery, added a barbaric but pleasing touch of color. Though the colonel provided a large mess tent and field kitchens, the savages preferred to do their own cooking at individual fires, eating in the balmy summer air, surrounded by dogs and children.

Horace Kinnear, as one of the treaty commissioners, was intrigued by the color and activity. Whenever there was a lull in the talks, he enjoyed strolling about the Indian camp, taking notes for a series of articles he intended to run in the *Illustrated Weekly News*. They were the first Indians he had ever seen.

By now, the Council was dissolved. The capture and death of two Council agents frightened off many of the members. Too, there was growing suspicion in some quarters that the headquarters of the subversive Copperhead movement was in Washington itself, the nation's capital. In addition, there had been fought early in July a great battle called Gettysburg. Although the results of the battle appeared inconclusive, many members of the Council felt that northward incursion by the Confederacy to be the high-water mark of the rebellion. Certainly, the South was unlikely ever again to be able to sustain such losses; the North, with untold reservoirs of manpower and arms, might be expected soon to recover, and press the battle again. Britain, too, was of like mind. Mr. Dillard-Hume, the ambassador's secretary, declined to attend any more meetings. Horace Kinnear, the last active member of the Council, tried vainly to obstruct the treaty talks at Fort Taylor, but abandoned those efforts when he saw the general attitude was against him. Ghost Bull eventually signed the treaty (he could write passable English script), while High Bear, Little Wolf, and many others "touched the pen," making a thumbprint on the eighteen-page treaty to guarantee peace along the Powder, the Yellowstone, and the upper Missouri. The Indians were disappointed, however, not to be able to secure a supply of raisin trees to furnish them with their favorite confection.

Awaiting transportation East, Horace Kinnear arranged with Colonel Garrett to talk with Mrs. Garrett, whom he understood had managed to secure David Chantry's store of photographs of the Sioux.

"Yes," Garrett said, "my wife knew Chantry—oh, very casually—when he was our trusty gardener while we were stationed in Columbus, some time ago. She interested herself in the young man and admired his talents—as a photographer, I mean. Consequently, when he came out to the Territory in your employ—"

Kinnear interrupted. "I had no idea, of course, that Chantry was an enemy agent! Imagine my surprise when I received word. It is not often I have been deceived in my life, but on that occasion I was royally hoodwinked!"

A shadow crossed Garrett's countenance. "Many of us were hoodwinked, I suppose. But at any rate—when Chantry first came out here my wife invited him to supper. He showed us some of his photographs, I remember. Later, after Chantry was killed in his attempt to escape, Mrs. Garrett prevailed on me to secure his camera wagon and his store of glass plates and prints from the Indian camp in the buttes. They are under a canvas now in our stable."

Later, Kinnear talked to Mrs. Garrett. The colonel's lady had an air of gentle sadness about her, in spite of her beauty. Colonel Garrett introduced Kinnear, then excused himself to oversee housekeeping items at the post, including cleaning up the parade ground, packing the Sibley tents and returning them to the quartermaster at Fort Abraham Lincoln, whence they had been borrowed, and settling the post once more into its routine efficiency. The Sioux had departed for their autumn hunt of the buffalo, and Fort Taylor looked much the worse for wear. An elderly corporal brought Kinnear and Mrs. Garrett tea and pound cake while an Indian woman dusted furniture on the outskirts of their conversation.

"And so you knew him," the publisher remarked, sipping Oolong.

Her sad eyes lighted. "He—David, I mean—was such a delightful young man! So sensitive, so cultured! There were not many like him out here on the frontier. We enjoyed him so, the few times we ever saw him."

Kinnear sighed. "His death was a tragedy, a great tragedy." He set the cup carefully down, munched reflectively. "Very probably, he died without knowing of the death of his older brother, Wade. I know David admired Wade greatly. Wade was one of Jackson's most brilliant lieutenants, killed in action at Culpeper last spring. Jackson himself called Wade 'a cavalry genius.' It is a shame that two such brilliant men, men with such talents, such futures, should have joined those who rose in rebellion against our Union."

Reverently, Mrs. Garrett lifted a stack of sepia-toned photographic prints to her lap. "Come close," she urged Kinnear. "Sit here with me, by the window, so you can see the pictures clearly."

Ample bulk perched on a stool, staring through hand-held pince-nez, he sat for a long time with her, studying each print as she handed it to him.

"I am astonished," he said soberly, "and delighted!"

"Are they not poetic?" She seemed caught in a private reverie. "I do not know any Indians, but there is something about these pictures that makes me feel I almost know these. Though it may sound peculiar for a woman to say, I seem almost to be among them, sharing their lodges, their council fires, singing, praying, hunting with them, living a strange but beautiful life."

"I have a kindred feeling," Kinnear said. He held each print carefully to the light, examining with the publisher's eye the detail, the play of light and shadow, the magnificent faces. An idea quickly came to him: the presentation of a great album to the President, and the possible consequent sale of hundreds of similar albums, photographs mounted on parchmentlike paper, the book bound in Morocco leather with titles in gold. That way, he could at least recoup some of the expense the Council fiasco had put him to. Museums would desire the book, libraries too, along with well-heeled private citizens. In the capital alone, he calculated, he could dispose of five hundred—perhaps a thousand.

"And look!" Mrs. Garrett cried. For a moment her sadness seemed to lift. "Here is a fine picture of David—Mr. Chantry—standing beside a tipi! See how tall he was, and how the sunlight catches the glints in his hair! His hair was very fine, and long—golden, some would have called it, though that is possibly an overworked word."

Kinnear adjusted his spectacles, bent over the print.

"Someone else obviously took the picture," he remarked. "Perhaps Chantry taught an Indian friend to handle the lens cap after he set up his camera and focused it properly." He pointed. "There is a young Indian girl standing beside him. At least, she *appears* to be an Indian female, though there is something a little different about her. But I suppose there *were* half-breeds in the camp. Maybe the girl's father was white."

"It is possible," Mrs. Garrett murmured.

Finally, they had gone through the entire stack. "There are many more in his wagon," she said, "and I selected only a few of those I thought best. There are hundreds more—glass plates and paper prints alike."

Kinnear put away the pince-nez, cleared his throat. "I suppose you appreciate the fact, ma'am, that all Chantry's pictures are the property of the *Illustrated Weekly News*? Though I was unaware of the fact I had been duped into financing his treasonable activities among the Sioux, nevertheless—"

She nodded. "My husband has explained all this to me, Mr. Kinnear. The only thing I would ask—"

"Your servant, ma'am."

"The only thing—" She searched through the stack of prints for the photograph of David Chantry and the young Indian girl. "I should like very much to keep this one."

"Of course, ma'am. And if there are others you desire—"

"No." Her response was quick. "This is the one." She touched the paper with a gentle finger, tracing an outline. "I wonder who she was, that girl? Somehow—it is very strange—I feel a kinship with her. I almost feel—it is silly, I know—that we, that savage Indian girl and I, share a common experience."

She was obviously moved, moved in a deep and mysterious way he did not understand. He had always been uncomfortable in the presence of emotion, so he reached for his hat and cane, nevertheless wondering. Colonel Garrett said they had known David Chantry only casually.

"Well," he concluded, "I want to thank you, ma'am. I will of course make all necessary arrangements to have the pictures and the glass plates carefully packed and shipped East. The wagon itself is of no interest to me, and your husband may dispose of it as he wishes."

Rising, she saw him out. When she spoke, she seemed to have regained her composure, though a lacy handkerchief was tightly clutched in her small hand.

"I am glad," she said. "Glad, sir, that David's pictures are in your hands. You appear to appreciate their unique quality. As a publisher, you are in a position to make them known to the nation, perhaps someday to the world."

On the porch, fragrant with summer vines, he bowed, put on his hat. "Do you know," he mused, "it would be strange, would it not, if by means of these marvelous photographic studies David Chantry, even with his misguided and disloyal efforts as an agent for the South, were to become better known, more famous in the long run— perhaps even illustrious—than his distinguished brother, Wade Chantry?"

Mrs. Garrett closed her eyes; the ghost of a smile played about her lips. "It would be an irony, I suppose, but a very appropriate one. After all, Wade Chantry was forced to kill other human beings in his search for fame. David only— only—" Her voice broke; she clutched the handkerchief tightly. "David respected and loved them."

Kinnear tipped his hat, walked briskly down the graveled path lined with nasturtiums. In the shadow of the porch lounged a tall man smoking a pipe, a man whom Kinnear recognized as Owen Garrett's civilian scout, who had acted as interpreter at the treaty talks. Kinnear raised his cane in salute. The man nodded pleasantly, puffing at his pipe. Then he leaned back against the rough-sawed boards of the commandant's house, looking thoughtfully at the distant mountains—the Wolf Mountains, Kinnear recalled. Someone had told him the Sioux called them the *Chetish*.

BIBLIOGRAPHY

1. Bourke, John G. *On the Border with Crook*. New York: Charles Scribner's Sons, 1891.

2. Brown, Dee. *The Westerners*. New York: Holt, Rinehart, and Winston, 1974.

3. Brown, Mark H., and Felton, W. R. *The Frontier Years*. New York: Henry Holt and Co., 1955.

4. *The Chroniclers* (The Old West). New York: Time-Life Books, 1976.

5. Foster-Harris, William. *The Look of the Old West*. New York: Viking Press, 1955.

6. *The Great Chiefs* (The Old West). New York: Time-Life Books, 1975.

7. Horan, James D. *Mathew Brady, Historian with a Camera*. New York: Crown Publishers, 1955.

8. Hyde, George F. *Red Cloud's Folk*. Norman: University of Oklahoma Press, 1937.

9. *The Indians* (The Old West). New York: Time-Life Books, 1973.

10. *Pioneer Atlas of the American West*. San Francisco: Rand McNally and Co., 1956.

Winners of the SPUR and WESTERN HERITAGE AWARD